Load the Boat

A Darla King Novel

By Rosalee Richland

Load the Boat

A Darla King Novel
By Rosalee Richland

Published by Wordsmiths4u
P.O. Box 3864
Bryan, TX   77805-3864

Copyright © 2013 by Wordsmiths4u

ISBN-10: 0985012943
ISBN-13: 978-0-9850129-4-6

The eBook version of *Load the Boat* is available online from most booksellers. Discover other titles by Rosalee Richland at: http://rosaleerichland.blogspot.com/ or find Rosalee Richland on Facebook®.

Dedication

This book is dedicated to the warm and welcoming community of square dancers worldwide.

Acknowledgments

Thanks to so many people who have encouraged the writing, completion, and publication of this book. Special thanks to folks in the Sam Houston Square and Round Dance Association, Circle Squares Dance Club, and Brazos Writers. And, of course, to friends and family, who make it both easier and all worthwhile.

Author Note

While Galveston, the highways, the ports of call for the cruise and other cities are certainly real, Clearton and Isquith and other locations in Load the Boat are completely fictional. Commander Cruise Lines and the ship Journey exist only in the pages of this book, as do the captain and crew. Square dancers are a warm and welcoming bunch, just as they are portrayed in this book. But the individual characters are totally the figments of author imagination.

Hopefully, you enjoy this adventure of Darla King and her friends. If you missed the first of Darla's chronicles, Right and Left Grand, take the time to read that book and catch up to see how the Clearton crew met up with Nick. Load the Boat is the second in the series. Follow Your Neighbor continues the saga and will be coming out soon.

If you're a square dancer or caller, you'll recognize the title of each book as a square dance call. If you have a favorite call you want to see as a title, shoot an email to RosaleeRichland@yahoo.com. You can also check out the Darla King Series blog at http://rosaleerichland.blogspot.com/.

In the meantime, hope to see you in a square!

NOTE: Oct 2013 edition: 09272013

Table of Contents

CHAPTER 1

A flash of light blinded me as I made my way through the maze toward the entryway of the cruise ship. An elbow jostled me from behind and I thrust my hand down to check that the suitcase I'd just set on the ground was still there. I'm sure that one will be a great shot, I thought. I turned back to the photographer. The wind whipped my short hair into my eyes, and I pushed it back with my hand.

"Would you take one more? I moved." I smiled my brightest, and I hoped most persuasive, smile toward the camera. The young man obligingly clicked again, with an obvious smirk. He probably got that request a lot. Then I saw more spots.

"Man, Darla, you could charm a billy goat into a bathtub. I've never seen 'em hold up the immigration process for retakes," said Sam Conners. Sam stood close behind me, which was a good thing or I never would have heard his wisecrack in the chaos. He made me laugh and I saw another flash and more spots. The flashes blinded me and I knew for a while I wouldn't be seeing much else besides the spots. The line continued to wind toward the row of officials. They would check our passports and grant clearance to the next stop on our way to the ship.

Sam, one of my traveling companions, is a good friend, as in fraternal and almost paternal. You could always count on him for quick humor. When the occasion warranted, he also came up with some rich wisdom. With the crowd noise around us, I didn't try to hold a conversation. I smiled my appreciation to him. We cleared the passport control stop quickly. The official barely looked at me as she handed me the all-important stateroom key. Called the "Sail With Us" card, it not only served as the key to my stateroom but would let me charge anything not already included in the cost of the cruise.

The official identification picture was taken by the cruise line staff as we checked in with our cards at the next stop. But we were still a ways from the ship itself. I could see the Gulf of Mexico in front of us and catch a glimpse of the Port of Galveston parking lot behind me. Neither one proved much to look at, and I was ready to get onboard. I couldn't believe how slowly we were inching along the boarding ramp to the cruise ship Journey. More photographers were taking pictures, and taking more pictures, and taking more pictures, presumably to be displayed and bought by all of us later on. Ever since I hit 40, I've hated pictures of myself. But I figured this was part of the whole cruise experience so I smiled through the flashes.

As we headed up the ramp, I struggled to keep track of my purse and my luggage. Even though I wasn't carrying my sound system, I had packed pretty heavily. It wasn't that I had a lot of bags to keep up with – it was that the two bags I did have each felt like they contained a brickyard inventory. When an official had opened one of them at the security station, I'd had a devil of a time getting it closed again. On top of that, I opted to self-carry rather than checking my bags and having them delivered to my stateroom. That no longer seemed like a great idea.

The line of bodies fitfully stopped and started, probably due to the picture-taking with multiple possible sea theme backdrops as well as the many official stops each passenger had to make. On one false start, I stepped on the heel of the young woman in front of me. She stumbled as her foot lifted halfway out of her strapless sandal and then hung up on the toe cap. Instinctively she reached out to steady herself. She managed to stay upright, but the short, chunky man in front of her didn't. He lurched to his right into the railing along the side of the ramp. As he went down I noticed he didn't try to break his fall with his hands. Instead he grabbed his satchel in a bear hug and landed in a shoulder roll so that he ended up on his back with the satchel on top of him.

"Hey, lady, what's wrong with you? Watch it!" he snarled. Both the young woman and I reached out to help him up.

"I'm so sorry!" she said. "Are you okay?"

"Leave me alone. I'm fine," he snapped, pushing his glasses back into place with his right hand as he clutched his satchel with his left. He had a strong accent, and it took a second for his words to register. As soon as I understood, I backed off.

In a blink, a ship's representative appeared next to the man. He reached to take the satchel so the man could get up. The man, still on the ground, pushed his hands away roughly. He had on a corduroy jacket with those leather-like patches on the elbows that were in style many years ago. It looked like he might have worn it for all those years, too. About 65 by my guess, he had white hair that was a bit wild and formed a scraggy ring around his head. He seemed to fit with the shabby clothes even though they were baggy on him.

His eyes jerked from one person to another as he stood up. He didn't bother to straighten his clothes, and under the heavy blazer his shirt bunched up around his neck. I took in the wild look in his eyes, his flyaway hair, his ill-fitting clothes, and his worn satchel. If it weren't that he obviously was getting on this cruise, I might have guessed he was homeless. Sam stepped up closer to me, chivalrously ready to protect me if I needed it. I didn't. It was over quickly. The ship's representative handled everything smoothly.

"Of course, sir. Are you okay? How may I help you? Do you need medical assistance?" He spoke calmly, clearly, and very professionally. His words were so crisp I could tell English wasn't his first language. Certainly, there was no hint of a Texas drawl, so I figured he wasn't a local from Galveston or elsewhere in the state. He allowed the man to rise on his own. Then he inconspicuously slid his hand under the man's elbow.

The passenger straightened his jacket, but didn't let go of his bag. The bag, like his clothes, was old. It was a leather satchel that could double for work or travel. That was the only bag with him. He most likely had taken the option to check luggage, which I was wishing I had, or else he traveled pretty doggone light.

"No need to wait here, sir. Let me escort you onboard," the ship representative said, as he propelled the man forward. They speedily threaded their way up the ramp and out of sight. Maybe I should take a fall, I thought, if it would get me up this ramp sooner. Instead, I extended my hand to the young woman I had tripped.

"I'm so sorry," I said. "I apologize for tripping you. I'm Darla King."

The morning light glinted off her blond hair, perfectly in place, as she shook my hand timidly. "No, no, don't worry about it, please," she pleaded. "It's all my fault. I feel so badly about that man's fall. I hope he didn't get hurt."

Sam moved up to offer his hand. "Sam Conners," he introduced himself.

"Mandy Myers," she responded. She seemed at a loss what to say next, so I spoke up.

"Don't worry about it, Mandy," I said. "He looked like he was just fine. And besides that," I smiled, "he got to jump line. He's already on the ship while we're still here. I think he came out great."

Mandy smiled at my attempted humor. She was attractive and nicely dressed. I have a great appreciation for women who can dress up and still look comfortable, which she did. Blonde-haired and blue-eyed, she had a kind of elegant style with the slim figure to accentuate it. I self-consciously fingered my unruly hair back into place again, feeling frumpy next to her. She appeared to be in her late twenties. Her nervousness could have made her look either younger or older than she was, so it was difficult for me to pinpoint her age. Plus, anyone younger than my forty plus years tends to look like a teenager these days.

"Have you been on a cruise before?" I asked her, making conversation to smooth over the incident as we moved forward.

"Yes, but not by myself," she said. "I came on one with my parents several years ago. It was a weird experience. I thought I'd enjoy it without some of the drama of that cruise." She made a face, but didn't explain what kind of drama she'd encountered. "I decided to treat myself to one for my vacation this year. Both my parents passed on this year, and this is kind of a memorial to them. Long story. This is the same ship we went on together – or at least I guess it is. It's the same name. How about you?" she asked.

"It's been a long time since I've been on a cruise," I told her. The honeymoon cruise I'd taken with Clint seemed a lifetime ago. Sam had been uncharacteristically quiet as long as he could stand. He joined the conversation as we inched up the ramp.

One of the friendliest people I know, Sam retired from serious ranching after he was widowed. A bit weathered around the edges, Sam remains incredibly active. He enjoys meeting new people and thrives on social interaction. He jumped into the discussion.

"Well, Mandy, I've been on many. There's always plenty to do on a cruise, so I don't think you'll have any trouble filling up your time. But if you get bored, feel free to stop by and watch some square dancing. We've got a big group onboard and someone will be dancing somewhere almost anytime that we're at sea. It's fun to watch and you can join in and learn some of the calls," he said with a big smile and wink of his eye.

"Square dancing? For adults? I thought that was just for kids. I remember we learned a little of it in school in phys ed," Mandy said with a smile back to Sam. She seemed less nervous with the change of topic.

"What you learn in phys ed class, that's just an itty-bitty taste of square dancing," Sam answered. "There's a lot more to it than you probably learned in school. I tell you, miss, we have a helluva lotta fun. Remember you're invited to stop by and see us if you want. Darla here's one of the square dance callers," Sam added.

I'm always surprised how people respond when they find out I'm a square dance caller. I tend to think of it like any other service profession, but most people react like I'm a celebrity or maybe an oddity. Mandy turned to face me and her eyebrows lifted.

"A caller? That's interesting. What do you do?" she asked.

"Come on to a dance and see," I offered with a smile. Then I continued, "I call out the moves the dancers do. I'll have lessons onboard, too, so you can do more than watch, you can try it out. Maybe you'll find yourself a new pastime." I noted that she was alone, and that seemed odd for someone so young and attractive. But what did I know? Maybe lots of passengers take cruises on their own.

"So what do you do Mandy?" I asked.

"I'm a librarian," she said. "I work in the main library at the University of Texas branch here at Galveston. I've been here about two years now," she added. My stereotype of a librarian kicked in. I thought maybe her profession explained why she didn't seem very outgoing. Of course, maybe it was just in comparison to my very outgoing nature that she seemed a bit timid. I like to call myself friendly and curious, but I realize other people might call me nosy.

We visited a little more as we slowly worked our way up the boarding ramp. It was light conversation – the weather, security procedures, and the size of this ship. The Journey holds about 2100 passengers, it's not one of the megaships. That didn't mean it wasn't big though. There were multiple decks and plenty of activities for passengers. When we finally made it onto the ship, Mandy smiled and waved as she went on her way.

"Can I help you, ma'am?" asked a trim, uniformed man, obviously with the cruise line. He was dressed like the crew member who had spirited away the rumpled man on the boarding ramp. In Texas, every woman is referred to as "ma'am" regardless of their age, but it still makes me feel old. Of course, at this point I could have looked old after the long wait on to board, but I didn't think that was it. I wondered if his use of the word was a nod to Texas customs or general customer service training he had received. After all, a woman in her mid-40s isn't likely to be called "miss" in any part of the country, so what was his alternative? This man seemed a little more seasoned than the crew member on the ramp, and I guessed him to be about my age.

"Yes, I certainly hope so. I'm Darla King. I'm part of the entertainment for this cruise. I was told I needed to meet with the other entertainers before we get underway. Here's my confirmation information." I explained as I dug out the paperwork and handed it to him. As he checked my paperwork, I gave Sam a hug and he went on his way, telling me he'd find me later.

"Welcome. My name is Joaquim Gonzalez. I am the Cruise Director. We were sorry Mr. Greenville couldn't come this year but we are happy to have you take his place. Danny here will help you with your bags and show you to your cabin

– you're on Deck 4." He motioned to the young man nearby as he continued. "Danny will also show you where the rest of the entertainers will be meeting. I commend you on your punctuality, Ms. King. You are actually the only one of your group who has arrived as yet."

His smile seemed to be permanent, if marginally sincere. With the smile firmly in place, he turned to the man behind me and began the routine again with, "Can I help you, sir?" and I realized I'd been gracefully dismissed.

"Thank you" was all I could manage to say before Danny took charge of my bags. I recognized him as the crew member who had escorted the odd man with the satchel onboard. Danny was dark-haired, brown-eyed, about 6 foot tall, and so muscular that he treated my leaden bags as if they were filled with feathers. He moved very quickly to the elevator, very businesslike and professional. I could imagine him handling things quietly and efficiently. Often, good service staff are virtually unnoticed. Danny's smooth delivery suggested that he indeed might be almost invisible as he moved through his tasks.

As the elevator closed, he pressed the "3" button and stared straight ahead, not inviting small talk. The elevator opened, and I followed Danny down the hallway. He stopped at a door labeled Lazy Lounge. He explained, "The entertainers are meeting in the Lounge here at 1:00 sharp. Your stateroom is at the other end of the ship and up one level. If you use the elevators at the end of this deck, you should not have any trouble finding your way." Danny pointed down the hall as he gave me directions. Then he was gone, the model of speed and efficiency. Unfortunately, that left me to get my baggage to my stateroom. Guess that is why it's called "self-assist." I glanced at my watch. A full morning already, and it was only 11:45. Good, I had a little time before I needed to meet the other entertainers at 1 o'clock. Instead of staying in the Lazy Lounge as I suppose Danny had assumed, I trundled down the hall to the elevator.

I found the elevator and eventually my stateroom. It was an inside stateroom and not exactly luxurious. I had the choice of upgrading my accommodations. Or I could have shared a cabin. It was much smaller than I had expected. Interior, so of course, no windows. I sighed. I should have known, I thought. I should have known it wouldn't be one of those bright, airy, open outer rooms that all the brochures show. I was after all working this cruise. Cruising for free as it were in return for my role in the square dance.

Slim had smooth-talked me into calling for him on this cruise, and I hadn't had time to think through the details. Now I was in trouble. When I get in small, closed spaces I can't breathe. This was definitely a small space! The lack of windows added to the "closed" sensation. I should have taken the upgrade option, even if it meant I'd just about break even on the cost and not come out with any profit for calling the dances.

I stepped back into the small hallway. At least it was roomier than my cabin. I took as deep a breath as I could and scolded myself. Here I was on a wonderful cruise, a chance for some relaxation and maybe some romance, and the first thing I did was complain. Straighten up, I told myself, just focus on one wall at a time, not on all four closing in at the same time. It's all mind over matter, I insisted. I stepped back through the doorway into my room.

Scanning around the cabin, I tried to find something to fool my mind into thinking it was larger. As I often do when I need to change my train of thought, I crossed over into imaginary scenarios. In this case, I imagined having a roommate in this tiny space. Picture Lucy and Ethel from I Love Lucy, I told myself. Can't you just see it?

I smiled at that scenario and felt better picturing Lucy's antics. I moved on to another imaginary scene. What about a romance? I tried to imagine the setting as romantic. It didn't work. All the space was functional, and there was very little room for walking around or even turning around. On the other hand, it would be cozy. My imagination covered the bunk with a patchwork quilt and converted the room into a pioneer cabin. The mental gymnastics worked and I found I was breathing a little easier, so I quit my mental tricks and quickly unloaded my bags. Especially all my square dance clothes. To keep from feeling my usual frumpy self, I wanted to be as unwrinkled as possible when I got on stage. I immediately put everything away. I stashed the empty bags under the bed to leave as much open space as I could. That would create more space in the small area I reminded myself to stop thinking about.

I'm usually a square dance caller and only sometimes a dancer. As either one, I mostly choose to wear the longer prairie skirts rather than the short full skirts of most dancers. My friend Carlotta, on the other hand, goes all out. She wears the traditional outfits and massive petticoats on her tiny frame. Despite her petite size, I was sure she would have more luggage than I did to accommodate her voluminous crinolines and fancy outfits. I was glad we weren't trying to share the small space of this cabin. More Lucy and Ethel scenes popped up in my mind.

Finished with unpacking clothes, I took my cosmetics and shower stuff into the bathroom. It was functional but even more limited in space. I like to think of myself as having curves rather than being overweight. One trip into this bathroom and a look at the small stall shower, I vowed to go on a diet! Minimal counter space, but I noticed that the mirror had handles. Sure enough there were some shelves behind it. I put the cosmetics, toothbrush, and other stuff in there.

I sank gratefully onto the bed to see if I could grab a quick power nap. It was relatively firm, and not too uncomfortable. If I could get over the walls closing in on me, the bed would do. Everyone had told me I'd love going on this cruise. And I was sure I would, once I got settled in. Especially whenever I wasn't in this cabin. But so far it hadn't been all that enjoyable. The close feeling didn't help any.

As I lay there, eyes closed, trying to imagine myself in an open field, I thought about the morning drive to the ship. Sam had come over to my house early this morning to carpool to Galveston. We'd gotten an early start. It's about a three-hour drive from Isquith to Galveston and Sam was good company. He never lacked for an opinion, that was for sure, so the conversation was lively.

On the way to Galveston, Sam and I had talked about our last experience with the Galveston port. We had been involved with a crime spree that made the news last month. I smiled at the coincidence that brought me and my friends from the Clearton Squares Dance Club here to the Galveston port so soon after our earlier adventures.

On the ride, Sam had kidded me about 'my' mystery and I couldn't deny it. Valuable stolen goods from across the state were eventually traced to the Port of Galveston. Unwittingly, I'd dragged Sam and my other friends from Clearton into danger. The thieves were eventually arrested, partly through the involvement of Sam, Carlotta, Doug, Nick, and me. Not exactly what you'd expect from a caller and some recreational square dancers, but our knowledge of square dancing helped crack the case. We might be the only ones who would claim that though. Having a team of amateurs assist state and federal law enforcement wasn't usually broadcast.

Sam told me I had to shoulder a lot of the blame for our involvement, and he was right.. He argued it was my background as an investigator and my innate sense of curiosity that got us in thick of things. However, I prefer to call it taking the credit rather than shouldering the blame.

Sam and I passed through some small towns before hitting Highway 45. It is usually a pretty landscape. The end of December though, the only green visible in the expanse of brown trees and grass was the occasional live oak on some of the ranches. And then some manicured lawns inside city limits. Even in the lower half of Texas the plant life feels the effects of winter. Sometimes we even get an occasional snow flurry or two.

Today was beautiful weather. Mid-50s, heading to the mid-60s, and sun shining. I had the feeling winter might be coming to an end. Maybe we'd have a mild January and February. Cows and horses were grazing, though forage wasn't too plentiful. I noticed they lacked the extra-furry winter coats that indicated a hard cold spell was on the way. Another two months or so, and this section of highway would be bordered with bluebonnets, and the land plowed for spring planting.

As we had made our way south and east, every so often we'd passed one of the large ranches that were a holdover from earlier days as often depicted in old westerns. These days, though, they looked modern. I saw more four-wheeler vehicles than horses. A sign of the times, I thought, when I saw placards indicating a couple of them were for sale. Despite a downturn in the national economy and the tough times for farmers and ranchers, many of the ranchers held on.

The ship's bells pealed and interrupted my replay of the morning's drive. I opened my eyes and looked around the box-like stateroom again. You're supposed to be resting, I told myself, not going over every tiny detail. Sleep! Nap! I closed my eyes and tried again, but the morning's events begged for my attention.

My mind continued its journey. The ride had been fairly smooth with only limited traffic problems, and we got onto Highway 45 with little problem. Sam had opted not to take the beltway to avoid the tolls. Everything was going smoothly and it looked like we would be making good time. That ended as we approached the Galveston area and exited the highway to head for the port. Clear from nowhere, an old model sedan, something like a Ford Fairlane, decided it owned the road. We were obviously driving too slowly to suit its needs. As it barreled past us, I noticed the car was gray primer and dirty white. I didn't get the license plate.

Generally, I associate wild and reckless driving with the younger bunch. My quick glimpse of the man driving as he just about forced us off the road suggested that the man was no youngster. His white hair gave him a faint halo as he stared straight ahead, not looking in our direction even once. Judging from my guess at his age, and the age and condition of the car, I was impressed with the speed he was able to maintain. I would expect to see him broken down on the side of the road. Instead he drove so fast it was like Sam and I were standing still.

Sam managed to keep our car mostly on the shoulder. His southern manners were momentarily lost and I heard language from his mouth I hadn't heard before. His language didn't improve much when he tried to pull back onto the road from the shoulder. It quickly became apparent that we had a flat tire. Sam pulled back to the shoulder. With Sam still venting, we set up to change the tire.

Why is it that spare tires are always under all the stuff you have carefully packed into the trunk? We managed to get everything out of the trunk. Sam changed the tire. Then we reloaded the trunk with only minimal loss of time. I was thankful again for the pleasant weather. But so much for our plans to arrive earlier than the rest and sail through security and boarding.

As we got back on the road and on our way, our moods gradually improved. We didn't see much of Galveston Island on our way to the dock, but some new construction was evident. I was eager to see the island, since it had gotten hit pretty hard by Hurricane Ike several years earlier. I wanted to see how it had fared. Even before Ike, Galveston had constantly struggled to retain its popularity as a tourist area.

Although the port had been here for generations, it wasn't used for cruises until it merged with the Port of Houston and expanded in the 1990s. When Sam and I arrived at the port of Galveston, the security officer directed us to the appropriate parking area and to the second pier. He pointed out that Sam could drive up to the pier and drop me off with the luggage, then park. I told Sam that wasn't necessary. I took every chance I could to get exercise, always hoping to shed a few pounds. Parking turned out to not be a problem. We quickly found the bus to the second pier. Sam noted our parking space number in his cell phone , and we were on our way.

We didn't have to walk far to get to the bus or from the bus to the terminal, so taking our bags with us wasn't a big deal. And I doubt I lost even a pound. The bus dropped us at the door to the security checkpoint. At the pier, Sam checked his bags. Looking back, he was smart. Only allowed to carry one bag, Sam had pretended one of mine really was his.

I had shipped my sound system to the cruise line ahead of time. The bags we carried were my personal belongings. Well, literally, Sam had carried the heavier of my two bags. I carried just my purse as I wheeled the lighter bag. It wasn't like my belongings were that expensive or dear. I just don't like the idea of them being tossed around. And then there are the stories of things going missing. It's probably just a control thing. Sam humored me as good friends do.

Going through security was a madhouse for the cruise, much as it would be if we were flying. The cruise was going out of the country so there were passport issues to deal with as well. The security procedures had taken forever and this was just on the way out of the country. I could only imagine what it would be like when we re-entered the United States. In retrospect, it probably would have been better if I had checked my bags. Although I marveled at the genius who thought to put wheels on luggage, I felt multiple bruises emerging on my legs from my rolling bag hitting them during quick stops.

Oh great. Now I was not only lamenting over what had gone wrong already, I was borrowing trouble from the future. As I lay on the bed mentally going through the tribulations so far today, I cheered myself by remembering I'd get a paycheck when we docked at the end of the cruise. And the cruise was free. This wasn't solely a pleasure trip for me, although I planned to have fun. The cruise was an unexpected, last-minute opportunity.

About two weeks ago I got a call from a colleague, Tom Greenville. He asked if I would do him a favor and take his place as a caller on this cruise. It was pretty good pay, sights to see in Mexico, plus a cabin for myself. Tom and I had called together many times. I enjoyed his funny, fast-paced style. I was honored that he thought I could handle a seven-day gig, but I told him I didn't think I was ready for it. I am relatively new at this caller thing, and still building my skills.

True to his nature, he laughed me into agreement. Two weeks later, here I was. Tom said I'd be sharing responsibility with two other callers including his brother, Slim Greenville. I knew Slim. The other caller would be Zach Jameson, who I didn't know. The downside was that the cruise continued over New Year's Day. Until Tom called, I had planned to celebrate with my college-age daughter, Heather.

I checked to see if Heather wanted to come along on the cruise. Sad to say, but she sounded almost relieved I'd be gone. Apparently she had already made New Year's Eve plans with her friends. She was trying to figure out how to tell me she was standing me up. Heather's 20 years old. I guess it's a normal part of her moving into adulthood. Probably not many 20 year olds want to go on a cruise with a parent. Or spend New Year's Eve with a parent. Her independence was happening more and more often. I wasn't quite used to it yet. In addition, she wasn't exactly excited about the idea a square dancing cruise. Dancing was my hobby, not hers.

When I discovered Heather didn't want to come along, I called a good friend from one of the clubs I call for, Carlotta Morris. I asked if she'd like to come on the cruise. I also invited two guys from the club, Doug Weathers and Sam. I had thought maybe Carlotta and I could share a stateroom, but she and her dance partner Nick Tricot had other plans. Doug and Sam had agreed to come, and were sharing a stateroom to save money. The group rate applied and the cruise hadn't sold out, so they all got a reduction to the cost.

Carlotta, Doug, and Sam make up part of what I think of as the Clearton Gang. Originally I called them the Three Musketeers. The addition of me and then Nick to our group of friends that name no longer fit. I'd gotten to be close friends with Carlotta, Doug, and Sam the last couple of years since I'd become the club caller. We all got to know Nick earlier in the year when he was the intended victim of the theft ring in our recent adventure. He was a dancer from the Stepping Squares club in Fort Worth. Anyway, all four accepted my invitation to join me on the cruise. Now instead of the Musketeers I thought of us as the Clearton Gang.

Despite the short time we'd all known Nick, he and Carlotta spent a lot of time together. Nick was driving down from Fort Worth and picking up Doug and Carlotta in Clearton. They drove to Galveston together. Sam had already been visiting friends up near my hometown of Isquith, and so he offered to share his ride. That way we'd only have two cars to transport the whole Clearton Gang.

Promotional flyers featuring the dance cruise had been sent out to other Texas clubs and nationally. Several dancers from various clubs I call for had decided to come on the cruise when they heard I'd be calling. There were other dancers from the Clearton Squares Dance Club too. In addition to Clearton, I regularly call for the Forsby Footstompers and occasionally for other clubs in the Houston and Austin areas. Altogether, I already knew about fifteen dancers from these clubs who would be here. The expectation was that there would be dozens of square dancers on the cruise. I didn't know who had booked the cruise, but there might be others from Forsby and Clearton. I called at a number of regional events, so I might even know some others.

So, here I was, barely two days after Christmas, on a cruise. Not that I would be free and clear to simply socialize and enjoy the cruise, mind you. I would, however, get to enjoy the stops and shore excursions and spend some time with friends. Hopefully, I would be able to relax. In the back of my mind was the suggestion of an idea that maybe Doug and I would be able to move our shaky relationship ahead a little. More importantly from a career perspective, this would be my debut as an international caller.

As I lay in the stateroom, it dawned on me that I was looking forward to this cruise, both to the places we'd put into port and to the rest and relaxation it would provide. And here I thought I'd been dreading it. No. It was eight days of tropical warmth, coming on the tails of a busy holiday season. Today we'd ship out, tomorrow we'd be at sea all day. The next day we'd put into port at Progreso, Mexico, with Cozumel the next. I was particularly looking forward to seeing Belize on the fifth day, which would be New Year's Eve. I figured the two days after that would be particularly restful, as we'd be at sea on our way home, and then the ship would pull into Galveston on the morning of the eighth day.

In the face of that realization, I moved on to thinking about what I needed to do. In the get-to-know-your-shipmates activities this evening, I would be calling with Slim and Zach at a square dance for both experienced dancers and non-dancers. Tomorrow, during our first full day at sea, the schedule called for workshops morning and afternoon, and an evening dance. There would be additional evening dances on various days we docked. The cruise would end with a 'trail out' dance on the last night. All in all, it wasn't bad because most of the rest of my time would be my own. A worrier deep down, I still wasn't sure how it was all supposed to come together. By nature, I prefer predictability and structure to my life. Not fully grasping how this cruise was going to work was a little anxiety-provoking.

My mind was racing and wouldn't let me sleep. I had about decided to give up on this nap thing and just get up. I was obviously too wound up to get any rest. I figured I'd try just once more. I started a relaxation exercise my grief counselor had shown me. I began at my toes, tightening each muscle then relaxing it. I continued the process up to my calves, tightening each muscle and relaxing it. Then I focused further up my body, tensing and relaxing each muscle. I tried to put the coming week into perspective and get some order to the cruise activities. I hoped that would help me relax enough to go to sleep.

I was enjoying new opportunities like this one in the new life I'd created for myself in Texas. New things were important as I moved into a new stage of life. But it didn't make them any easier to embrace when they came with such uncertainty. I like to be prepared. It's hard to be prepared when you don't know what you're preparing for.

It's not like I've always wanted to be a square dance caller. In fact, I haven't always wanted to be anything in particular. I've been a wife and an attorney and a civil servant, and dabbled in a number of other vocations and avocations. I've been, and still am, mom to a beautiful, wonderful, thoughtful, intelligent (most of the time) daughter currently off at The University of Texas. I suppose you could say I'm still an attorney, too, in the sense of 'once a lawyer always a lawyer.' But I haven't practiced in years. My most recent profession prior to calling square dances in Texas was in Florida. I was with the State Attorney's Office as an investigator. While it called on my lawyering skills, it didn't actually require any specific court time. It was a profession where my natural curiosity was an advantage, even if it did bring me into some rough spots.

My life took a sharp turn a little less than five years ago. It pretty much derailed any directions I thought my life might be headed. Clint, the love of my life, my husband, father of my beautiful daughter, and the man I planned to grow old with died in the line of duty. At the same time, all hell broke loose at my office. I was in no condition to handle it. I pretty much fell apart and took my responsibilities down with me. I left the job with hard feelings on both sides. As a result, I seldom keep up with any of my colleagues.

I regretted the situation at work and failing my coworkers, but not nearly so much as the situation I had created at home. Heather and I had each fallen deep into our own types of grief. It was months before I even realized I'd left my then 15-year-old daughter to cope with the death of her father with no emotional support from me. We have rebuilt our bridges since then. Unfortunately, there is still some remaining baggage even after therapy, change of scenery, and new beginnings. Heather and I are taking it one day at a time. But I still carry a load of guilt for how I dealt with Clint's death all the way around.

I finally surfaced from my depths of self-pity following Clint's death, thanks to a very good therapist. I stepped out of my self-imposed isolation to an activity that was familiar and safe for me – square dancing. I had square danced before I was married. Clint and I had both been active dancers before Heather was born. Then life got in the way and we never found the time to dance. I had always found the square dancing community to be warm, friendly, and supportive. After his death I chose dancing to make my reentry into life.

I never expected to become a caller. Another caller suggested it. I love to sing, so I decided to give it a chance. I never expected a lot of things I've encountered in my life. Like this cruise for example. I thought it was fitting that the ship was named Journey. Not just because we were traveling on it, but because this was a new step in my personal and professional journey.

It had been an unpredictable day so far, and my brain insisted on reviewing it even as I doggedly continued my relaxation exercise. Something seemed to be digging at the back of my mind and wouldn't let go. Until I figured out what it was, I doubted I would get any peace. So without bidding, my mind started over again. Sam's arrival at my house this morning, our predawn departure. I replayed the drive to Galveston and that crazy driver and our flat tire. I thought about the tiresome security requirements and the time spent prepping to board. Oh, and then there was that incident with the grumpy man who fell on the boarding ramp.

Finally, I dozed off somewhere toward the end of rehashing the man's fall on the ramp. As I slipped into sleep, I wondered idly why he seemed to be more concerned about the contents of his bag than he was for his glasses or even himself. Maybe it contained his laptop and he was afraid it would break. Maybe, but the bag wasn't a computer case by design. He didn't exactly strike me as a techno geek. There was something familiar about him, but I couldn't be sure what. Thankfully, that was the last thought I had before my mind finally caved in and let me drift off.

I awoke with a start, realized it was about 12:30 and I would have to hustle to get to my 1 o'clock meeting. I freshened up and bumped my hip as I turned around too fast in the small bathroom. I wondered how many bruises I would have as mementos by the end of the week. I grabbed my keycard, my purse, and my camera and headed out. I would have to figure out how to use the cabin safe at some point, but I didn't have time right now.

CHAPTER 2

"Is that you, Darla?" I heard as I paused in the hallway to check that my stateroom door was locked.

Turning around in the hallway, I saw Slim Greenville and another man walking toward me. Slim may have been slim once upon a time, but as with most of us, he had put on a little weight with age. He sported a baseball cap, probably to hide his slight balding.

"It's me, Slim." I smiled and gave him a quick hug. I turned to the younger man with him. "And you must be Zach."

"Zach Jameson at your service," responded the man with Slim as he gave me a hug. Judging from his age, I guessed the reason I didn't know Zach was that he had been calling even less time than I had. And he must have started at age 16! Hmmm. The cruise hadn't even started and between Danny, and now Zach, I was beginning to feel old. A very nice-looking man, tall, with sculpted shoulders showing through his shirt, he obviously found time to work out between gigs. How do people find time to exercise and work out when I couldn't, I wondered guiltily. A thought popped into my head from somewhere. Perhaps Zach and the young woman from the boarding line might have something in common.

Zach was nice-looking alright. That is, if I ignored the tattoo on his arm. I couldn't quite decide what it was, and didn't want to stare. And I might not get to figure it out, since I probably wouldn't see the whole thing. For square dances, men always wear long sleeves, even in the Texas heat. Wouldn't want the ladies to touch a sweaty arm, or in this case a tattooed arm, would we? True to the tradition, Zach was wearing a long-sleeved shirt, white with a western rose on the yoke. The sleeves were rolled to his elbows, though, and the tattoo peeked out just beneath the sleeve. I wasn't a fan of tattoos, and I seemed to be seeing them everywhere and on everyone these days.

"Nice to meet you, Zach. Been calling long?" I asked.

"Zach's been calling with some other callers in New Mexico for a while. Then he started calling with me, and recently he has taken over some of the clubs that Tony used to call for," Slim explained. A mutual friend, Tony was the person who suggested I take up calling. He had retired recently after calling for over 20 years. I heard that he had to retire due to health issues, but had lost touch with him in the past few months.

It was not surprising that Zach was able to find clubs in need of callers. As the population of callers and even the dancers ages, a number of clubs in Texas, and maybe everywhere, are without regular callers. All in all, it was good that Zach and other young callers were ready and interested in stepping up to take on some of the work. Square dancing is a long-standing form of American folk dance. It would be terrible if it were to fade away.

As we walked along the hallway, Zach chimed in with a smile that went all the way to his eyes. "I caught the square dance bug by going to dances with my parents. The excitement and enjoyment of the dancers was contagious. Of course, you have to know the moves to call them, but I'm a caller more than a dancer. My parents still square dance and know some other callers in New Mexico – Dwayne Piston, Buddy Cezach. You ever heard of them?" he asked, his enthusiasm high.

"I've seen their names, but never met them or heard them call. But then I haven't been to many of the national conferences yet. So they got you into calling, huh?" I replied, guessing where his story was going.

"Yup. When my parents told them I liked to sing they brought me up on the stage as a little tyke. When I got older it seemed like a fun part-time job. I got to meet a lot of different people. Like many callers, I have a day job. I still have fun calling, though. It doesn't interfere with my regular job as a high school teacher and coach. Calling on a cruise ship is a new experience for me. Actually, I've never even been on a cruise before," Zach explained. His enthusiasm seemed a bit dampened by anxiety – or maybe I was just reading my anxiety into it.

"I've only been calling for a few years myself," I offered. As we stepped onto the elevator I continued by sharing, " I have never called on a cruise ship before either," to let him know that he wasn't alone if he was having some misgivings.

We got off the elevator and approached the lounge that Danny had showed me earlier, joining a variety of other entertainers inside. About twenty of us, it looked like. Some were likely the cruise staff and the cruise line's regular singers and dancers. Some of the others, I assumed, like us, were only hired for this one cruise.

I was glad to see there were some sandwiches and other goodies on a side bar, as well as something to drink. Food tends to be aplenty on a cruise, and that apparently goes for the entertainers as well as the guests. I headed over and snagged a sandwich quarter. I guess the caterers who cut the sandwiches this way figure the sandwiches will go further if they're cut smaller. Either that or it's a nod to healthy eating through serving size. Serving size didn't stop me, and I added a couple more sandwich quarters of what looked like multi-grain bread, watercress, spinach, and tomato. There were surprisingly tasty and filling.

"Attention please! Can I have your attention please?" The man who had introduced himself to me as Joaquim earlier shouted at the gathering group, apparently trying to get the chatter under control.

"We have a very limited time here to go over the responsibilities and expectations for the cruise before we embark. I will try to make it short." He distributed schedules of the various activities and who should be where when with what. The cruise had just about everything musical, from chamber music to dancing to DJs to excerpts from Broadway. And for this cruise, square dancing. At least two or three activities were possible for passengers each night. And then some were available during the days. Definitely something for everyone's taste, I thought. For those less musically inclined, there were a comedian and a magician. Other than the entertainers, I knew there were also exercise and spa activities, as well as a game room, ping pong, and other activities, all floating out to sea on the Journey!

I looked around the room, curious. I noticed that as a group we ranged in age from under 20 to much older than me. One man looked to be in his 70s or so, a little stooped over, and looking tired. I imagine I looked a little tired as well, and made an effort to stand up straighter. My guess was that he would be with the chamber music group. On the other hand, the young guy dressed in jeans and western shirt I guessed was one of the DJs. The one with the cage and rabbit, and the young voluptuous lady on his arm, well, I hoped he was the magician. The tall hunk with the cowboy hat and ostrich boots, I pegged as the country-western DJ or maybe a singer.

I figured that as time went on, I would find out just how close to the mark I was in my mental guesswork. Joaquim, the veritable professional, continued with his litany of rules and directions, most of which I missed while musing about my comrades. I started listening again. He introduced the lead singers and dancers from the cruise company. He also introduced some of the others. I chided myself when he introduced one of my 'probably' DJs as Justin, the piano player.

"For the regular cruise staff, we do expect you to mingle with the rest of the passengers, and particularly today when most of them will be on the decks and socializing as we proceed out to sea. For the rest of you, that is a request only. The regular crew is expected to help with our lifeboat drill at 5:30 today. The others of you," he looked toward our little group, "will be participating in the drill." He then dismissed all the continuing cruise staff, who supposedly knew what they'd be doing. That left only the piano-playing Justin, the magician, the hunky cowboy DJ, and us. He paused, then continued with a slightly less authoritative tone.

"Folks, I'm sorry to say that somehow at the security checkpoint, there was a problem. With the hurried transfer of some staff and entertainers from another ship, some of the bags were left open. It is possible that your CDs, DVDs, or other items are among those that ended up loose. I hope those of you who have CDs and DVDs can quickly ascertain if you have all of yours in your luggage. If not, we have collected all the loose ones. If you cannot find something of yours, let me know and I will try to help you locate it or obtain a substitute." Joaquim explained this all apologetically as he gestured toward a large bundle of about 150 discs. "In the meantime, if your equipment was labeled as such, it has been moved here. If only labeled by your stateroom, it will be delivered to your staterooms tonight."

"As you get yourself acclimated to the ship, please feel free to partake of the refreshments on the sidebar in case you didn't have a chance to eat," he said. His ever-present professional demeanor slipped and his discomfort with having to tell us about this slip-up showed through. By way of dismissal, he suggested that we check our gear, check out our designated locations, and enjoy the cruise.

As he was leaving, he added, "We do hope you enjoy the cruise. Danny will be here to help with any problems." He gestured to the crew member who had escorted me to my cabin.

Slim, Zach and I exchanged looks. We all milled around, helped ourselves to the food or visited with the other entertainers. The hunky cowboy introduced himself as Mark. One man arrived just as Joaquim was leaving, and Joaquim had a private conversation with him. I wasn't sure if it was a reprimand for being late, a summary of what he had told us, some combination, or something altogether different. As I tried to find my sound system in the maze of equipment, he stopped by and introduced himself to me. His name was Chance. It was easy to remember, since it was only by 'chance' that I was on this cruise. He explained that he was a country singer. In turn I told him my role as a caller. As most folks do, he expressed some surprise at my profession.

The boxes that had been shipped ahead or come through security were scattered everywhere. It was one very big mess, and did not speak well for the cruise line in my mind. I sure hoped they did a better job with the passenger luggage, or I figured they'd be hearing about it from unhappy cruisers. Once I located all the gear I had shipped, I checked my sound equipment. The main components, speakers, and extra microphones seemed to be intact. Most of the CDs seemed to be in the sleeves where I recalled putting them as I readied for the trip. I did notice one by 'Snooping Dog and the Cubs,' what appeared to be a rap group. I knew that wasn't mine, and I took it up to Danny. This left me with one empty disc pocket and unfortunately my list of music was in my cabin. I had no clue which one was missing.

"I think this one got stuck in my bag by mistake," I told Danny. "It'll take me a little longer to figure out which one I'm missing. Maybe if I just look through the 'random' ones you collected, I can figure it out." Some of my CDs were commercially produced, but not all. Some weren't in fancy printed cases, just blank CDs in clear cases. These would have my scribbled scrawl to indicate the songs by track. If the missing CD was one of the handwritten ones, it would be easy to spot.

Danny shook his head, but not in refusal. He was also apparently disturbed by the state of affairs but maintained a practiced smile. He shrugged as he pointed to the stack. "Happy searching. Just add that one to the stack. I promise you this is an unusual occurrence. Another ship barely made it into the nearest dock. The staff and entertainment crew were shuffled all around with very little notice so we could remain on schedule. That really made a mess for all of us. I am sorry. Please let me know if I can help at all." As earlier, Danny struck me as a very efficient, helpful employee.

I looked over at the stack and decided that it wouldn't be very productive to search through it right now after all. I walked over and browsed the loose discs briefly. I figured if I waited until the other entertainers pulled theirs first, it would be easier to find mine. I noticed at least three other discs by Snooping Dog and his crew as I added mine to the stack. Must be a popular group. I wasn't surprised I hadn't heard of them. I'm not too much of a rap fan, and the name sounded like that might be what it was. There were no pictures on the case, so I couldn't tell the age or gender of the group.

Maybe after the rest of the folks pared down the pile it wouldn't seem so insurmountable to find my one missing CD. I reassured myself that the likelihood of anyone taking square dance discs was slim. Most of the CDs that callers use aren't much good to anyone else. Each song is usually on the CD twice. Once would be instrumental only, for the caller to provide the calls in real-time. The second time would be the same music but the calls would already be voiced. That way, dancers could practice without a live caller if they wanted. These double-down discs were mostly commercially produced, but some callers recorded their own the same way. Most callers now used computerized song lists, or CDs as I did. I wasn't quite sure who would use DVDs in the entertainer group. I supposed maybe DJs were getting more creative or contemporary. We did live in an age where technology was associated with being progressive.

Slim fired off questions in rapid succession as he joined me in surveying the mess of CDs on the table. "So, Darla, did your equipment make it? Pretty sloppy of security to not close all the bags, huh?" He flipped idly through the discs on the table. "Some of these CDs aren't even in cases. You all ready for tonight's dance? Got the CDs you need to call a few? I've never heard of this 'Snooping Dog' dude, have you? There's enough CDs of his group, though, to be a publicity gimmick or a give-away! Somebody must like him." Slim was clearly upset. Talking non-stop, at this rate, was not normal.

"Looking at this mess, I'm feeling kind of lucky. I'm only missing one CD but I'm not sure which one it is," I replied. "If I can't tell which one it is, I figure I won't miss it. Other than that, I guess I'm as ready as I can be."

"I don't know about you," said Slim, "but I'll feel better after I get everything set up and check out my sound system. First I guess I need to change my shirt, maybe mingle a bit, and talk up the dance tonight. I didn't get a chance to grab any lunch, so those sandwiches sure look good. I understand that for anything we want, we use our stateroom keycards. Apparently, nobody other than the casino uses cash or credit cards." Slim barely stopped to breathe between sentences. He also didn't stop to wait for a response. He just grinned his trademark smile and waved as he walked toward the door to head to the deck area. I noticed he picked up a plateful of sandwiches on his way out.

I thought about just how much mingling I could do. Small talk isn't my strong point, I don't like it, and I don't do it well. According to the schedule Joaquim just handed out, champagne would be flowing on all deck levels from 3 until 5 o'clock as part of the 'meet and greet' activities before pulling out to sea. The champagne might help me schmooze, but for now I was just hungry. Following Slim's lead, I grabbed a couple more of the quarter-sandwiches. This time I took some with what appeared to be chicken filling. In deference to my vow to diet, I piled some carrots on my plate as well.

After I munched my goodies, I made my way to Deck 5 and over to the Dreams Dance Club where the schedule said we would be calling dances. Zach was already there, and together we checked out the acoustics and set up his equipment on the main stage. Now it would be ready for use later on. He indicated it looked like he was missing a few CDs, but he'd figure out which ones later on. We planned to use only his sound system tonight, so I put my equipment at the back of the stage to check later.

A few crew members stood around looking busy, though it didn't really look like they were doing anything constructive. I had yet to see Joaquim or Danny without a smile in place for more than a fleeting minute, but I noticed these crew members weren't practicing their smiles at all. Nor were they dressed the way I expected. They wore the standard black work pants, but instead of a crisp cotton shirt they had well-worn undershirts that showed heavily tattooed arms. What is it with tattoos these days?

As they talked, I sometimes recognized a word or two in Spanish or some language that sounded like Spanish. My Spanish wasn't good enough to get the gist of what they were saying. My impression was that Zach and I had interrupted a private conversation among the group. Slim came in as Zach and I finished setting up the equipment.

"Whoa, you guys are way ahead of me. I better set up and check my equipment. I also need to check I have all the CDs I want to use. Do we use the whole room, I hope?" he asked, looking around. The Dreams was a large all-purpose room. There were dividers sticking out a little from the wall. It looked like these could be pulled out to separate the room into smaller sections.

"For tonight's welcome dance we're using the whole room," I answered. "Zach said we could all use his system tonight. Tomorrow we split up for the workshops. Then we'll need our own equipment. Those partitions over there will create three rooms," I explained. "There's a schedule and diagram on the corner of the stage. The DJ doing country western will be in the other, smaller room across the way. Hopefully, there isn't a lot of interference between his music and ours."

Slim nodded and then looked over at the crew members, still in conversation but not doing much else. Looking back our way, he raised his eyebrows at Zach and I. We both just shrugged our shoulders. We still had over an hour before the festivities and drill, so I headed back to my room to try to rest up and change clothes.

Part of me dreaded going back to my matchbox of a room. On the other hand, I had been too anxious about the cruise to sleep well last night. Then I had to get up early this morning to make the trip to Galveston. My short nap in the cabin today had left me feeling groggy more than anything. On top of that, I had a feeling it was going to be a very long afternoon and evening. And for some reason, I was already getting stressed out. Mingling and small talk tended to drain me of energy, so I needed to start with a full tank. Despite my claustrophobic nature, retreating to my cabin seemed the best option. It also meant I could check my music list with the CDs in my case to see which one was missing.

I thought about taking the elevator to Deck 4, but with so many people gathered at the elevators, I took the stairs. When I got to the room, I pulled out my music list, but realized I'd left the discs with my sound system back in the Dreams Club. I just couldn't seem to get it all together. Other than that, there wasn't much to do in the room, since I finished unpacking earlier. I lay down on the miniature bed and took some deep breaths. Just as before, after a few mental calisthenics, I eventually slipped into a restless nap. I awoke with a start, my brain not up to speed, when I heard someone knock at the door and call my name.

"Darla? Darla, are you in there?"

The voice was tentative, but it clearly belonged to my friend Carlotta. I was glad that she'd been able to make arrangements in her life to book this cruise on short notice. I'd known Carlotta several years now. As with Sam, we became friends because I'd become the caller for the Clearton Squares Dance Club. Some years younger than me, Carlotta positively bustled with energy and enthusiasm. In her mid-30s, the high-energy petite redhead always looked cute and perky, no matter what. Carlotta and I hit it off immediately and had become good friends. Our friendship strengthened earlier this fall when we shared the harrowing experience of being kidnapped. All because my curiosity got us involved with a theft investigation.

"Yep, Carlotta, it's me. On the way," I called out. I rolled off the tiny bed and crossed the few feet to the door. When I opened it, I saw Carlotta's face flushed with excitement and eyes wide. She had her life preserver in her hand.

"Come on, Darla! Everyone's up on Decks 10 and higher. The champagne and hors d'oeuvres are wonderful. Everyone is getting ready for the ship to leave dock! Let's go. We don't want to miss it! Don't forget your life preserver.

They said we have some kind of drill as soon as we take off," spewed Carlotta. Her red hair spiked out all over her head as usual, and she exuded energy.

"And hello to you, too, Carlotta!" I laughed. Carlotta runs on fast and faster. She laughed in return and gave me a quick hug, then grabbed my hand and pulled me into the hallway.

"Hold on," I protested. "I need my purse. But I don't think we need our life jackets. I understand that we just go to where our station is. We can drop yours back in your room on the way." The information sheet in my cabin explained that the cruise line no longer drilled with life jackets. Instead of going to the boats, we would simply go to locations where we would assemble based on where our staterooms were.

"Well, okay, but hurry, and I guess you need this too," she said, handing me my name tag.

"Where'd that come from?" I asked.

"It was in this plastic mailbox next to your door. Come on—Nick, Sam, and Doug are on deck holding a space for us. We can wave to the landlubbers like nobility setting out to sea!" she exclaimed.

As I grabbed my stuff, I checked my watch and about fell over. It was nearing 5 o'clock already. I had slept almost 3 hours and I wasn't even dressed for mingling or tonight's dance. Oh well, I'd just have to go as is. Not off to a great start, I thought. Thank heavens Carlotta had come by my room, or I would have missed the lifeboat drill.

I followed her to the elevators and then we headed to Deck 10. All the time, she kept up a steady stream of words. She had run into Slim and he had told her my cabin number, she said. Her cabin was 6215, just a few doors down from mine toward the front of the ship, but she was on the Deck 6, not Deck 4. She hadn't gotten the number of the men's cabins yet, but she thought they were relatively close to her cabin. No one from our little group had upgraded to the higher decks or staterooms with a balcony. From what she'd seen through my door just now she thought her room was a bit larger than mine. It also had a large picture window over the ocean. That sure would have helped my claustrophobia.

Take a breath, Carlotta, I thought. I'm still waking up. I considered asking her if her room was big enough that I could share it with her, but decided that wouldn't really be fair. She came on the cruise expecting a room of her own. I could imagine all her colorful petticoats taking up most of the open space in her cabin like so many super-sized scoops of cotton candy. And besides that, I really didn't want to come right out and ask where Nick was sleeping these days.

It was a good thing we'd had friends to hold us a spot, because the deck was ringed with passengers with champagne flutes waving gaily to the people on the pier. Carlotta and I wound our way around the perimeter of the deck looking for familiar faces. I spotted them at the same instant Doug turned around to look for us.

"There they are," I told Carlotta. "Over there by the lady in the big red hat." We headed toward the landmark of questionable taste. As we walked past different groups, I could hear smatterings of different languages. Living in Texas, I was used to hearing English and Spanish. Now I was hearing other languages as well. I wondered how many people flew in to take this cruise.

"Darla, great to see you," said Doug. I gave him a quick hug and slid in beside him. I turned and quickly said hello to Nick with a quick hug and Sam. I've known Doug longer than any of the other three. In fact, he's one of the reasons I ended up calling for Clearton Squares. More importantly, since I moved back to Texas, we've had an on-and-off relationship of sorts. Right now we were in the on phase. I was hoping for a chance to nurture the romance with him during the cruise. He slid one arm around my waist and lifted up the other in a wave to no one in particular. I chuckled to myself that the scenery behind the few folks below us was mostly industrial. I didn't bother to take a picture.

"You all set for the dance tonight?" he asked, a smile on his face.

"Well, sort of. I checked on my sound system when I got onboard to make sure all the pieces arrived. I haven't tried it out yet. Oh, and one CD is missing. They had some kind of a problem in security with the stuff that was shipped and luggage in security. After the lifeboat drill, I'm going to look for it. I was going to do that earlier, but I fell asleep instead," I confessed. "I might have to beg, borrow, or steal something from Slim and Zach, but I think I'll have enough of my own music." I looked around to see if Slim or Zach was around, but didn't see either of them. That was alright. I was happy to stay in Doug's arms.

"So did you get your luggage yet?" I asked Doug, but directed my gaze to include Sam, Nick and Carlotta as well.

"Not yet," Doug answered. "I don't think it will be at our rooms until after dinner. The others nodded and then looked at the pier as it appeared to move away from us.

"Look at the view! Can you believe this?" Carlotta's excitement was contagious, and we all watched in awe as the cruise ship effortlessly maneuvered out of the port and the city of Galveston faded away. Sirens sounded and we all headed for the stairwells. Crew members looked at our keys and told us where we needed to go. Because our group was all booked in the same general region of the ship, we stayed together.

We were directed to the Dreams of all places, so I already felt at home, and we stood together as we waited for instructions. Several crew members were located throughout the room. One crew member stopped to chat with any family with children. A voice, presumably the captain, welcomed us through the public address system. He explained that this was a federal requirement and directed crew to check to be sure all staterooms were empty. When the crowd was in place, the public address system continued with relevant announcements. Basically, the voice told us that this would be our emergency station in case of an emergency signal. On cue, the siren gave three short bursts. It startled me and I jumped slightly, but most of the folks took it in stride. A good number of them were repeat cruisers and used to this drill, I imagined. A crew member demonstrated operation of his life jacket.

The captain then stressed the importance of basic personal safety. He called attention to various hand sanitizers and the need to wash hands frequently for the good health of all. He explained that with concern for the spread of germs, none of the crew would be shaking hands. I thought that was taking things a little too far, myself. He thanked everyone for their cooperation in the drill. The siren gave one short blast, and I was proud I didn't jump this time.

"That's the all-clear signal, folks," said the crew member. "You can all head on out. Remember that this is your emergency station. The first seating of dinner tonight will start at 6:30, but the food court on Deck 10 is now open again. Have fun and enjoy your cruise!"

As people started to file out of Dreams, it occurred to me this was an excellent chance to publicize square dancing. I regretted not having put on the clothes I'd wear tonight. With a smile plastered on my face, I started shaking hands like a hometown preacher following a rousing revival service.

"Hi, I'm Darla King. I'll be calling a square dance here in the Dreams Club tonight. Stop by and try it out." I repeated variations of the same words while everyone tried to exit. My friends laughed some, but Sam joined in. The others hung back until most of the crowd has exited, then we made our way out of Dreams and went to our rooms. We were assigned to the early dining option and would meet there. That gave me about 30 minutes to freshen up and change my shirt, still delaying dressing for the evening's dance. Once on Deck 4, I managed to find my room, smiling at other passengers as I made my way.

Dressed and stressed, I returned to Deck 3 and located the Galaxy Dining Room. Several dining room staff waited for passengers. As I walked up, a gentleman, maître'd by his uniform, wished me a good evening and asked for my stateroom key. He then directed a waitress to escort me to table 357. Slim and Zach were already seated at the large, round table. I joined them, and shortly thereafter, Nick, Carlotta, Doug, and Sam arrived. Four others joined our table as well. It ended up they were also square dancers. They were from a club in Oklahoma and friendly. Not unusual—most square dancers are friendly.

Between ordering and courses, we all conversed. Obviously, the major topics were the cruise and square dancing. When I couldn't smile anymore and was starting to worry about the dance, I headed for my stateroom. I stayed just long enough to change into my dance clothes. I donned a western style denim prairie skirt, western shirt, and calf-high boots. I freshened my makeup and tossed my hair. My straight short bob made it easy to get ready, but is nothing spectacular. Generally, my hairdo is much more likely to be termed practical than cute. It really wasn't much to fuss with.

CHAPTER 3

Once I was dressed, I headed to the Dreams Club for the welcome dance. I was a little worried, and unsure how many people would come. I had met a few of the guests as I mingled and then the couple from Oklahoma at our table. I had no real idea of how many people would come to square dance on a cruise. Slim had looked over the guest information the cruise line had given him. He told me that there were about forty identified as experienced square dancers. They had specifically booked with the square dance group. With four couples per square that would give us about five squares, not counting any new dancers. And it was possible that some hadn't booked through the square dance option.

As I headed to the Dreams, I saw the guy I had spotted earlier in western gear. He still sported western boots, cowboy hat, and very large belt buckle. He caught my eye and waved as he disappeared into the smaller venue behind the Dreams. I had looked at information on the ship's layout before I came onboard so I'd have less chance of getting lost once I got to the ship. I remembered that in addition to the Dreams, this deck also held a large casino, two nightclubs with singers or DJs, at least a couple of bars and shops, and a theater where there would be shows at various times. The room he ducked into was the country western nightclub. I patted myself on the shoulder that I had pegged him right during my earlier guesses about entertainers. I looked at the setup for the two musical venues so close together. I hoped the acoustics would be good enough so we wouldn't be competing.

Tonight's square dance would use the full space of the Dreams Club. The idea tonight was to appeal to all passengers, whether they were already square dancers or not.

It was also an ice breaker to help everyone get acquainted with others on the ship. That was why the dance area was not being divided up into smaller sections tonight. We would divide it up tomorrow, when we started calling dances by ability levels.

On land, square dance classes can last several months, but many callers are used to hosting open nights called 'fun nights.' The idea of a 'fun night' is to teach enough calls during an evening to manage a few simple patterns and introduce non-dancers to the sport. The hope is that they will like it and take lessons. Lessons wouldn't really occur on the cruise, but we'd be using the fun night concept to lead dances that would appeal to all levels of dancers. Later on, we would hold workshops so that new dancers could get additional instruction and seasoned dancers could get better.

Some dances would actually be limited to seasoned dancers or at least folks who had finished lessons. But a few events, like tonight's dance, would be open to anyone who just wanted to have fun. I hoped that Mandy, the young woman from the boarding ramp, would stop by and give it a try. She looked like she needed a little fun, she was alone, and square dancing needed an influx of younger dancers. On the other hand, admittedly, I wouldn't be disappointed if the grumpy man with the satchel didn't make it.

After the welcome show in the large auditorium down the hall, the loud speaker directed guests to the various activities for the evening. I was surprised, as guests slowly filtered into the Dreams, at how quickly the dance floor filled up. Obviously a good number had listened to the announcement, were at least curious about square dancing, and had made it past the casino and bars. I noticed that some did go into the adjacent night club. Zach, Slim, and I moved to where we had set up our equipment on the stage at the end of the dance floor and the evening began.

"Welcome to the Dreams Dance Club square dance! I'm Zach, this here is Slim, and the lovely lady is Darla. We will be your callers tonight and for the rest of the cruise. For tonight at least, we will start with some basic square dance moves and see where we can go. We will try to give the experienced dancers a chance to strut their stuff before the night is over, but in the meantime everyone is invited to dance. Come on now, get out there on the floor! Start out by forming two circles. One circle needs to be inside the other. Don't be shy. Line up boy-girl, boy-girl," Zach was smiling and laughing, waving the guests who seemed hesitant onto the floor. His mood was contagious and the passengers were laughing despite any nervousness on the part of those trying something new.

"This is supposed to be fun, so just treat it as playtime and don't worry if you step on someone's toes. On second thought, if any of you gents have steel tips on your boots, you may want to worry! Make sure that men and women are alternated in the circles. The inside circle faces out, the outside circle faces in. That's it folks. You're almost square dancers already!" Zach continued his directions, his tone both directive and supportive. His good looks, athletic build, blue eyes, and dimpled smile didn't hurt when it came to crowd appeal. He wore a long-sleeved shirt buttoned at his wrists, as I anticipated, completely covering his tattoo.

Slim and I helped get the dancers in one circle or the other. With some, that took additional prompting. Cruise ship personnel had assured us that they would provide extra males if we needed them. Joaquim had reassured us about that at our entertainers' meeting today. I assumed this meant they would require some of the crew to dance. The hitch was that we needed to determine if we should call them on the promise. I think it is pretty well true in every form of dance that women are more interested than men. So, no surprise, there is generally a shortage of men in square dancing. Sure enough, we needed about three more men to even it all out so I made the call to Joaquim to let him know.

Zach filled time by going into the history of square dance and the traditional costumes, using Carlotta and some of the other women who were in square dance garb to make his point. Carlotta often got chosen for this type of exhibition because she's petite, cute, and all the petticoats and frills look good on her. She loved bright colors, shiny fabrics, and wearing the traditional square dance 'big skirts' so she was a walking ad for square dance apparel. As Zach finished up and Carlotta returned to the circle, several of the male guests tried to shift their positions to get closer to her. This was also a pretty common occurrence. Since she and Nick had became a couple, the other men didn't stand a chance.

Three male crew members showed up and looked for us to tell them what to do. I was a little taken aback. Two of them were the same discontented crew members who had been here earlier when we came to check everything out. On the positive side, now they were dressed in the standard crisp uniforms and did have on long-sleeved shirts so, like Zach, their tattoos were nearly hidden. One of them had a tattoo that peeked out from beneath his cuff and crawled a little ways up his hand, but it wasn't too bad. If they would just smile once in a while, they might even fit in. The third man was less sullen and didn't have any tattoos that I could see.

All three of them looked awkward and uncomfortable. I could tell they were not particularly thrilled with the idea of square dancing. A little rough around the edges, to say the least, but they would fill the bill. I placed them where they needed to be in the circle, tried to get them to smile, and gave Zach the sign to start up.

"Everyone join hands and circle left. Now circle right. Now circle left. Now, let's start dancing! The first thing you need to know is that men, your partner is the lady in your right hand. Ladies, your partner is the dude in your left hand. No matter how many times I move you around, remember, your partner is not any particular person, but the person who is to your right for the guy and to your left for the lady. Now for the test! Drop hands with anyone who's not your partner, and hold up the hand of your partner!"

Slim and I circled behind the dancers helping them get it right. It's amazing how hard it is for adults to know their right hands from their left hands. When everyone was holding hands with their partners, Zach continued.

"Great job, everyone. Turn and face your partner – that's the person you're holding hands with. Now, walk forward to your partner, then sideways so that you pass each other on the right, then back to back, and then backwards to your starting point. Good! Try it again, but this time just walk backwards to your original location." Zach kept his tone light and encouraging. Slim and I were on the floor watching and encouraging folks as Zach called instructions. One of the crew volunteers was definitely a reluctant dancer and I almost considered pulling him out, but that would have created a scene. Instead, I just made sure he knew I was watching him and nodded to him in encouragement. I occasionally prompted him where he should end up, thinking he might be having trouble understanding English. As I walked around, I saw Mandy had come in and I smiled at her.

"Pass going forward right shoulder to right shoulder and back up left shoulder to left shoulder. That's called a do-si-do. So do-si-do your partner." As Zach explained this, he motioned me to the platform and we did a do-si-do to demonstrate. He continued to move the dancers around for a while, introduced them to names of dance moves, and finally gave them a break. Slim moved into place on the stage and, after five minutes or so, called everyone back together. He changed the dancers from large circles to groups of four couples.

"We call this squaring up," he said. "Raise your hand if you haven't been square dancing in the last five years—or ever!" he added with a smile, and suggested that the experienced dancers share squares with less experienced dancers. In square dancing, each move is completed by eight dancers in a square, one couple per side. With experienced dancers in every square, they would be able to help out. Once the squares rearranged themselves, he repeated the same calls that Zach had introduced. Then he added some more so that dancers moved around the square and changed partners. Some of the experienced dancers helped the newbies along. More important, no one got upset if the square didn't end up with everyone in the right place. By the time it was my turn to call, Zach and Slim had covered about twelve different moves.

"Howdy! You are all doing just great," I started out. "Do your brains hurt yet? I am only going to teach you one more move tonight for this part of this tip. A tip usually means two songs, the first is often just used to warm you up or teach you a move that you need for the second song. Most times, the second one is a singing call, which means the words fit the timing of the song, and it only lasts as long as the song. This time, we're going to learn one more move, and then take another break to rest those aching brains. After the break, we'll do a tip for all dancers. What does a tip mean?" I quizzed them. I had to encourage people to holler out the answer, but finally got a little response.

"After that," I said, "we'll do one tip with the experienced dancers so you can see some fancy dancing—no pressure there, folks! Now, the move I am going to teach you is actually on the Plus program of dance moves. That means dancers don't usually learn this move until they have been dancing for some time and have mastered other moves. But you're all doing so well, I know you can handle it!" A little nervous laughter floated around the dance floor.

"So why do this now?" I didn't give them time to answer this time. "Well the name of the move is Load the Boat! I thought we ought to learn to Load the Boat since we're already on one," I offered in answer to my own question. That got me a few laughs.

Slim raised his eyebrows at me. Load the Boat wasn't easy to teach. I just smiled back at him and kept to my plan. I was hoping that the experienced dancers were spread out enough to help others learn the move, but there was really no way to tell. Usually I could identify experienced dancers by the outfits they wore, but tonight almost everyone was in casual clothes. A few, like Carlotta, wore traditional clothes so I could guess at a few experts here and there. Although the move looked complicated, it wasn't as difficult as it looked. Much of the movement was for show, and as long as everyone knew where they were supposed to end up, it would work. I planned on focusing on where they should end up and not on the moves they needed to make to get there.

"Okay, to start, each square form two facing lines. Oh wait! Hold up. I forgot, I need to tell you how to make the lines. Each couple facing me or with your back to me, you're called head couples. Okay, head couples join hands with the couple on your right and shift over to make lines with the open end toward me." Maybe this wasn't such a good idea after all, I thought. But it was too late! I continued my instruction, taking care to think ahead what I needed to tell dancers who didn't know square dance basics.

"We will focus on the four people on the ends of the lines to begin with and we will focus on where each dancer needs to end up. I want each end person to look at the person across from them—that person will be your partner when we finish the move, and you'll be at the opposite end of the square together. Look at the opposite end of your own line. When you are through you will be standing where that last person is, but facing in. If you forget the move, just go where you should end up, okay?"

Load the Boat is a fairly complicated move, with different sets of partners doing different moves, so I tried to go slow and explain as I went along. I went through the instructions and practiced the move several times. I held my breath, and amazingly enough most of the squares seemed to be able to follow. But we were only half way there, and we had only done the easier part.

"As you may have noticed, some people are adding the sound effects of a boat whistle," I told the dancers. "As Zach said, we're just having fun, so feel free to toot your tugboat horn! That's customary in this move." I walked them through the last half of the movement and ended with, "I believe you've got it!"

I noticed that Slim was looking a bit relieved at my simplification and I smiled at him. I was glad both he and Zach seemed to approve, since some callers are sticklers for accuracy and would have frowned at my way of teaching the move. With my simple version, though, most folks got it. A few experienced dancers were doing turns inside the squares for flair, but it didn't seem to confuse the new dancers.

"Now are your brains tired?" Groans and laughter greeted my question. "I think you all have it—let's put it together. Load the boat! Okay! Great job!" I was thirsty and ready to take a break, and I knew the dancers were, too. "Take a break and then Slim, Zach, and I will call a tip for everyone using the moves you've learned tonight. Don't worry if you don't feel ready yet, jump in anyway. It's all for fun and we'll help you out!"

As everyone headed for water, I made it a point to go over to the three crew members who had joined us and thank them individually for being gracious enough to help out. Two of them just grunted, but the third guy shrugged agreeably. "You know, I thought this was gonna be awful, but it really wasn't such a bad duty to pull. At least nobody was yelling at me!" he said with a genuine smile. It sounded like he was used to people yelling at him.

"We really do appreciate it. As you might have noticed, some folks are leaving during the break so you can get back to your other duties if you need to. Can you tell me your names so I can be sure to let Joaquim know that you were helpful?" I asked with a smile.

The friendly one answered first. "Jim Falcon, ma'am. If it is alright I may just hang out here in case you need me. This is the lightest duty I've had in some time!" Unlike the other two, who spoke with an accent, Jim drawled like the best of Texans. He was slim, tall, and awkward, but he would likely grow out of that with a few more years on him. I'd noticed he moved like a skittish colt on the dance floor, but seemed to catch on to the moves quickly.

"Pete Crhhhh," mumbled one of the other two. At least that's what it sounded like. "Will," replied the other one, who didn't even bother to try for a last name. He was the one whose tattoo extended to the top of his hand. They both spoke with accents, and I made the assumption that they were from Mexico given the cruise itinerary. They didn't seem particularly social, but then not everyone likes to dance. I figured first names would have to do. Joaquim would probably know who he sent anyway.

I waited until Slim and Zach squared up the dancers and found a place for Jim in a square. When I turned around, I discovered the other two had disappeared without another word. Although the plan had been for three callers to take turns for this tip, we decided that Zach and I would help on the floor. Slim called a tip of two singing calls for all the dancers. He included, bless him, the Load the Boat move I'd taught and the other calls we'd gone over during the evening. He called to traditional square dance music—in this case, 'Rocky Top' and 'Mountain Music.' Slim had a good voice and the tip went well. When he finished the two songs, he announced another short break.

During this break, I finally got to chat with Carlotta, Nick, Sam, and Doug. As I walked over, Sam was talking to Mandy. As I walked up, Doug gave me a hug and teased, "Darla, I don't know how you pulled out the Load the Boat move. Thought for sure we would sink! Good thing you simplified it some." The others nodded and smiled. Sam tipped his hat to me. I laughed and then saw Zach's signal that it was time for us to start.

Zach and I each called a tip, with a shorter patter call to review or introduce a move, and then a singing call. As I ended my tip, I realized that with the breaks, it was getting late, and we only had time for one more tip cycle. As I walked around, I smiled and chatted with the dancers. I recognized some and made small talk with others. I also realized that at some point, Jim had left the dance. I knew that after the break Slim and Zach would both call before me, so I had a little time. Something was nagging at me, I just couldn't figure out what it was. I headed out the door to the deck to get some air along with some time alone to figure out what it was.

It wasn't the dance itself that was bothering me. The dance was actually going more smoothly than I thought it might. Surprisingly, other than during the breaks, I couldn't hear the music from the dance hall next door, either. No, it was something about those two crew members that just didn't ring true with the other cruise line employees I'd seen. I just wasn't sure what it was. When I got outside in the fresh air, I walked to the railing and closed my eyes to concentrate on the feeling.

"You doing okay?" Doug's voice startled me. I thought I had managed to duck out of the Dreams without being seen. I was feeling a lot more stressed than I usually would calling a dance like this one. I felt like I might be in over my head, calling on this cruise. It concerned me that I might not do a good job at it. But that wasn't what was bothering me. Something else wasn't right. The two crew guys had set off all sorts of red flags with me. Not just because of their negative moods and sullen responses. And it wasn't the tattoos, either. I don't particularly like tats, but I also don't usually react quite so negatively to them. There certainly are lots of male square dancers with tats. And some callers too, like Zach. It was good to see Doug, but I wasn't ready to discuss my unidentifiable gut feeling.

"Fine. I just needed some air," I said to Doug. Even to my own ears, I didn't sound fine. A little sharp. I tried to soften it up, but Doug responded before I could say anything.

"I should guess so," he said. "Teaching that move to a bunch of newbies has to take it out of you!" The calling had been exhausting, but it wasn't the reason I needed air. I let Doug think so, but I didn't really know what the real reason was. Just a sense of foreboding. From my past experience, I was pretty sure I needed to pay attention to my intuition. I was just as sure that it would get me in trouble if I didn't.

"Yeah, I can't take too much time off. I have to get myself back together before I go back in. Gotta look great on stage," I said.

"You look great to me." Doug chimed in a quiet, throaty voice.

"Very chivalrous of you," I said, and started to feel a little better in response to his flattery despite the fact that I doubted it was true.

Doug could be chivalrous, all right. He was charming, smart, and compassionate, too. An all-around good guy.

He'd been in military intelligence in the Air Force and was stationed in Florida when my husband was killed. He got assigned to the investigation of my husband Clint's death. It had been a messy case with officers from the Drug Enforcement Administration, Coast Guard, and Air Force pulled in to cooperate. I met Doug at a rough time in my life. He knew what I'd gone through dealing with Clint's death. When he retired from the Air Force, he moved back to Clearton to manage his family's horse ranch. When my career went south, I moved to Isquith to be closer to Clint's parents, which I thought might help Heather.

The two towns weren't far apart by Texas standards. Ironically, my in-laws retired to Florida shortly after that, so I should have stayed put or moved back. Instead I was determined to make a new life for myself and Heather so I stayed in Texas. Doug and I kept in touch. It was when I finally got back into life and started dancing that he mentioned that he was also a square dancer. I started dancing with his club, the Clearton Squares. Then I got interested in calling the dances. After I got into calling, I still kept in touch and occasionally managed to get down there for a dance. A few years later, when the Clearton Squares club was looking for a caller, I volunteered. After that, Doug and I spent a lot of time together. We were comfortable with each other. Most of the time.

Doug and I had similar values and interests, and a little shared history. At times that was enough to make me think we could be more than friends. We'd had an on-and-off romantic relationship for a year or so. The off part was mostly due to me. I was still carrying around a lot of emotional baggage and couldn't seem to open up to anyone at more than arm's length. I was discovering that intimacy required getting closer than that. But it was hard to get closer when I kept finding reasons to run in the opposite direction. I was hoping that the new year and this cruise would bring me a new perspective on things. Perhaps instead of keeping our relationship 'going,' it could spur it to 'growing'!

I could tell by his voice that Doug was trying to move that way now. I was determined to respond in kind. The problem was I needed to figure out how to keep myself from standing in my own way. I searched for a snappy comeback to his compliment, but couldn't find one.

"Thanks, but it's not really the look, it's the stress and my calling I'm worried about," I replied. "I'm worried I don't have the experience or ability to call for this cruise. I'm used to the same clubs on a regular basis. I'm getting more comfortable calling at the larger regional and state dances, too. But that is only one weekend at a time, and for short periods of time. Both Slim and Zach seem lightyears ahead of me, even though Zach hasn't been calling that long either."

"Here, let me help you out," Doug answered as he moved behind me and leaned toward my neck. Next thing I knew he was massaging my shoulders. His closeness startled me, and I jumped a little. I expected him to pull back at that, but he stayed put. When he spoke, his voice was barely loud enough for me to hear him. "You do feel tense. Let go and relax with me."

My stomach flipped. My mind raced. How the heck was I supposed to relax with his hands on me? Do I keep it light? Or respond to the clear overture? My relationship with Doug or, heck, with any man since Clint's death, has been up and down. My fault, in most cases. I just can't figure out how to open up and get close to anyone. It scared me, and that was all there was to it. In the middle of everything else I had to think about tonight, I couldn't deal with our relationship right now after all, I decided. I went with the light approach.

"Thanks. I appreciate the massage, and it will have to do for now. Back to work." I laughed nervously.

"Doesn't have to end. We could just put it on hold for later." His tone didn't match mine. It wasn't light. It was heavy and low. My stomach flipped again. His meaning was clear. He hadn't moved, and his whisper was aimed directly at my ear. I pulled away and turned to face him. His eyes were serious, but his mouth sported a crooked smile. There was barely room for a piece of paper between us. I guess he saw my hesitation, and he backed up a notch and raised his voice to a conventional level. "But if you insist…."

When I had come out on deck, I felt middle-aged and used up. I had misgivings about…something…oh yes, a couple of crew members. Now my face was flushed like a teenager's and I wasn't worried about anything except the moment. It had been a long time since I flirted and I wasn't sure I remembered how. Apparently not. I resorted to a smile and silence. He put his hand under my chin and gazed into my eyes. I felt my emotional barricades kick in and I tensed up. He leaned in and brushed my lips with his, then did it again.

"I really have to head back in," I said quickly with a catch in my breath.

"Yeah, I know. Just a minute." He moved smoothly and this time placed a firm kiss on my lips. He lingered just long enough to get its message across, then I felt the air on my mouth. He leaned into the bend of my shoulder and I heard him inhale deeply before pulling away. There was a teasing smile as he said, "Didn't you need to get back to work?" I did, and I sure hoped the air conditioning and fans were working. I also hoped that nobody noticed how flushed I was. I hadn't succeeded in cooling off on deck. In fact, I was feeling hotter than when I came out. And more nervous.

As I walked back into the Dreams after the refreshment break, Slim was just finishing up his first tip of the wrap-up dance for all dancers. Zach started into his patter call, and

Slim met me as I arrived at the stage. "Wondered where you were," he said under his breath. "You all right?"

"Why does everyone keep asking me that?" I hissed back. "Yes, I'm fine. It looks like the crowd is thinning, though. How about I skip my individual tip and we call the last one together?"

"I like that idea," Slim responded. Zach was about to start the second song of his tip, and popped in his next CD and introduced it as it queued up.

"This one might be familiar to some of you Baby Boomers in the crowd," he said. "It's called 'Calendar Girl' and was made popular by Neil Sedaka. Of course, from now on people will say 'made popular by Zach Jameson'!" He frowned at the CD player, which would not play. After a couple of tries, he gave up and quickly popped in another CD.

"Sorry, folks, a small technical problem. Guess you'll have to wait for tomorrow to hear that sentimental journey. Instead we'll dance this call to…" he glanced back at the CD he had jammed into the player "…Kevin Fowler's song 'Hard Man to Love.'"

After Zach finished that call, Slim clued Zach in that the three of us would trade off during the final tip using the moves we'd covered. Slim selected 'House on Pooh Corner' by Nitty Gritty Dirt Band and Glen Campbell's 'Galveston Oh Galveston' for our finale.

Usually one caller is responsible for both songs of a square dance tip, often one patter call and one singing call. While it's unpredictable when you have more than one caller calling together, I enjoy the challenge. This time all three of us sang both songs of the last tip, trading off calls, and I had a great time. With the help of experienced dancers on the floor, it went well. Judging by the laughter and talk, it sounded like everyone was having a good time, and that really was the idea.

I noticed that Mandy had not only joined in but seemed to be catching on quickly. She was laughing most times when I located her on the floor. Doug and Sam seemed to have taken her under their wing. She was in a square with the Clearton Squares dancers as Sam's partner this time around. I looked around for Doug, but didn't spot him. Slim, Zach, and I called the final dance for entire group, then squared up the experienced dancers only.

"Okay, you regulars, before we call it a night, you'll have the chance to show your moves on the next few tips," Slim announced. "The rest of you, you might want to stick around and see what happens when I call full speed! No break this time, square 'em up!"

"Thanks to you all," I added. "For those of you new to square dancing, remember to check your daily schedules for open dances and workshops. Now everyone stick around and watch the pros!" My announcement was met with general laughter around the floor. Even the most experienced dancers know there aren't any really any pros. Squares will always make mistakes and break down, especially when the dancers are showing off for a bunch of newbies.

Zach did two singing calls, inserting the calls into the words of the song. He had a great voice and the applause when the tip ended was great. Other than the minor snag with the Calendar Girl CD that wouldn't work, everything went pretty smoothly. I was kind of disappointed that Zach had to replace that one with an alternative CD. Most folks, regardless of age, are familiar with the Neal Sedaka classic, and it's fun to dance to. The snag with the CD also reminded me that I still needed to check all my CDs and figure out which one was missing.

It was around midnight when we finished and, despite my nap, I was barely holding on. Zach, Slim, and I secured our equipment. I was glad we would be calling all our dances in the Dreams Club, so we wouldn't need to move the equipment each day.

"Zach, you did a great job. And Slim, you were fabulous as always. Did you happen to see when the last of those three crew members left, Slim? The one named Jim stayed after the other two. He seemed to enjoy dancing," I said as we worked.

"Nope. I had expected them to be somewhat resistant. They didn't stand out after all, even though two of them seemed a little sullen. I lost track of them early on. Too bad we don't always have someone on call to supply us with extras dancers when we need them!" Slim laughed. "I think it went off really well for the first night. The experienced dancers seemed like a good group. Our dances the rest of the cruise should go pretty smooth, though we may need to add in a few Plus tips," he continued.

"Well, yeah, I could tell we have some good dancers that would enjoy the challenge of Plus tips. But, even in the experienced dancers I noticed some of the older folks having trouble with the speed of that last tip. We'll have to pay attention to the floor and be sure to have some stuff everyone can dance to," I said.

Sam came up to the stage and joined us. "Darla darlin', you did a great job with the Load the Boat! Even though you simplified it, at least it gave some of us a chance to feel like we were really dancing, not just workshopping. We're heading up to the midnight buffet. Did you work up an appetite?" he asked.

As he spoke, he indicated the small group of Nick, Carlotta, Doug, and, to my surprise, Mandy. It wasn't just that she wasn't one of the Clearton Gang that surprised me. She seemed much younger than the others. I thought she would have enjoyed one of the DJ dances with a younger crowd, or the country western venue next door, or with Zach. But she looked very comfortable standing a little too close to Doug. I told myself I was not jealous.

"Hello, again, Mandy. I see Sam made sure you met the whole gang from Clearton. As I'm sure you've figured out by now, this is Slim and this is Zach," I said, introducing my fellow callers. Both opted for the standard square dancer's hug.

When everyone petered out of greetings, I said, "Sorry, Sam, you guys go on. I feel like I've been run over by a truck and I gotta get some sleep. Man, I do hope I'm not coming down with something."

The group wished me a good night, Doug gave me a quick sideways hug along with a questioning look. I just shrugged and made my apologies again. They traipsed off to find the midnight buffet. Slim and Zach decided to go with them, although I don't know where they got the energy. I kind of hoped Zach and Mandy would hit it off. Then she'd have a good time on the cruise, of course. It had nothing to do with the fact that I didn't like her standing so close to Doug. And I wondered why Doug hadn't come over by himself to talk to me after his earlier overtures to me. Or why he didn't seem more disappointed that I wasn't going with them. I gave up. I was really too tired to try to figure it out.

I gathered up my gear and headed back to my stateroom. I hoped that a good night's sleep would help shake this uneasy feeling I couldn't explain. Actually, I really just hoped that I could get a good night's sleep in that teeny tiny box of a cabin. I knew it wasn't motion sickness that made me uneasy. The Dreams Club was airy enough that it wouldn't be my claustrophobia kicking in there. I'd started feeling uneasy even before Doug met me on the deck, so it wasn't anything with him either. Being me, I had to figure it out. And, being me, I knew I would have to do something to get rid of the feeling. That was the part that usually got me in trouble. I might have been better off with the flu.

A Darla King Novel

CHAPTER 4

I slept somewhat fitfully, still not adjusted to the small quarters or the ship's movement. I know some people love the rocking motion of a boat and others need drugs to be able to function, but I fall somewhere in the middle. That night, I was sure I could hear the ship's engine growling. I swear I heard the waves slapping the side every now and then, too. On the other hand, I didn't think I could be hearing both from my inside stateroom so I chocked it up to overactive imagination.

After I woke up, I kept my eyes closed and tried to imagine I was in my bedroom at home. It didn't work. My brain knew I was cooped up in a room that was very close and had no windows. I got up around eight o'clock and grabbed some breakfast on the Lido deck instead of in the dining room. I enjoyed some time to myself and engaged in some people-watching.

I still felt uneasy, but decided to chalk it up to a carry-over from the holidays. I also rationalized that it might be that this cruise reminded me of the one Clint and I had been on for our honeymoon. Memories can be good, but sometimes they do overshadow the present.

I headed to the Dreams to get ready for morning workshops. In the hallway I spotted the older man who fell on the boarding ramp. He was still clutching his satchel, and still dressed in the same outdated blazer. He was clearly upset in discussion with one of the ship's officers. I assumed it was the Purser when I noted his spotless white cutaway jacket. Curiosity got the best of me, as it usually does. I moved closer to them and fiddled with my shoe so I could hear their conversation.

"Mr. Jarcourt, I apologize for this inconvenience. I assure you, if you will fill out this form and list all the items that you are missing and their respective value, we will allow you to replace the items in our onboard stores or compensate you. We will do whichever is most agreeable to you," the Purser explained patiently. As with most of the crew I'd encountered so far he seemed to be handling the problem, whatever it was, very professionally. I guessed him to be my age. If this was his career, he probably had been doing this for some time.

"You don't understand. You just don't understand," the man said as he stormed off. He almost collided with me in his haste and anguish. I didn't know what he had lost, but he certainly didn't seem appeased by the Purser's reassurances and offers for compensation. The Purser looked genuinely distraught and a little anxious that I might have similar complaints. I flashed him a reassuring smile as I straightened up and continued to the Dreams to find Slim and Zach and get set up for the workshops. Clearly, this cruise was fraught with problems for stuff that had been shipped, and possibly for luggage handling as well.

"Hey guys! How are you doing this morning?" I offered as I joined the Slim and Zach back in the Dreams. I noticed that someone had put up the room partitions. We'd need to each take our own equipment to the section where we would hold our workshop.

"Hi Darla! I'm doing okay this morning. Zach, here, he is getting himself all worked up over the fact that his 50s CD didn't work last night. It was in his handmade CD case, but the disc wasn't his after all. I guess his CD slipped out during the security fiasco. Then someone put the wrong one back into his case. I told him to just tell that Joaquim dude to replace it," said Slim. Zach's head came up from searching through his stack of discs.

"Yeah, but I like 'Calendar Girl' and there are a couple of other songs on there that I planned to use. I'm frustrated I can't find it. Other than that, Darla, I guess I am okay—so far having a good time. I stayed up for a while with some of the passengers, first at the midnight buffet and then at one of the nightclubs. I probably stayed a little too late. I'm sure I will feel it by mid-afternoon. It's probably what's making me grumpy right now," Zach said as he stifled a yawn.

As I looked over at the stack of CDs he was going through, I was amazed at how many he had with him. "I guess you certainly have a variety to choose from. You're pretty serious about calling already," I said.

Slim nodded in agreement. Like me, he probably only had the ones he needed and we'd hear some of them multiple times I was sure. Zach laughed, and in explanation added, "A friend of my dad's got me into the calling thing. When he retired, he gave me all this stuff. I am still trying to figure out what all is here and what works for me. I guess for this morning I will stick to the ones I usually use for the Basic program. I'll keep to the tried and true. Maybe I'll get more adventurous with the Mainstream group."

Square dance movements are taught by program. The first program is called Basic, the second is Mainstream, then the Plus program, and various levels of advanced dance movements. Zach was leading the Basic workshop in the morning and the Mainstream workshop in the afternoon. Slim, as lead caller, got his choice and had opted to do Mainstream and Plus workshops in that order. That left me, as substitute for the absent Tom, with a Plus workshop in the morning and Basic in the afternoon. We helped each other sort out the sound equipment and get set up in our respective sections.

Folks who had never square danced would learn the Basic moves, so I'd have the very new dancers this afternoon.

Some of them might also have taken the morning one with Zach. This morning I'd have experienced dancers taking Plus. Those who had already taken Mainstream classes could take Basic or Mainstream, but would probably take the Plus workshop from either Slim or me. That meant I'd have to plan for a variety of skill levels. Sam, Carlotta, Nick, and Doug might be in my Plus workshop in the morning. They definitely would not be in my Basic group in the afternoon. On the other hand, Mandy might be in my Basic group if she didn't take Zach's workshop in the morning. My brain hurt and I stopped trying to figure it out. I plowed on with my setup.

Because I had the Plus-level workshop first, I was in the smallest of the three sections of the Dreams. After I arranged and tested my equipment, I checked to make sure I had all the CDs I needed for the workshop. I limit CDs for Plus tips to ones I know well. At dances, callers usually only call Plus tips three or four times during the entire dance. But for this workshop I would be using songs with Plus moves in every tip. That meant I needed to have at least four ready to go at the start of the session. The room should be large enough, I thought, but if all the experienced dancers showed up it would be a tight fit for five squares. One wall was curved. That could be confusing to the dancers, so I used that wall as the one I would work from. With the Plus workshop, if I made a mistake the veteran dancers would definitely know it was a mistake, so I better be on my toes. Expectations would be high.

"Morning Darla, how is that stress this morning?" With my mind on planning, I hadn't noticed Doug come into the room. He gave me a hug and a smile. His hug lasted longer than most. He left his arm around my waist as he added, "Missed you last night at the buffet. The food was phenomenal. But I do think you were the wiser to opt for sleep. I'm beat!" He released me but stayed in close range.

"I'm sure you enjoyed the buffet. And I enjoyed my sleep so it all worked out fine," was my retort. I mustered up a smile though I wasn't sure how to respond. I was thinking I should learn to enjoy Doug's affectionate attention when he stepped back slightly. He turned toward the door as Carlotta, Nick, and Sam entered. His internal radar must have been working better than mine. I hadn't heard either him or them approaching. It amused me that we seemed to travel as a pack, but that's part of the social aspect of a dance club, I guess.

"So did you guys get into any trouble in my absence last night?" I asked with a smile. I looked straight at Carlotta and she laughed. Sam answered for the group.

"Nah, Darla, without you, life is calm and serene. It's your curiosity that brings on the trouble," laughed Sam. "You might be interested to know, though, that two of the men who helped us out at the dance last night worked the buffet. Or at least pretended to work, I'd say. They seemed very interested in our new friend Mandy. So much so it seemed to make her a little uncomfortable." He shook his head.

"You're right, Sam," continued Doug. "She commented on it a couple of times. She couldn't figure out why they hung around and watched her. They definitely made her nervous, especially the guy with the tattoo on his hand. Did you hear her talking about the last time she was on a cruise with her parents? There was some kind of incident, with smuggling I think, and she can't help but be reminded of it this time around. The way she told the story, I was surprised she came on a cruise again."

"No, I didn't hear the story. Smuggling, huh? Drugs coming into the country from Mexico I would guess. Very little goes out of the U.S. into Mexico. When we boarded, she mentioned she was taking this cruise to honor her parents' memory, I think. Do you remember, Darla darlin'?" Sam wrinkled his forehead in consternation. I said I didn't remember much, other than the bit about her parents, and thought it would drop there. It didn't.

"She's surely young and pretty. That's likely what the crew was drawn to, don't you think? Or did it seem more threatening than that to you?" Sam asked, though he didn't really sound convinced.

"I don't know, Sam," Doug answered. "They certainly made her nervous for sure."

I looked over at Carlotta and Nick for confirmation, and they just shrugged. More dancers came in and people started to socialize. We ended our chat and split up to visit with folks as they came in. Joaquim and some of the wait staff brought in bottled water and juice. Then we were ready to go. With the Plus group, there would be no extra dancers needed. With experienced dancers, both men and women can usually dance both parts. I let Joaquim know, and he went to check with Slim and Zach. Really, only for Basic would 'extras' be able to help. At the other levels, dancers would be expected to bring a certain amount of knowledge with them.

"Okay, good morning and let's square 'em up! We're gonna start with a singing call to get everyone warmed up. That will give me a chance to see if there are calls we need to workshop a little—or a lot, as the case may be. So bow to your partner, and your corner, circle left." I started the music and cued in a singing call that had a variety of Plus calls. Not surprisingly, no one had a problem with Load the Boat, but some of the squares broke down with Relay the Deucy and Teacup Chain. I worked on Relay the Deucy for the second half of the tip and called a break. Then we reviewed that move and worked on Teacup Chain. After that I did another singing call. At some point I noticed that Doug had left, or at least I couldn't locate him on the floor.

"Ok, you're looking good! Let's take a break!" At the far side of the room, Slim slipped in the door and walked over toward me. I met him halfway on my way to get a drink.

"Hey, Slim, what's happening in your room?" I asked.

"Not much, Darla. Looks like a pretty good group in here. Figured I'd check it out while we took a break. I also wanted to check on how your refreshments were doing, and let Joaquim know if we needed anything else. Be sure to give me a list of what you covered this morning and any words of wisdom. I'll have the Plus group this afternoon and will probably have lots of the same folks. And do watch out for this wise guy!" he added as he shook hands with Doug.

"Hey Slim! Darla's doing such a good job of taking us through our paces, I may have to skip out on your sessions this afternoon and take a nap," Doug joked in return. After he shook hands with Slim, he hugged me again. Carlotta and Nick joined our little group, followed by Sam and a lady whose name tag identified her as Zoe. I wasn't surprised that Sam had himself a partner so soon. As a single widower with a great sense of humor, he rarely if ever had trouble finding a dance partner.

Sam wasn't exactly old enough to be my father, but close. Semi-retired, he had time to take this square dance cruise, and he'd been a dancer for decades including a stint as past president of the Clearton Squares dance club. Probably he had held every post in the club at some time or another. He'd even held offices for the state and national square dance associations. His wife died ten years ago, during the time I wasn't dancing, and I never knew her. He had two kids, both adults. Neither of them lived in Texas. Somehow, I didn't get the impression he was very close to them. He certainly never talked about them. I couldn't imagine not being in touch with my daughter Heather for any length of time.

After his wife's death, he'd given up some responsibility with the club. He was still active, and I'd gotten to know him in the last couple of years since I began calling for the club. Sam was strong on common sense, gained from a long life of experience on his ranch. It was the ranch where he had grown up as a child and which he now managed as the owner. He had a sharp, curious mind and a strong, wiry body. Over 6 foot tall, he towered over most others and that made him easy to spot in a crowd.

"Yeah, right, blame it on Darla! You burned the midnight oil with the rest of us Doug, and you'll just have to pay the piper," Nick contributed with a laugh. I apparently had missed a good time the night before. I raised a questioning eye to Carlotta and she just smiled and winked. I guessed I'd have to wait until later to find out the full story of the evening.

Less than six months ago, none of us had known Nick. He'd been attacked more than once during a series of mysterious events when we were around. None of us had been sure of his motives early on. But he and Carlotta had gotten to be quite close in the past few months and were now pretty much inseparable. They were no longer singles for all intents and purposes. I still didn't know Nick well, but I trusted her judgment that he was a good guy.

"Sorry to break this up, but it's time for me to get back to work," I said. I went back to the mic and gave the usual roundup call, "Let's square 'em up. We have just two more tips this morning." I did another full tip with both a patter call and a singing call, then workshopped Spin Chain Through and Spin Chain and Exchange the Gears. The last two are confusing movements. I made a mental note to tell Slim to review them again in the afternoon. As the tip came to a close I ended with "Thanks a lot folks! You've been a great crowd this morning. Don't forget, Slim will be calling Plus this afternoon. He'll be at this same location beginning at 2 o'clock."

As I made a quick list of the calls I had covered and which ones Slim might want to work on, the usual Clearton crew came in my direction with laughs and smiles. I valued the friendships I'd made with this group of folks. I knew I could count on them whenever I needed help or a friend. As if to verify my thoughts, Sam automatically helped me with the sound equipment. There was a place to lock it up behind the stage, but I needed to break it down. That way it would be easy to pick up and move to the smallest section of the Dreams Club, where I'd be calling the Basic workshop this afternoon.

"So Darla, you gonna be able to work us in for lunch in about 30 minutes in the main dining hall?" Sam asked as I locked the cabinet. I noticed Sam's partner Zoe had come with the Clearton dancers and was visiting with the others while Same helped me.

"Sounds good. I'm assuming I have time to get freshened up in that 30 minutes? Or is there some other party going on? Will I be missing out again, like last night, if I head to my cabin for a minute?" I asked. Many people don't realize it, but square dancing is an aerobic activity. Often dancers work up a sweat just like they might if they worked out or used a treadmill. And calling is a performance in itself, even when I don't feel the stress I was feeling on this cruise. A clean shirt was definitely in order.

Sam drawled his response as we walked into the main portion of the Dreams Club. "No other party, and you won't miss anything but some downtime, darlin'. You worked us hard this morning and some refreshing is definitely in order for me!" He looked sideways at his companion briefly. I gathered the motivation for his freshening up was really a lady named Zoe and had little to do with my calling. I realized I hadn't actually met her, so I introduced myself and gave her the standard square dance hug greeting. Turned out Zoe was retired. She was accompanied by her daughter and grandson on this cruise.

"Darla, you did a great job! Are you still feeling a little stressed?" Doug asked as he put his arm around my shoulders. I was getting mixed messages from him. From the his earlier overtures to his absence from the workshop when I'd looked for him, and the fact that he'd been dancing with Mandy for many of the tips last night. But then, in fairness to him, when it came to mixed messages I gave as good as I got. There was probably an explanation for it all, and I was prone to reading too much into everything anyway.

"I think I may be getting into the groove here. Certainly I should be feeling less stressed than the last time I called this many dances and workshops back to back. At least this time I have no mysteries to solve," I said. I smiled and shuddered at the same time as I recalled what I liked to call the Clearton Caper. It started when Nick had been attacked, then Carlotta and I had been threatened and kidnapped, and the case wound up at the Galveston port.

"You got that right! No more mysteries for us. Though I have to admit I got to know all of you as a result, and that's been a good thing," Nick responded with a touch of emotion as his eyes focused on Carlotta. "We'll see you at the dining room at noon," he added as he and Carlotta headed off.

As I waited on the elevators with Doug, Sam, and Zoe, we were joined by Slim, Zach, and many of the other guests, including Mandy. Mandy was the only one going down so she took a different elevator. The guys got off on their deck with a "see ya in a bit" and I got off on Deck 3. It might have been my imagination, or should I call it paranoia or jealousy, but it almost seemed like Doug had moved away from me a little when Mandy joined us waiting for the elevator. When the elevator doors closed, he moved closer and started rubbing my back again. And I, of course, jumped slightly. Poor guy, I reprimanded myself, I can see why he's so confused about our relationship. I want him to be attentive to me, but not too attentive. I don't even know where the line is, so how can he?

Lunch was uneventful other than the overabundance of food that is typical of cruises. Zoe joined our group and we all ate too much, talked about eating too much, and then had dessert! At least the rest of them would be working off some of the calories square dancing this afternoon. While I would be active, I would not be getting the same level of exercise standing there calling. I looked around to see if I could spot the crew members who had helped out, especially Jim, but didn't see any of them.

I had a little time before the Basic workshop, so I excused myself and headed off to check on my still-missing CD. The missing CD was one with a handwritten label in a clear case. It was one that I had created myself. Joaquim wasn't in his office, but I left a message telling him about the label in case he noticed it in the stack of extras. He seemed to be one of the hardest working staff on this cruise. He had to both keep track of the entertainers and be sure everyone was entertained. And so far, he had done so with a smile. His couldn't be an easy job.

I had a few minutes and felt a need to touch base with Heather. I had turned off my phone to avoid international charges and any data roaming. Instead of the phone, I made my way to the ship's equivalent of an internet café to send an email. It would still cost me, but not nearly as much as a phone call from sea. The library cum business center had several rows of computers for those who just couldn't live without. I inserted my stateroom key and quickly signed in to my mail account. I was surprised and happy to see an email from Heather.

"Hi Mom, I know that you are going to check email and worry about me, so I figured I'd beat you to it! I'm fine. Micah and I are hanging out and trying to recoup from the semester and the holidays. Still plan to go out on NYE, but should be pretty low-key. So don't worry about me. And, Mom, have some fun. Love ya." I smiled and realized that while she may not be predictable, I obviously was. I was absolutely certain her New Year's Eve plans weren't low-key, but knew she was trying to reassure me. I shot back a reply with "You got me!" and a few lines about the cruise so far, mostly about the food and dancing. I told her I loved her, hit 'send,' and read through the rest of my messages before I signed out. Nothing that couldn't wait.

I headed back to the Dreams and the afternoon workshop. The Basic workshop went well with the usual beginning calls, many of the same ones we had covered in the open dance last night. I recognized some faces, with new ones thrown in. Both relaxed and serious ones. I had about four squares most of the time, with a few people sitting out at different points, so about 35 in the workshop altogether. Couples, singles, singles hoping to become couples. I was glad to see Mandy come. Apparently she enjoyed last night's welcome dance. She seemed to catch on pretty quickly. She laughed and kidded with the others in her square. That was a good sign too. I wasn't quite as glad to see Doug show up halfway through the workshop and step in as her partner for the remainder of the afternoon.

The workshop ended, and I was pretty beat. I was almost glad that my friends were off somewhere and I could just sit for a few. I half expected Mandy to come up and chat after the workshop since she had attached herself to our group, but she didn't. Then again, neither did Doug. They both seemed to disappear while I talked to some of the other dancers. Zach stuck his head in with a "Catch ya later!" and so did Slim. We'd have another dance tonight, trying to balance Mainstream and Plus depending on who came to dance.

After I packed up, I decided to take some alone time on the deck. I sat on the deck and soaked up the sun a bit away from most of the other activities. Quiet and alone, I found myself thinking about Clint, our life together. I reflected on all the things I do that might have contributed to the fact that I am alone and lonely a lot of the time. I thought about all the times Doug had made overtures, with me being unresponsive or outright cold. I liked Doug, and sometimes it seemed like our relationship could move forward, but…yes, but. A picture of Paul Harbinville popped into my mind. Paul was the FBI agent I met when we inadvertently got involved with that theft ring earlier in the year. Why on earth would I be thinking about him now?

Well, truth be told, Paul was the kind of man to drool over. He was tall, well dressed, good looking, and obviously worked out. But I'm not a woman who drools, I reminded myself. I'm the down-to-earth, in a relationship for life, old-fashioned type. Carlotta thought he'd been flirting with me during the series of events that brought us all together, but I didn't see it. She'd sternly told me my flirting radar must be broken. No, even if he was to die for, I was not getting involved with anyone else in any way associated with the criminal element. Losing Clint through violence on the job had been lesson enough in that department.

My unruly mind jumped back to my relationship with Doug. Paul and I had only one dinner alone together, and that was really just so I could try to pump information out of him. Man, was Doug upset about that. My drowsy mind fogged up, mixing Clint with Doug and Paul. The salt breeze made my eyes tear up a bit. As I watched the blurry water meet the sky at the horizon, I firmly closed my eyes and emptied my mind. Then I dozed off.

"Ma'am? Excuse me, Ma'am. Mr. Gonzalez suggested I find you and see if this is the CD you were missing? Ma'am? Are you alright?" Danny, Joaquim's assistant and the crew member who had helped me yesterday, interrupted my sleep. I had never dozed off as easily and as randomly as I was doing on this cruise. Whether it was because of the boat's rocking motion or my lack of sleep in that little hatbox they called a stateroom, I seemed to be drifting off with the sandman any chance I got. I seldom napped when I was at home, but I'm a creature of routine. When I get out of my routine, I have been known to compensate by sleeping—a lot. Although not in random spots and times as I'd been doing on this cruise. Whatever. I suppose it's a better coping strategy than some others I could think of.

I answered Danny groggily.

"Um? Oh yes, I'm fine. Just a little too much sun I think," I offered, and continued, "let me look at it" as I accepted the CD. I noted the labeling on the case, Calendar Girl 50s Selection, and told Danny, "No, this one isn't mine, but I think I know whose it is. Okay if I take it for him? I'll bring it back to Joaquim if I'm wrong."

"No problem. We are just trying to get these all sorted out," he sighed. He was still polite and professional. But it sounded like this was a never-ending process that was getting tiring fast. That, or he was distracted with something else on his mind. I guess running a top-notch luxury cruise could be just a tad more distracting than calling square dances.

He left the CD with me and walked away. As I gathered up my things along with the CD, I wondered how he had found me. Had he walked around every deck? This was a big ship, and this was a quiet deck with very few passengers laying out. I shook my head at the absurdity of it all.

Curious if this was Zach's CD, as soon as I got to my stateroom, I pulled out my CD player and popped it in. Yup, this certainly was a selection of 50s songs, including Sedaka's, with singing calls on alternate tracks. Well, at least Zach would be happy to have his CD back. Joaquim on the other hand probably wouldn't be thrilled when Zach gave him the other one. To know that he had just exchanged one CD for another unclaimed CD wasn't really progress, and the one he was getting back apparently didn't play to boot.

While I was listening to Zach's CD, I closed my eyes to try to forget what a small space I was in and darned if I didn't nod off again. When I woke up I was hungry. I stole a look at my watch and wondered if I could still make it to the dining room. Probably not, and at any rate I wasn't in a mood for a formal night after the hectic day. But I did long for the social aspect of dinner and was disappointed I had slept so long that I couldn't eat with my friends in the dining room.

I rationalized that I wanted something a little lighter than a full cruise meal anyway. Not to mention, I could manage to avoid all the photographers that way, a plus given the way my hair looked after the afternoon's naps. So I headed up to Deck 11 to the largest food court I have ever seen. I smiled at various guests, but I didn't see any of the Clearton Gang or dancers I knew up here. I didn't see anyone I recognized from my workshops, but as I ate my meal of a burger and nachos I did some of the people-watching I enjoy so much.

The usual cruise crowd milled around and my imagination made up stories about them as it usually does. There were several seniors who looked like a group traveling together, maybe from a church. A few families with kids of varying ages, probably on family vacations. In one of the groups I saw what looked like a strong family resemblance both in their faces and gestures, so I guessed at a family reunion. Hmm, I bet that couple over there is on their honeymoon, the young couple who can't keep their eyes or hands off each other as they leave the eating area. As I looked around for other likely candidates to keep my imagination busy, I saw Mandy coming over. She was carrying a tray of food but managed a small wave without dropping anything.

"Hey, Darla, can I sit with you?" she asked, pulling up a chair without waiting for my response. "I've been enjoying square dancing so far, and you're a great caller!"

"Thanks," I responded. "How are you enjoying the rest of the cruise? You didn't want to do the formal dining tonight?"

"I decided to pass on the formal deal this time. I think there's a dressy night toward the end of the cruise. Maybe I'll feel up to it then. As for the enjoying the cruise, well, some good and some not. I don't remember if I mentioned to you that I'm sort of taking this cruise in memory of my parents. They both passed away this year," she said, somewhat wistfully.

"Yes, you did say something about that when we spoke on the boarding ramp. And about a cruise you took with them. How many years ago was that?" I asked.

"Gosh, it was almost ten years ago, and I think it might have been on this very ship. At least, the name sounds the same. It was one of our few family vacations, and I remember I looked forward to it so much. When I think about my parents, of course, it makes me sad sometimes. I am enjoying the cruise mostly other than that. Well, except for the problems with my cabin," she added.

"This ship doesn't seem that old to be the same one. I think it is one of smaller ones in the fleet from what I read. So I guess it might be one of the original ones," I offered. "What problems have you had with your cabin?" I asked.

"When I got to my assigned cabin, they had to move me. My bathroom wasn't working. Apparently the ship is fully

booked so they had to scrounge a cabin for me. I heard some
of the other passengers saying their luggage was lost. I was
afraid my luggage would get lost in the shuffle, but that part
seems to have gotten settled fine. Oh, and then the room safe
in my new cabin doesn't work. No one can get it open, so I
have to leave anything of value at the Purser's office or carry it
with me whenever I go anywhere. It's sort of a pain," she
explained. She bit into a piece of pineapple.

"Mmmmm, this buffet thing is great," she said, slightly
muffled. "All the food seems so fresh."

"They can't get your room safe fixed?" I asked.

She swallowed and swiped at her chin, catching some
wayward juice from the pineapple. "Apparently not. One of
the Assistant Cruise Directors came by a couple of times and
can't get it to work," she answered.

"Assistant? Do you remember his name? Danny, maybe?
The one we met on the boarding ramp?" I asked.

"Yeah, that's the one. He said my cabin is one they don't
usually put a guest in. It is an exterior, but the window is
directly behind a lifeboat and the view is blocked. It only has
a single bed, plus it's right near the elevators and gets noisy,"
she explained. She shrugged and continued to eat her plate of
fruit.

"Well, at least you have window," I said, feeling sorry for
myself about my interior accommodations once again.

We visited about her work and other small-talk topics.
She didn't mention anything else about the trauma that had
occurred on that cruise with her parents. I didn't ask because
she'd seemed so sad when she talked about them. She didn't
mention how her parents had died, and I didn't ask her about
that either. I didn't tell her much about me, and she didn't
ask. I finished my meal before she finished hers, but I sat
with her until we were both ready to go.

"Glad you joined me for dinner. I have to run now," I said. "Will you be coming to the dance tonight?"

"Hope so," she said, and we took off in different directions. I went to my cabin and changed my clothes yet again. Then I headed back to the Dreams Club for the next installment of square dancing. Carlotta caught up with me in the reception area outside the club.

"Hey, Darla. We missed you at dinner. I bet you fell asleep, huh? Have you had a chance to take in any of the other entertainment?" she asked. I made a face at her. She knew very well that I hadn't had time to do anything else with my full day of work, but I knew she was just teasing me.

"Not hardly," I answered. "Barely had time to eat and, yes, catch a quick nap. Did some people-watching up on the Lido deck and visited with Mandy Myers a little. What about you? Did the magician make Nick disappear? Every other time I've seen you, he's been at your side."

"Oh, he and Doug and Sam are at the pool cooling off, I think. I had a chance to catch some chamber music. I don't think chamber music is Nick's cup of tea. Oh, and one of the other passengers at the concert was talking about the DJ who was on the country-western side last night."

She laughed and continued at her usual breakneck speed. "Have you seen him? He's easy to spot between the boots and the big hat. They said he was pretty good and had some DVDs as well as CDs. The DVDs apparently have a western motif and serve as backdrop to the music he plays. I think he's part of the entertainment for New Year's Eve, so we'll get to see and hear him then if not before. Of course, unless we're at your dance instead then," she added in a whoosh.

"I don't suppose anyone mentioned if one of the DVDs he used was of a group called 'Snooping Dog' or something like that?" I asked her, thinking back to all the CDs and DVDs that had been in that pile yesterday. "We've found some unknown extras scattered around and I might be able to ask him about them." Before Carlotta could respond, an anxious voice interrupted.

"What did you say? Why did you ask about snooping and scattered ashes? What are you talking about?" interrupted the man from the boarding ramp, who I had heard Danny call Mr. Jarcourt. His face was red, his clothes rumpled, and he was still clutching his beat-up satchel.

"What? No, we were talking about a DJ. I didn't say anything about ashes. Oh, I guess you heard me talking about scattered CDs. Um... are you interested in music or dancing?" I asked him. I was a little taken aback, and more than a little confused, but I valiantly tried to be friendly and polite.

"Never mind, never mind. Sorry I bothered you," mumbled Mr. Jarcourt, as he skittered out to the deck.

"That is a very strange man, Darla. I've seen him several times and he is always running, well walking quickly, and mumbling. What is his problem?" Carlotta asked, shaking her head.

"I'm not sure. I thought for a minute there he had something to do with the mixed-up CDs, but I guess not. Anyway, don't desert me for the DJ tonight at the square dance. I could use the company of friends to break up the tension of the all day and night grind. And besides, I want to hear about the buffet last night. And we have to plan our day in port tomorrow. I'll get a break from work while we're docked," I added, thinking that some vacation time on this cruise was definitely in order.

"We'll be there. I understand Mandy was at the Basic workshops today. Was she in yours this afternoon? What did you visit with her about at dinner? Doug's been dancing with her a lot and said she plans on coming to the dance tonight, too." She hesitated and then changed the subject. It seemed like she was a little awkward telling me about Doug and Mandy being together. She rushed on, "Look at the bright side, tomorrow morning we dock in Progreso, and you get a break from calling. You get to be a tourist, just like the rest of us."

"Sounds heavenly…. For now though, I better see what Zach and Slim have in mind for tonight and give Zach his missing CD." I shrugged, smiled, and went into the Dreams Club to get the lay of the land for the night's dance. I tried to shake off Carlotta's comment about Doug and Mandy and put a smile on my face.

"So Zach, look what I have for you—your Calendar Girl CD!" I announced with a flourish.

"Really, Darla? That's great, you're the best! I love all the songs on that CD and just figured out how to do without it tonight. Now I don't have to make do! Where'd you get it?" Zach asked, his pleasure apparent in his face and sparkling eyes.

"That crew member Danny brought it to me. He said Joaquim thought it might be the one I was missing. Someone apparently turned it in. Did you get the other "Calendar Girl" CD back to Joaquim?" I asked.

"Not yet," he said. His eyes darted to Slim and back.

"You know," I continued, "Carlotta just mentioned that one of the DJs was using DVDs. Is it possible that the reason it doesn't work in your CD player is that it is really a DVD?"

Zach chuckled and, I swear, blushed. "Yup, Darla, I came up with the same idea so I decided to try it in my DVD player. It was definitely a DVD and not a CD!" With a wink to Slim, he added, "I don't think it was the background for any DJ though. The girls on this DVD weren't exactly dressed for boot scootin', if you get my drift. Certainly not what Sedaka sang about, but possibly what he really had in mind." He and Slim apparently had an inside joke going on.

But Slim wasn't laughing. In response to my confused look he explained, "Not the best quality, Darla, and definitely not background videos. Unless you like porn, plain and simple! Now, Darla, just so you'll know, before we knew what they were we stopped by the lost CDs and picked up a couple of those 'Snooping Dog' ones to check them out. They were all DVDs not CDs. All the ones we picked up are the same. Well, at least the first few minutes are the same. That's all I would let Zach here play." Slim seemed embarrassed by the whole subject.

"I guess that Joaquim can forget anyone coming forward to claim them," he continued. "Probably, when all is said and done, I'd bet money that all the unclaimed, loose DVDs turn out to be porn. Someone ought to be strung up for making things like that!" It was clear Slim felt strongly about porn films. Zach just seemed to be amused by the whole thing, but chimed in to change what was obviously a touchy subject.

"Hey, but it's not our problem," he said. "Joaquim and the Captain or somebody can figure out what to do with the DVDs and whatever's on them. Maybe they'll just burn them or bury them at sea. Our problem is we have a square dance to call! I'll start off with one of my faves from that CD you just gave me. What do you guys want to use?"

We agreed that by alternating who was calling tips, and occasionally throwing in a Plus tip, we could split up the work. In between, we would help out some of the new dancers by dancing ourselves when we weren't calling. We decided to do more patter calls than singing tips tonight because it was easier to review the moves without the confining structure of the song verses.

Normally, at many dances, every third tip was a Plus tip. We decided to start off that way and see how many dancers we lost when it was time for a Plus tip. If there weren't a lot of Plus dancers, then we'd go to 'Announced Plus,' with only two or three Plus tips all night. If it looked like just about everyone was dancing Plus, then we would throw in a few more. Zach requested not to call Plus tips, so Slim and I would trade off on those. Slim elected to take the third tip, so that put me calling second after Zach.

I started going through my CDs and located one with contemporary country music. I figured that would be a good change of pace after Zach's 50s number. As I watched folks start to drift in, my mind wandered back to the pornographic DVDs. Who would bring such a thing on a cruise ship? Or at least why so many of them? Did they belong to a passenger, a crew member, or to one of the entertainers? We'd have to do something with them. I was curious how Joaquim would handle their return.

Personally, I've never quite understood the draw of porn. But obviously other people did. There was a demand for it. Based on the number of Snooping Dog DVDs I'd seen in the stack, there weren't really enough to be a major distribution attempt. I had a mental image of porn distributors as greasy and sleazy, but I hadn't seen anyone who fit that description onboard.

Logically, I couldn't believe someone would bring DVDs to Mexico or the Caribbean to sell. Not because I had any faith in human nature, really, but simply because it didn't seem to make sense. Having worked in the Florida State Attorney's Office for several years, I was familiar with smuggling and black market routes. It would make more sense that someone would bring porn into the U.S. to distribute, not out of the U.S. But that didn't seem the case, after all we had just left dock when they were found.

My background with criminal cases kicked in and it occurred to me that this was probably a federal case. Trafficking in pornography would be under their jurisdiction and clearly the DVDs were onboard when we were in U.S.

waters. If this was a case at all, I reminded myself. Maybe my imagination was just running rampant again. It could be someone just brought DVDs for their friends. I laughed at myself, and remembered the 'church group' I thought I saw when people-watching during dinner. Could they be a swingers or wife-swapping group instead? I was thinking it through when Sam walked up and interrupted me.

"Darla, are you in pain? Didn't anyone ever tell you not to scrunch up your face like that? It will freeze that way!" offered Sam with a smile and a hug.

"Hi Sam! I was just thinking. Didn't you see the smoke coming out of my ears?" I kidded back.

"Must be some pretty heavy thinking there. Don't you remember that you're supposed to be relaxing in between work on this here cruise?" he answered. "Or do you know what it means to relax? Darla, you don't have another mystery brewing, do you?"

"Sam, remember I mentioned the mess up with the CDs, and all the ones not claimed? Well, it ends up that some of them aren't CDs at all. They're DVDs and we just assumed they were CDs. Sam, they're porn," I explained.

"I knew it! You can't go anywhere without tracking down a mystery, can you? Well, 'fraid I can't explain the draw of porn myself. At least now. But of course I was a little more interested when I was a teenager." Sam winked and looked as much like a teenager as someone his age could muster. "Maybe we should get our Clearton Gang together and see if we can figure it out. We could become a regular crime-solving posse. Hooboy, that would be something! But you and Carlotta gotta be sure not to become targets again," he laughed.

"Absolutely not!" I laughed, too. "Why, I'm just a plain old square dance caller. Zach's signaling that we are about to get started so I've gotta get to work. You better go find your friend Zoe for the first tip." With a hug, I left Sam and joined Zach and Slim on the stage. Slim got the group's attention.

"Welcome folks! Second night in a row we are square dancing! Some of you look familiar from the workshops today. We have high expectations, even for some of the new dancers! Remember, this is recreation, so let's square 'em up, and have some fun! Zach will be calling the first tip, Darla will call the second, and I'll come back up here for the tip after. I'll be calling Plus on that third tip, by the way, so plan your partners accordingly. Take it away Zach!"

Slim jumped off the stage and we both started to look around to see if we were needed to finish out a square, either as partners or separately. Tonight we wouldn't be calling on Joaquim to make sure everyone had a partner. It would be up to us to fill in as needed. If some folks ended up sitting out a tip, we'd try to rotate them in for the next one. In a workshop setting everyone needs to dance to learn the moves. At a dance people are responsible for finding their own partners and forming their own squares.

As I looked around, I noticed that Doug was partnered with Mandy. Once again, I was again surprised to feel a twinge of jealousy. Maybe that twinge was what I needed to get past my fear of intimacy. I also noticed the crew member Jim from the previous night's dance. He stood by the door and watched the dance. Well, maybe he really had caught the square dance bug. Or was he one of the ones who made Mandy nervous at the buffet last night? Zach finished up and called for a quick break. After the break, I took over, reining in my imagination.

"Okay, now most people don't really associate square dancing with 50s rock and roll. Zach just showed you that any kind of music works. This tip, we are going to dance to county music. Same moves, a little variation, and again, just plain fun! Square 'em up!" I continued calls from the Basic and Mainstream programs with a medley of country music as the background for my patter call.

"You are all looking great! Now for a singing call!" I called to 'Ridin' My Thumb to Mexico' with the calls interspersed with the lyrics. It's one of my favorites, and includes a fair number of different moves without being particularly complex. It seemed very appropriate given our destination. I ended by announcing, "Great job. Take a break, and Slim will be up to call a Plus tip next!"

I transferred the microphone to Slim, but he didn't make any other announcements before turning it off and laying it on the table. When I hopped off the stage, Zach handed me a water bottle. I accepted gratefully.

"Nice choice, Darla. I like that song myself!" Zach commented. "So are you gonna be able to dance this one, or just sit it out?" he added.

I looked around for Doug, but didn't spot him immediately. "I don't know. My usual partner is around here somewhere but I don't see him. You want to dance this tip with me?" I asked.

"Sorry, Darla, not for Plus. If someone needs a partner during Mainstream, I'm happy to help. I haven't mastered the dancing or the calling for Plus yet. I never do have a chance to get to go to the workshops," he responded with a shrug. And that would be the case on the cruise as well, I thought. Whenever Slim or I were doing a Plus workshop, Zach would have another group himself.

"Guess I will wait until the next Caller Convention and take the lessons there," he added. That would be in the spring sometime. It was an opportunity for callers from all over the country and internationally to get together and refresh our calling skills. And there, since we were the only people, we honed our dancing skills as well.

As Slim called out "Square 'em up," I spotted Doug heading my way and waving me to the floor. "Here comes my partner, Zach! Catch you later!" I met Doug halfway. We exchanged a quick hug before he guided me into a square with Sam and Zoe, Nick and Carlotta, and another couple. Their name tags indicated that they were from the Dallas Darlins and Dudes, but I didn't recognize them. Al and Amy Adams.

Everyone hugged and said hello, Slim started the music, and we were off. I noticed that Slim kept with the usual plan of patter first followed by a singing call. When Slim finished his singing call, and it was time for a break. And time for me to head back to the stage to plan my next call.

I cut short my usual thank you's to everyone in the square so I could go check with Slim and Zach. Before I ran off, I asked Doug, "So, can we dance the next Plus dance together too?"

"Well, I don't know yet. Sure if I'm still here. I promised Mandy the next two tips so she can get some practice. Then she wanted to head over to the country and western venue. But I'm not sure. If I am around, I'll come find you, Darla." I was happy he looked a bit uncomfortable. I wasn't happy that he might go with Mandy and leave me partnerless. But I didn't let it show.

"No problem. I was just wondering. It's no big deal." I answered, trying to sound as casual as I could. I wasn't quite sure what I was feeling or should be feeling but I wasn't happy. It was a little disconcerting to realize that I counted on him to be my dance partner even when we couldn't decide if we were a romantic couple or not. The situation with us was definitely at that awkward stage. I didn't have time to worry about it now. I gave him a smile and a hug and headed to the stage.

Zach was up, and planning to call to a contemporary pop song. I busied myself and talked to Slim. I turned sideways to the dance floor so I wouldn't be able to see Doug dancing with Mandy. Slim asked if I was doing okay, and I just shrugged. When Zach called to square up, we discovered that a square in the back needed another couple. Slim and I joined in that square. I stopped worrying about Doug. One thing about square dancing, you can't dance and remain preoccupied. You have to pay attention to what you are doing. That Zach was a good caller helped.

The next tip I called, and there seemed to be one or two less squares. We were well past the two-hour mark as Slim got ready to call the Plus tip. When I finished my tip, Slim came up to me and motioned Zach over. He had noticed some folks tiring out and fading away. We could all tell the crowd was slimming considerably. It really wasn't very surprising. After all, some of the dancers had been to workshops during the day, as well as the dance tonight. Plus on a cruise there are multiple distractions easily accessible that pull folks away from the dance. Everyone who remained still seemed to be enjoying themselves, however.

"Darla, Zach, how about after this Plus tip, we split up a tip with three singing calls and call it a night? I heard a bunch of folks are heading over to the country western room or just plain calling it quits to get a good night's sleep before heading out early in the morning to see the sights," Slim suggested.

"Sounds like a plan to me!" I responded. I was beat and an early night sounded good.

"You bet!" Zach echoed.

Slim called to square up, and announced the plan to the remaining dancers. I looked around for Doug, but decided he was AWOL. Zach and I flipped through our CDs to figure out what we wanted to do for the finale. We came up with my patriotic CD. Patriotic songs always seem to go over well with dancers and, after all, we would be docked in Mexico in the morning. During a short break before the final tip, we clued in Slim about the songs and then ended the night with the patriotic trio and about five squares still on the floor. Not bad really for a full day of square dancing.

We ended with the traditional thank you's and started to pack up our equipment. Tomorrow was a day off from workshops. As dancers drifted out, Sam and Zoe joined us at the stage. "Darla Darlin' that was great," Sam drawled, his arm around Zoe's waist.

"Thanks, Sam! I gotta tell you though, I am sure glad that we have tomorrow off. I'm beat!" I responded as we packed up our stuff. "So, where's the Clearton Gang?" I asked. I hoped I sounded nonchalant.

"I haven't been keeping up with 'em. Was it my night to watch 'em?" he quipped. "Well, speak of the devil, here come Nick and Carlotta now. I think Doug and Mandy went to check out the country western dude," he added. "The four of us decided to head up to the Barrio Bar for the rest of the evening. It's a nice quiet place. Why don't y'all join us?"

"Not yet, you don't, Darla. We gotta go explain to Joaquim about these DVDs. He really should check all the DVDs out, especially the Snooping Dogs, and lock up the ones like these," interjected Slim, holding up the offending disc. "I think it's important that all three of us go so he knows we are serious. And we can be witnesses for each other in case there is any trouble about it later. I hear trouble seems to be YOUR middle name, Darla!" he said, with a smirk on the last part.

"Well, then why don't you folks take care of business and the three of you can join us in the Barrio in a few. I for one hanker for a long cold one!" said Sam. We all indicated agreement, and the four of them headed in one direction and we headed for Joaquim's office, DVDs in hand.

Joaquim looked both embarrassed and quite taken aback as Slim explained that the DVDs contained porn. This immediately turned to panic when the idea was suggested that the rest of the DVDs, maybe even some that he had tried to return to people, might also be porn. He indicated he would notify the Captain, and then whoever it was they determined to be the appropriate authorities. In the meantime, he said he would immediately lock up all the unclaimed CDs and DVDs just to be sure. He didn't want to be considered as trafficking in pornography. That taken care of, we headed to the Barrio to join the Clearton crowd. Well, the Clearton crowd minus Doug, who was apparently still in the country western club dancing with Mandy.

"Phew, did you order us drinks too? Calling is a thirstier occupation than dancing, you know!" Slim kidded Sam as he slid into a chair and punched Sam's arm.

"Took care of you, Slim. Pitcher is on its way. If you want something besides beer, though, you're on your own. Now, Darla, you sit right down and relax a spell, ya hear," was Sam's invitation. He looked around at the group. "Do we have plans for tomorrow while we're in port?"

Carlotta chimed in and said, "I assumed we're all going ashore at Progreso. There's lots to do, and Darla, Doug said to tell you that he plans to come with the rest of us." She hesitated, then said, "Don't know if Mandy will come with us or not, I saw them dancing together tonight."

"Great! I'm glad we're all headed in together," I answered, ignoring her hesitation and implied question about Doug and Mandy. After all, what did I know anyway? "I've never been to Mexico, so I am looking forward to it. I read up on some of the ruins and such. And the beach looks beautiful in the pictures."

That successfully shifted the conversation away from Doug to the range of possible excursions and sights, and the next few days of typical cruise activities. Somewhere along the way, Zach disappeared, probably to find a crowd that was a little closer to his age, I figured.

Once we all agreed to meet up on the exit deck in the morning, I managed to sneak out quietly. I was struggling with my feelings and wasn't really in the mood for conversation. I still wasn't sure what to think about Doug, or more specifically, Doug and Mandy—or even more specifically, Doug and me. It was certainly logical that since I was working, he would need a dance partner and be a 'good Samaritan' by helping out a new dancer. The question was, did I care?

In dance clubs, when we held lessons, experienced dancers often acted as partners and guided new dancers through the ropes. We called that being an 'angel.' But here, Doug wasn't part of the host club doing lessons. There were plenty of other singles to pick up the slack and partner with Mandy. On the other hand, Mandy was young and attractive and I was feeling middle-aged and washed out. Unless I was really a bad judge of age, she was much younger than Doug or me. If Doug compared me against her I was feeling sorely like I might lose out.

Not for the first time, my brain collapsed under the weight of my own insecurities and indecision. I decided to head back to my box of a stateroom and see if I could outwit the claustrophobic walls and get a little shuteye.

As I headed to my cabin, I wove my way down the two flights of stairs. I thought I knew where I was going, but the halls of the ship were color-coded and this color didn't look familiar. I kept walking. Eventually I turned a corner and saw the familiar royal blue of the staff offices. I recognized Joaquim's office and knew which direction I needed to head to find my cabin. As I passed his office, I heard moaning and stopped to see if everything was okay. The door to Joaquim's office was splintered and Joaquim was on the floor. He moaned again and rubbed his head.

"Joaquim, are you alright? What happened? How do I call the ship doctor?" I was slinging questions at him as he lay there and not exactly giving him a chance to answer. Whatever it was had obviously just happened, so I scanned the office and hallway to make sure we were alone.

"No need for a doctor," was his first response. Then he tried to sit up and went back down again. He reconsidered and managed to say, "The intercom system is over there. All you have to do is press #10. That's the sick bay. I don't feel so good."

I did as directed and relayed the information I had. I told the person on the other end that Joaquim looked like he had been hit in the head. The person on the other end said they were on their way.

"So what happened?" I asked again, as I waited with him.

"After you, Slim, and Zach left me, I was interrupted with an, uh, emergency," he responded with much hesitation. "After that, I came back here. I started to check through all the DVDs and CDs. I wanted to take out all the Snooping Dog ones and any that weren't labeled commercially. They should all be over there on the desk. I heard someone trying the door. I'm embarrassed to say in light of the other, uh, emergency, I ignored it. I was getting ready to put the CDs and DVDs that I thought probably really were music in the drawer over there before I took the rest to the Captain. I got up and my back was to the door. The next thing I knew I heard a crack and then I was coming to on the floor," he explained with another moan.

"Joe, are you okay? Hello ma'am, I'm Dr. Matisse. Step aside so I can check him out before we move him." Dr. Matisse slid from friendly to brusquely professional and back again with ease as he turned to Joaquim. "The stretcher will be here in just a few minutes and we will take you to sick bay at least for the night. I notified the Captain and Danny, so don't worry about any of your duties. Both will be here shortly; they're pretty much finished up with that…," he looked from Joaquim to me and back to Joaquim as he hesitated and then continued, "that other situation for now." I got the impression he was talking in code due to my presence, and I assumed Joaquim's "emergency" and the doctor's "other situation" were the same. My ever-active curiosity wondered what it was.

"No, don't you move. Let me check you over first," he said to Joaquim.

While the doctor knelt by Joaquim and checked his reflexes and such, I restrained my curiosity enough not to ask more questions. Probably it was just an unhappy cruiser, I thought, possibly that Mr. Jarcourt again. But I didn't leave. I slid over to the desk. Some of the CDs and DVDs were scattered on the floor, but it didn't look like all of them. I wondered if Joaquim, or Joe as the doctor called him, had time to put the other CDs and DVDs away in a safe place or if they were now missing. I didn't immediately see any Snooping Dog DVDs among the mess on the floor.

"Ms. King, can you tell Danny and the Captain about the DVDs?" Joaquim asked as Danny and the Captain arrived within minutes of each other. They acknowledged me with a nod, but huddled with the doctor for information. Some orderlies arrived with a stretcher. They got Joaquim on the stretcher, and then they were gone. Once he was out of the door, the Captain turned his attention to me.

"Ms. King, I am Captain Rios. The doctor said that Joaquim probably has a concussion and that you could possibly explain this." His Mexican accent was evident as he waved his arms toward the mess on the floor. "I would like some explanation," he added brusquely. I realized he thought

I was responsible for the scattered CDs, and possibly Joaquim's condition. I wanted no part of the blame.

"Captain, I'm one of the entertainers. A square dance caller in fact. I assume Joaquim told you that there was a problem when we boarded with the equipment and security, and some of the CDs and DVDs got loose?" I asked, hoping that he really had been informed of this.

"Yes, Ms. King, I understand about that. I apologize for any problems that caused, but what does that have to do with this?" was his response, a bit impatient to say the least, and again waving his arms toward the mess.

"Well, like I said, I'm one of the square dance callers. One of the other callers tried to play what he thought was a CD of his. But it ended up it was a DVD. Not just a DVD, but it was pornographic," I realized I wasn't presenting the information in a very organized manner, but I hoped he could follow me.

"Slim and Zach tried a number of DVDs by Snooping Dog and somebody, and they were also porn. We notified Joaquim about this after the dance tonight. That was about two hours ago, I guess. When I found him just now, he said someone broke in and knocked him out. The CDs and DVDs that were suspicious appear to be gone. So I guess whoever did this…" I swept my arm in a motion that took in both where Joaquim had been laying and the scattered discs, "…took them. Unless Joaquim had time to lock them up as he intended. The rest are scattered. There may be more that are porn in those for all we know," I explained as succinctly as I could. "The CDs were in an orderly condition when we left him," I emphasized.

Captain Rios and Danny both looked a little stunned. Out of the blue, Captain Rios asked, "Just where were you and your two caller friends during all this? This is not the only alarming incident this evening, and not the most serious," he said.

I was a bit taken aback that he asked me for an alibi, but I responded civilly, "We were in the Barrio Bar with some other friends. Slim is probably still there. I left to get some sleep and got lost on my way to my room. I heard moaning as I passed by, so I looked in and found Joaquim. We were trying to do what was right, letting Joaquim know about what we found."

"I'm sorry, ma'am. As I said, this is not the only incident we need to deal with tonight, so if I seem a bit abrupt, I apologize. Danny and I will take charge here." He signaled Danny to collect the items. "I will talk to Joaquim, who I am sure will verify your story." I got the impression he wasn't sure at all. "Thank you, and good night." He turned and walked away.

Danny signaled for me to exit without so much as a word. I was more than a little bit put off, not to mention confused, and left the office shaking my head. Obviously, whoever those DVDs belonged to couldn't claim them. Slim was right about that. But why go to the trouble to assault someone to get them back? And just what was the other situation that had occurred tonight? How did it relate to the porn if at all? At any rate, the Captain certainly wasn't going to be on my faves list.

I finally made my way back to my tiny stateroom and, as confused and tired as I was, it didn't take long for me to fall asleep. Even the boxed-in stateroom and small space couldn't compete with a full day of dancing and calling, not to mention the unfolding mystery of the discs. But before I fell into the bunk, I checked the locked door one more time just to be sure I was safe from anyone looking for trouble.

CHAPTER 5

The ship was scheduled for a full day docked in Progreso and the Yucatan, so no workshops or square dances today. I was looking forward to a day off to have some fun and relax. After my night of surprisingly sound sleep I woke up with a new attitude. To hell with worry and romance, I thought, today is just a day for fun and friends.

Dressed in walking shorts and comfortable shoes, I read the ship's brochures while I waited for the others to show up on the exit ramp. Progreso is located at the northern tip of the Yucatan peninsula, the brochure explained. It's a small beach town most known for its Mayan ruins. The brochure made it look so picturesque. It also explained that most of the town's growth in recent years has been the result of cruise ships and tourists. Progreso sits on a limestone shelf that very gradually goes out to sea. They built the pier exceptionally long to get past the shelf and shallow water. This allowed the ships to dock rather than use tenders.

From the brochure it looked like the old village and ruins sit right alongside fancy restaurants on a seaside promenade known as El Malecón. The brochures talked of tranquil beaches with no currents or tides, palm trees, friendly local residents, and fresh seafood, and of course, the Mayan ruins of Dzibilchaltún and Xcambo. Sounded like the perfect recipe for a relaxing day. More than that, the weather was sunny and calm with a slight sea breeze to keep the sun from being hot. And because it was December, the sun and moderate temperatures were wonderful.

"Hello Darla. I said, Hello Darla!" Carlotta's excitable voice usually couldn't be missed, but apparently I'd missed it today. She was shouting in my ear before I realized she had arrived.

"Sorry," I said. "Guess I was just wrapped up in reading about where we'll be going today. Anyone else on their way?"

"I talked to Nick at breakfast. The guys should all be here soon," she said.

Doug and Nick arrived, and Sam followed soon after with Zoe in tow. No Mandy, and I didn't ask. Doug gave me a hug and a friendly 'good morning' and then we started through the disembarkation process to walk down the long pier. Exiting the cruise ship was somewhat hectic. But what can you expect with just about everyone trying to get off the ship at the same time? Slowing up the process were the photographers, some dressed as Mexican dancers. We all declined the pictures, but many of the passengers stopped. I wondered just how many photos were never purchased.

We reached the end of the pier and stalled for a few minutes. There were guides with signs for excursions, taxi drivers, and the passengers all milling around. I really wasn't sure who was leading our group. I had left all that to Carlotta and Nick.

"You know folks, Zoe and I, well we've both already been here before and done the ruins. We're thinking that we may just do some shopping and hang out at the beach. You know, just have a relaxing day. Why don't we all meet back at that cantina over yonder, La Oficina, at about 4ish for happy hour?" Sam suggested, as we stopped to plan our next moves.

"That works for me," Nick responded.

"Sounds like a plan to me," seconded Doug. Carlotta and I smiled and nodded.

The four of us headed toward the buses to Dzibilchaltún, which was described in the brochures as a great Mayan city with a variety of memorial stones and structures in a round enclave. Doug and I walked arm in arm, as did Carlotta and Nick. Nick chattered on and on about the various places to see and the memorial stones with writing on them. Doug and

Nick figured out transportation that would enable us to go to Dzibilchaltún as well as on to El Corchito. The brochures described El Corchito as an ecological preserve operated by local fishermen. The fisherman work to nurture the mangrove swamp by reinforcing canals. The canals then function to improve water circulation and encourage the growth of native plants.

I was sorry that this cruise had come up so quickly. It meant I hadn't had time to do a lot of research beforehand. It seemed like Nick had found time, though. He had the most interest in the ruins and memorial stones we'd be seeing there, but Doug was fascinated by the idea of the ecological preserve. El Corchito wasn't a usual shore excursion, so in the end they talked to a number of taxi drivers before making a final arrangement.

Apparently Nick had checked companies on the internet, so he knew which ones were recommended. Carlotta and I didn't care. We were along mainly for the ride, the relaxation, the adventure, and the shopping. Some of those peasant tops and full skirts would work really well for me. They might make for an alternative to the prairie skirts I favored, at least on the cruise.

As we rode a bus to the ruins, Doug put his arm around me and occasionally squeezed my shoulder. We exchanged comments about Sam and Zoe, the scenery, the great weather, and the places and people we were passing. It was a short ride to the ruins, and then we were there buying tickets to get into the site. Inside, we walked, climbed, chatted, and walked some more.

Nick ooh'd and ah'd quite a bit and talked to us about the architecture and the general structures of the buildings. Clearly, Nick was in his element. Who knew an actuary with an insurance company could get so excited about Mayan ruins and history? I am not usually a history buff, but his excitement was contagious. Learning about the archeo-astronomical happening during the solstice and the equinox was fascinating, and the beautiful pieces in the Mayan World Museum were equally as impressive. Of course, there was also discussion of the Mayan calendar, and why the world didn't end in 2012.

We stopped often to take pictures. We took some of Nick and Carlotta, some of Doug and I, others of all the combinations possible when one person has to click the shot. Periodically we stopped likely candidates to ask if they'd take one with all of us in it. We returned the favor for other groups.

"Enough, enough! I call 'uncle' and I need some hydration," Carlotta quipped as she feigned fainting and Nick caught her. I had to marvel at how well suited they were for each other despite the fact that I never would have picked out the quiet analytical Nick to go with my vivacious friend.

"Okay, how about water all around? I'm buying," Nick responded as he returned Carlotta to a standing position and let go. He walked over to the nearest vendor, just a few feet away.

"I hope you guys aren't completely dying here. Nick just really loves this stuff," Carlotta said under her breath. "It's all he has talked about since you told him about the cruise, Darla, the various Mayan ruins we would get to see."

"No problem, Carlotta. The next stop is more my speed and you three will probably be bored to death there. Won't stop me," Doug responded.

"Hey, I am enjoying seeing something new, learning something new, and not having to be on stage all day. Ruins, preserves, whatever…but what is taking him so long with that water?" I asked.

We turned to see Nick actively involved in an animated discussion, in Spanish no less. He obviously had gotten distracted from his task. He hadn't gotten the bottled water yet. With a sigh and shrug, Carlotta went to get the drinks. We sat on some benches around the entrance, close enough to watch him in his conversation while we drank. Almost immediately that triggered the inevitable question of where to find the restrooms, at least for us two ladies. We left, came back, and rejoined Doug, still without Nick.

As we waited, I finally had a chance to fill Doug and Carlotta in on Joaquim and the status of the pornographic DVDs. Even with all that conversation entailed, and all their questions, it took Nick long enough to return that we were getting a little impatient. We could see Nick still chatting away, so we ventured over to his side. We figured our presence might be a subtle hint. It worked.

"Uh oh, I am so sorry. Well, I'm not really. This here is Memo Jimenez and he is one of the patrons who helps maintain this site. He also has worked extensively to document the history. Fascinating stuff!" Nick explained.

Memo smiled and nodded, and said in English, "It is not always we meet Americans who are this excited about our history. Most are like you. They walk through and visit the ruins, because that is what you are supposed to do, right?" He then shifted to Spanish and clasped Nick's shoulders with a word of farewell. I was impressed by Nick's fluency in Spanish. Memo turned back to us, "I hope you all have a wonderful day. You are lucky to travel with a man of such enthusiasm."

"Water right? We wanted some water?" Nick asked as Memo walked away. We all laughed and Doug held up his almost-empty bottle.

"We've finished ours, thanks, but you better grab one for the road," Doug said.

It was time to move on to El Corchito. We found our taxi driver and he asked if we wanted to stop for lunch before El Corchito. It was a little after noon, and about four hours after the early morning breakfast. We all agreed that some food was in order. Juan, our driver, took us to a little café. He assured us the food was both excellent and safe for Americans' digestive tracts. It was time to have our first taste of real Mexican food, and not the TexMex stuff we were accustomed to in Texas.

We ordered local specialties such as cochinita pibil tacos with pickled red onions and a plate of panuchos filled with marinated turkey meat. The black beans with bacon and lots of chiles came with the meal. In addition, we had a choice of grilled shrimp with garlic, fried whole fish with white rice, and a lettuce and tomato salad with lime dressing or fried chicken tacos with green sauce and fresh cheese. To drink there was cold watermelon juice or tamarind water. Between us, we just about sampled the entire menu.

"So, Nick, the other possible places we could have gone were Chichen Itza, Uxmal, and Xcambó. Dazzle us with your knowledge of those sites while we're eating, so we know what we missed," I suggested.

"Well, Darla, back in its heyday, Xcambó was a fish distribution center for a number of surrounding villages." Nick started out on his narration, then smiled. "Or are you serious? Are you just kidding me about my overachieving research? I could probably spend a month here and not see everything I'd want to. But we wouldn't have time for your shopping or Doug's preserve!" he added with a laugh.

"No, really," I replied. "I'm enjoying your travelog. I guessed you must have researched all the possible places we could go because you didn't know which one we'd choose. I'm interested."

"Well, just remember, you asked!" he said. Nick proceeded to talk about everything he'd learned all the way through the rest of the meal.

When we finished eating, Doug said, "That was good. I definitely need to walk around the preserve and check out the plants to work this off. That's if we don't fall asleep first."

"Whew, you are sure right!" I agreed. With that, we paid the bill,, found Juan, and headed for El Corchito. We heard some yelling and some sort of commotion as we entered. Oddly, there was the passenger called Mr. Jarcourt, still clutching his bag. Carlotta and I just looked at each other. She rolled her eyes and I shrugged my shoulders, not quite sure what he was doing. We seemed to keep running into him, but then again he was hard to miss if he was anywhere in the vicinity. He saw us behind him and came toward us quickly. Looking very nervous, he looked directly at me and said, "Why are you following me, lady? What did I do to you? I can report you, you know, for stalking?"

"Following you? I am not following you—this is just a popular place to come for cruise passengers, honest. We both just happen to be here at the same time," I said, a little concerned and a lot confused.

"Look, I don't know who you are, but the lady is with us, and our being here has nothing to do with you, you understand?" Doug didn't know the story, but he stepped up to defend me.

"Oh, oh, oh. Misunderstanding, then," was Mr. Jarcourt's response. He continued to clutch his bag and look around nervously, his eyes darting right and left, before he pushed past us and was gone.

"That is one very strange man," was all Carlotta could say once again, as she shook her head.

Doug put his arm around me and gave me a squeeze, murmuring, "Just let it go." We spent about an hour in the preserve. We walked, read plaques, looked at wildlife, and talked to the docents who were available to answer all of Doug's questions. It was a beautiful setting, very calming and, well, romantic. But the inevitable practical side of me reminded me that we really needed to head back toward Progreso. I still wanted to get some shopping done and we were supposed to meet up with Sam.

I convinced the others and we found Juan chatting with some other drivers. Juan got us back to the town and we stopped in several stores before heading for dinner. Carlotta and I managed to find some adorable blouses and skirts. I found an onyx dog for my daughter as a souvenir. Thinking of her, I made a mental note to check my email again when we got back onboard. Carlotta picked up a few souvenirs herself. All the while Doug and Nick chatted and made faces at us.

We walked down to the beach and walked on the sand, sandals in my hand. As we watched the approach of sunset, I realized I was actually relaxed and enjoying Doug's company again. I sighed and he moved a little closer as the four of us met up with Sam and Zoe at the café for happy hour. I noticed that he watched me through dinner, eyes looking a little on the heavy side, and I smiled back. The mood at the table was lighthearted, helped by the tangy margaritas. Sam and Zoe talked about their day at the beach. They had watched people parasailing and talked about that as a possibility at a later stop. Doug checked his watch.

"You guys have another one," he said to the others. "Darla and I are going for a stroll on the beach."

He grabbed my hand and pulled me up. I tensed up, then forced myself to relax and enjoy the anticipation of a romantic stroll along the moonlit beach. When we were out of earshot, I said, "We can't be late." Boy, was I romantic or what?

"Yes, Darla, I know that. We have some time. Do you want to be here with me or not?" I could hear the frustration, and I didn't blame him.

"Of course I want to be here!" I did, didn't I?

"Really?" The edge was still in his voice, and his eyes challenged me.

"Really," I said and moved a little closer to make my point.

"Really?" This time his voice was soft and suggestive.

We walked under a pier and stopped to look out at the sea. As he turned to face me, Doug encircled my wrists with his fingers and pulled my hands around his waist. I felt his body press full length against mine. It forced me against the rough wood of the pier supports. He brought his face close to mine, his eyes looked into my eyes. Slowly, giving me every opportunity to stop him, he pressed his lips to mine. I tasted the salty flavor of his mouth. The soft touch of his full lips contradicted the sharp scratch of his beard. As an afterthought, I realized he hadn't shaved today. The musty, enticing smell of his sweat overpowered any other scent.

He pulled away slightly. His hands kept mine behind his back. Our eyes locked for moment, but I lost focus when I pulled him closer to me. Our lips touched, barely, close enough for me to taste him. When I licked his lips, I felt his body tense. My right hand was suddenly free as his left hand went behind my head, pulling my face closer and harder into his. He pulled me tight into him. I felt his body hard against mine.

He let go and stepped back. His wet lips glistened in the moonlight. Suddenly self-conscious, I wiped my own lips dry with the back of my hand. I dropped my gaze to the sand.

"We've gotta get back to the ship, you know," I said self-consciously. I really didn't know what to say or do.

He stepped away and held up his hands like he had a gun in his back. "Darn it, Darla! What the hell am I supposed to do? I know you have some emotional baggage, but we all do. Welcome to the club, and deal with it. But stop giving me the green light/red light game," he snapped in frustration.

"Sorry, Doug. I'm sorry. I'm just confused. I'm not playing with you, really," I mumbled.

"Whatever." He sighed. "Let's head back, you're right. After all, we have to get back to the ship. The others are waiting for us." He took my hand and we walked back to the cafe. It was a very strained walk, not the leisurely pace of our earlier walk from the café. Neither of us said a word.

"Hey, you two," Carlotta called out when we approached. "Wondered where you went. Ready to go?"

"Yes," Doug said. His tone was clipped, but Carlotta was the only one who seemed to notice. She raised her eyebrows at me, but I didn't respond. I gave a slight shake of my head, enough to let her know not to pursue it. We all gathered our things and headed back to the ship.

The distance to the ship seemed miles longer than it had when we left this morning. Carlotta, Nick, Sam, and Zoe kept up a cheerful conversation. I hoped it wasn't too obvious that Doug and I said nothing. We finally made it up to the passenger landing inside the ship. The others split off, and I turned to Doug before heading to my cabin. I stopped as I was about to speak when I saw his attention shift to something over my shoulder. His face transformed into a scowl.

"Ms. King, may I speak to you for a moment, please?" The voice was slightly familiar, but I didn't immediately place it. That was until I turned around and looked into the dimly lit face.

"Paul?" I stammered. "What are you doing here?" As soon as I asked the question, I realized I knew the likely answer. I had already thought, hadn't I, that the DVD mix-up could be trafficking of pornography, which would be a federal crime. And Paul Harbinville was the most recent face of federal law enforcement I'd run across.

Doug snaked his left arm around me. He put out his right to shake hands.

"Doug Weathers," he said. "We met back in Clearton last year."

Paul shook his hand and nodded. A man of few words. From Doug's body language, it was pretty clear Doug was not going to abandon me. Paul turned, motioned for us to follow, and led us out to a secluded section of the deck away from the noise of the boarding passengers and anyone who could overhear us.

"I was wondering if either of you have spent much time with Ms. Mandy Myers," he said in his very authoritative, no nonsense manner. So much for small talk.

I volunteered that I had met Mandy upon arrival at the ship. I added that she had come to some of the dances. I avoided looking at Doug. I figured he could volunteer his relationship with Mandy if he chose to. I was kind of interested in hearing his description myself.

"Excuse me, but why do you want to know about Mandy?" Doug asked. I could feel his challenge in the question. I realized there was more in play here than just Paul's simple question. Doug was aware I had gone out with Paul one time. Lord knows what ways Paul had of getting information about Doug and me. A back-and-forth conversation continued for about five minutes between the two of them. I didn't say a word. I really didn't know what had transpired between Doug and Mandy. I knew it couldn't be anything criminal.

I watched them verbally spar with some amusement. I swear I could feel testosterone levels rising. Doug released me and squared himself in front of Paul, subconsciously I think. As a result, he placed himself in a defensive and protective posture. Whether on behalf of me or Mandy, I couldn't tell.

Finally Paul broke the standoff by offering a tidbit of information. That was all he ever offered, really.

"Don't get defensive, Mr. Weathers. Ms. Myers is the one who suggested I check with you and Ms. King. Her cabin was broken into and ransacked last night. I am just trying to find out what is happening here. She seemed to think you might be able to help clear this up. Something about a crew hand named Willie and the square dance the first night. What can you tell me?" he asked, appearing a little peeved with Doug's defensive dance.

"What? Her cabin? Is… Is she okay? She's not hurt is she?" Clearly concerned, Doug spit out all the questions at once. I was concerned, too, not only for Mandy but also for Doug's excessive alarm over her.

Paul reassured us, "Yes, I believe she's fine. She was agitated, a bit excited, and not making much sense. She rambled on about having taken this cruise or having been on this ship once before with smugglers and other unlikely problems. The ship doctor gave her a sedative. She is in sick bay, but she is physically okay. Unfortunately, I can't say the same about one of the crew. He's dead. She says she found him in the trashed cabin when she returned there last night."

"What? Someone dead in Mandy's cabin?" I interrupted, now a lot more interested. Paul noticed the kick in my energy level and smiled a little. He probably was amused that I would perk up at the mention of a mystery. After all, that's how we met and all he knew of me. At least that was all I knew he knew, anyway.

"We're still trying to figure everything out. I would ask for your discretion and cooperation. Please don't say anything to anyone else. Once again, then, Mr. Weathers, what can you tell me about Ms. Myers? What about members of the crew and the dance on the first night? Any idea what she was trying to tell me about smuggling?" asked Paul.

He was playing his cards close to the vest as usual, I thought. Feeding out little bits of information at a time. Surely he knows about the porn discs. I didn't really see how that would relate to Mandy. I wasn't in a hurry to break the news of another situation to deal with. I suspected he already knew. I wanted to see if he would tell me first.

"I don't know much," Doug said. "I'm sure Darla can fill you in better than I can. I'm going to go see if Mandy needs anything. Where is she again, Mr. Harbinville?" I noticed that while I called him 'Paul,' Doug used the more formal 'Mr. Harbinville.' Not even "Agent Harbinville." I didn't know if he intended respect or coolness.

Paul reiterated that she was in the medical suite on Deck 2. He didn't try to stop Doug from leaving.

"Let's find a place to sit," Paul said. He located a couple of deck chairs and separated them from the others. We both sat down.

As we settled in, I explained about the first night. I told him how some of the crew had helped out at the dance to fill in where needed for additional men. I remembered that there were three of them. I also remembered that one of them seemed to actually like square dancing. Jim, I thought, was the name of the one who had enjoyed it. I didn't remember the other names. I did remember they were hesitant to tell me their names. The other two seemed less inclined, but didn't really stand out in any way. I did mention the tats and that they both seemed a little sullen at the assignment.

Paul asked about the tats. I related that I'd noticed them earlier, during setup that day. I did my best to describe the one that extended on to the man's hand. That was hard to do because I never did figure out what the tattoo was supposed to be. I didn't remember seeing those particular crew members much since the first night. And I told Paul that as well.

Paul was silent for a while after my narrative. It was as if he hoped the silence would encourage me to provide more information. Silence didn't work with me. I'd raised a teenage daughter. Besides, that was all I knew about Mandy or the crew members.

"Your turn," I said. "What brings you onboard? Why are you asking about Mandy and the crew? We weren't in American waters last night when this happened. Mandy is in sick bay from what you've said. But you still got here awful fast." Another thought occurred to me. "Oh dear, I hope the crew member wasn't Joaquim Gonzales. Was it? I found him attacked in his office last night."

Paul shook his head. Maybe it meant "No, not Joaquim." Maybe it was because I'd asked him for information even though I knew he couldn't give it. Maybe because I was again in the thick of trouble and mixed up in his investigation.

"You know I can't give you the full story," he said. "But it is appropriate for me to tell you why I'm questioning you. From the information we have, when the ship was in preparation for boarding, and crew was being boarded, they were short a few people. Some crew were supposed to be transferred from another ship. That ship encountered problems and that led to some unforeseen scheduling problems. Another ship docked unexpectedly at the same time in Galveston. The Captain explained that in order to have at least the minimum crew for this cruise, the cruise line moved three crew members from another ship to this one at the last minute. The three are Jim Falcon, Pete Cruz, and Willie Lopez. Do those names sound familiar?"

"Yeah, Jim's the one who liked dancing," I said. "He came back for at least one workshop. The names Willie and Pete sound familiar. They may have been the other two I met. They weren't particularly friendly. They had been down in the Dreams earlier when we were setting up the equipment."

"Did you happen to see Jim, Willie, or Pete hanging around Mandy? Were they trying to get friendly with her?" was his next question.

"No, sorry. I can't say that I have seen Willie or Pete since that night. Like I said, Jim did come by a workshop. He also poked his head into the dance club last night. He didn't seem to be hanging around Mandy. I really only saw Mandy that day we boarded. Then when she was at a square dance or workshop. Oh, and then she joined me for dinner last night." I stopped talking and Paul didn't say anything.

"Oh, wait!" I did remember something else after all. "I remember hearing that one or two of them were giving Mandy a hard time that first night at the midnight buffet. Don't know who. Sorry, that's it. That's all I can tell you about those three."

He went with silence again. I guess it worked after all, because I found myself adding, "Well, one other thing. When we were boarding, Mandy mentioned she had been on a cruise before with her parents. She said there was some kind of 'drama.' She didn't say what it was. She mentioned it again last night at dinner. Just a mention, no details. Is that maybe what she was talking about when you saw her?" I asked.

My mind was working in overdrive. Paul hadn't answered my question about Joaquim, not really. I thought he would have told me if Joaquim was the one killed. So I figured it must be one of the three borrowed crew members. It didn't take a genius to figure out that he probably didn't die of natural causes.

"That might relate," he said. "What can you tell me about her previous cruise on this ship? It seems that might have something to do with all this," he added. All this, I thought, implies that he knows more than just one incident. I still hadn't told him about the discs, and he hadn't mentioned them. How long would we play this game, I wondered.

He didn't seem quite his usual arrogant self, so I softened up. I gave him what little information I had about her prior cruise with her parents, but I didn't know much. She had implied that it might have been traumatic for her. She had as much as said she was taking this cruise in memory of her parents. She seemed to want to get past the experience of their deaths close together this year. But it happened some ten years ago. I didn't quite see what connection it could have now.

"Darla, I guess that's all the questions I have for now. I've got to go see the Captain, check with Ms. Myers again, and get myself some sleep. I may need to talk to you and your friends again. Especially your Mr. Weathers. I hear he has been spending quite a bit of time with Ms. Myers." Like I needed to hear that, I thought. And where did he get that choice bit of information? "For now, please keep our conversation to yourself," he added.

"Paul, you never answered my question. Was it Joaquim?" I had to be sure.

"No," he said as he turned and started to walk off. I guessed I'd be better off with full disclosure. After all, he was the FBI.

"Paul, wait. I assume that being you, you already know everything I do and more besides. But I better come clean," I said with a smile. "I don't want the feds to come after me." He raised his eyebrows and had a glint in his eye that indicated maybe I did want this fed to come after me.

"I'm too tired to fence, Darla. What haven't you told me?" he said obviously torn between being frustrated or amused.

"Do you know about the mix-up of discs and the pornographic DVDs?" I asked.

He shook his head again, and this time sighed along with it. "Don't tell me you're mixed up in that, too? You just seem to get in the middle of everything, don't you? Yes, we know about the DVDs. In fact, that's what brought me to the ship in the first place. I swear, if I didn't already know you, I'd think you were part of the whole thing."

A smile played across his lips. "Lucky for me, I do know you! We'll talk more later." It almost sounded like a threat. Then he turned and really did walk away.

I had once again missed dinner, thanks to Paul. That didn't leave much else for me to do except head for my cabin, reflect on the rapid changes in my moods over the course of the day, and wonder about Doug's dashing off to Mandy. I could tell my eyes were starting to brim with tears. I wasn't sure if it was because of Doug, a death that saddened me and would spoil my wonderful cruise, or sheer exhaustion. No sooner did I head toward the same door that first Doug, and then Paul, had exited through, and there was Carlotta.

"Hey, Darla, someone said you and Doug came out here … girlfriend, are you alright?" Her initial jovial tone shifted to one of concern as I felt my tears roll over onto my cheeks. "You come with me right now. We need to wash your face and get you into a better place! What did Doug do?"

"I'm okay, Carlotta, really. Thanks, but you go back in and spend time with Nick. A lot happened before we came back to the ship. And then some other stuff after Doug and I came out here. I'll tell you about it later. I just need to get a little rest. Doug went to be with Mandy. I'll be okay," I reassured her.

"To be with Mandy? He left you for Mandy! That cad!" I could tell Carlotta had gotten the wrong impression. I tried to explain, but I didn't have time to get a word in to explain. She rolled on, "And you think I would leave you to feel sorry for yourself over the breakup? Not on your life. Besides, as far as Nick and I go, spending too much time together makes it hard to figure out what to talk about. Not that we spend all our time talking...," she added with a wink.

I laughed, and let her lead me to the nearest lounge restroom. When Carlotta's on a mission it's pointless to fight it. As usual, she kept up a steady stream of conversation, which was comforting as I sure wasn't ready to talk.

"Take it easy, Darla. Don't worry about anything. This is only the third day of the cruise. And this IS a cruise you're supposed to be enjoying! A new year is coming up. It's bound to be one of your best. You're just stressed out right now. You're tired and you were in the sun too long today." She laughed. "Heck, I was in the sun too long myself. When we were coming back onboard, you'll never believe who I thought I saw. Some guy who looked a lot like that agent, Paul. You know, that FBI hunk who had the hots for you earlier this year? Can you believe it? We both know he isn't on this cruise, but I swear my mind made him up. I just don't know why! The sun has weird effects sometimes. You'll get over your mood if we just go have some fun." She finally wound down and gave me a chance to talk.

I laughed, and said, "Carlotta, that wasn't the sun. You did see Paul Harbinville. He's onboard. I told you I'd tell you all about it later. I guess now is later." She stared at me. I couldn't tell if she thought I was still sunstroke or if she just couldn't believe we were apparently involved in another adventure.

"Girl, you got a lot of explaining to do!" she said. After she worked on my face to conceal the fact that I had been crying, we went to one of the quieter areas on the ship. At the library I tried to explain what had happened and what had stirred up my feelings. I explained about Paul telling Doug and me about the crew member dead in Mandy's cabin. I explained that Doug had gone to see if Mandy was okay. As I retold it, I realized his response was probably not all that surprising or upsetting. Doug was a compassionate man. His compassion was part of what I liked so much about him. Halfway through the tale, I remembered Paul's cautionary request not to talk. Yikes, I thought.

"Oh, by the way, Carlotta, you know you can't talk about this, right? Even to Nick," I asked. "It's a federal case and I'm not supposed to tell anybody. Of course, you're not just anybody," I laughed.

"Gee, thanks. You give me a juicy piece of gossip like this and I'm just supposed to clam up. Good thing for you I work at the newspaper and am the next best thing to a journalist. I can keep my sources and my secrets under a lid. But don't tell me any more I can't talk about. Let's talk about the even juicier part anyway. What's up with you and Doug and Mandy and Paul? I just love a good romantic triangle!" she laughed. After a second, she quipped with a scrunched face, "Or is that a square?"

"Carlotta, I just don't know what kind of relationship I want with Doug. I like him, sure. I like his attention and his touch. I just don't know if I want anything more with him, with anyone right now, or if I want it and it's too scary, or what! Until now, most times Doug and I have only seen each other for a day or evening at a time, and then not for a few weeks in between. He gave me lots of space, and it didn't become an issue. Now, on the ship, we see each other all the time. There's an expectation of romance. It's harder and more confusing than I expected. I don't know how to deal with Doug in these close quarters. Here we are in a setting that is ripe for romance. I feel like I am blowing it." It was my best attempt to explain what was going on with me, and of course, led to more tears.

"Wow, Darla! That's freaky! I knew you had issues about getting close to someone, but try to relax and take it at face value. You have to take things at your own speed. Maybe

Doug was just being protective of Mandy, you know? Or protective of you? Maybe he wants more from you, but that doesn't mean you have to give it. Certainly, you don't have to rush into anything. Look, tomorrow when we dock in Cozumel, Nick is going snorkeling and really wants to go scuba diving. I don't do either. How about you and I hang out together, and just be tourists? Hang out at the beach, do some shopping, and relax. No guys. Not even Sam, assuming he would leave Zoe's side. I swear they're attached with Velcro! For us, just a girl's day out before we bring in a new year in a couple of days."

"You sure, Carlotta? That sounds great to me but I don't want to pull you away from Nick," I responded. I dabbed at my eyes one last time and stood up, ready to go to my cabin or to get some food. "You ready to go, Carlotta?" She nodded and we both headed for the elevators. We spotted Sam and Zoe waiting at the elevator, arm in arm. Carlotta poked me and pulled me into an alcove, giggling.

"Velcro," she whispered. She managed to get a smile from me.

We waited a few minutes to give us time to get a straight face, then made it to the elevator. Sam and Zoe were long gone.

"Okay, we will meet at the Purser's office about 9:30 in the morning—a little later than the stampede this time," suggested Carlotta as we headed in different directions. It occurred to me that I hadn't seen Danny or Joaquim since we had come onboard. I made a mental note to check on Joaquim before we went ashore in the morning. I still didn't know for sure which crew member had been found in Mandy's cabin. I was relieved that it wasn't Joaquim. He seemed to be hardworking and nice. I guessed he probably was not paid near enough for the aggravation he was dealing with on this cruise.

I took time to grab a quick shower and get changed before heading back to Deck 11 for a light meal. It had been a long day, and it hadn't gone on a positive note so far. As I pulled out my jeans and t-shirt, I wondered if I had brought enough clothes for all the workshops and dances. It was possible I'd need to do laundry before the week was up. I'm not a fashion plate like Carlotta, and generally I don't worry about what I wear. But when I call, I do try to look professional. And I did want to look nice. I was surprised how many dancers had brought their traditional square dance outfits along on the cruise. It made me feel I needed to step up my wardrobe. Not because Paul was here, of course, but just to keep up with the dancers. I ran a brush through my hair, and was ready.

When I got to the food court on Deck 11, I grabbed a salad and some pasta. I chose a seat so I could listen to the band playing on deck and watch the dancers. The band was playing popular music, not too fast, not too slow. Most everyone was in jeans, but some were still in bathing suits. Others wore shorts. I envied some of the ladies, girls really, who had the cute figures needed to parade around in a bikini. Never slim, the years had added some additional curves to my figure. I ate and watched the small crowd. The energy level was low, due I'm sure to all the energy expended in Progreso.

I had just about finished eating when I felt a hand on my shoulder. "Hi Darla! I see you went for the healthy fare," Slim noted as he sat down. He had a plate that was stacked high, and most of the food wasn't green.

I smiled and offered, "Yeah, we ate well in Progreso so I figured I would eat lite tonight. Did you get off the boat or have you seen it all already?"

"Been there, done that, got the t-shirt. At least all the touristy stuff. I've done this route so many times…. Last year I made friends with some of the crew. They let me in on a fairly small beach that isn't very crowded. Last year and this, there were only a handful of tourists and another handful of the younger crew members letting off steam. Truth be told, it's a bit rustic but the water is clear, the beach is clean, and it's quiet." He shrugged and smiled as he finished his explanation. "And what did you do?" he asked.

As Slim attacked his plate, I related our day, the ruins, the preserve, the shopping, and the food. Needless to say, I didn't say much about Doug or even mention that the FBI was onboard or why.

I was beat. It had been an exhausting day for me, both physically and emotionally, and I just wanted to get some rest. I said a quiet goodnight to Slim. I hopped on the elevator and headed straight to my stateroom. I really hoped I wouldn't run into anyone I knew. Carlotta would likely want to cheer me up some more. I was just not sure I could cope with more cheering right now. Mostly, I hoped I didn't run into Doug or Paul again. I almost wished I had a disguise to go incognito. Fortunately I didn't need it, and I got to my stateroom door without interruption. Surprisingly, I was asleep in no time despite the small cabin. Maybe this cruise would cure me of my claustrophobia!

CHAPTER 6

Eventually the cabin won our ongoing claustrophobic battle, assisted by my rollercoaster emotions, and as a result, despite my exhaustion I slept only fitfully all night. In the morning I wasn't feeling bright-eyed and I looked more like red-eyed. I finally gave up trying to look good without pounds of makeup. Hungry, I decided to sneak up to the upper deck for some breakfast with a bare face, hoping no one would see me.

I chose stairs for the first few decks to get some exercise. After the first few flights, though, I made my way to the elevators at the end of the ship. I figured since we disembarked mid-ship, most of the passengers would be using the center stairs and elevators. Obviously, others had the same idea. The elevator took a while. Most were going down while I was trying to go up. For a fleeting moment I contemplated taking the stairs for the next six flights. About then the elevator saved me by arriving, thankfully, empty. Deck 11 was pretty sparse as most of the passengers were on the lower decks trying to disembark and get in a full day of snorkeling, ruins, and nature parks. Today we docked in Cozumel, and I could feel the ship was already stopped.

I made a pass through the buffet line and found a table in the corner by a window overlooking the beach. It looked like we were going to luck out on the weather yet again. It was sunny, and a little breezy, but it hadn't felt cold when I stuck my head out. I chose to eat healthy again this morning and I was just finishing up my fruit cup when someone walked up beside me. Looking up, I was surprised to see Mandy.

"Hi, can I join you?" she asked.

"Sure, I'm about finished but I'd be happy to stay and visit," I said. "Are you planning to go in to port today?" I wondered at the coincidence. This was the second time she joined me.

"Yeah, I thought I'd go in later, but I'm not in any hurry. I'm taking things slow," she said.

"Oh?" I asked, inviting her to expand.

"The cruise just isn't turning out to be very relaxing, and I keep having problems with my cabin," she responded.

"That's an understatement! I heard about the episode in your cabin. Are you doing okay?" I asked. She looked harried and tired, definitely anxious.

"Well, yes, I guess I am. But I can tell you, I don't plan on going on any more cruises ever again," she said with a shudder.

"I guess with the incidents on this cruise and the last one, I can understand that. What exactly happened on that earlier one?" I asked. I still had trouble seeing how something that happened ten years ago related to pornography and a dead crew member, but I was curious. Well, some people would call it nosy.

"Oh, it was quite well known at the time. It was about ten years ago, and on this same cruise line. Maybe this same ship, I'm not sure, but the same name. I came with my parents and we had a great time. That was right up until the next-to-last day while we were at sea." She stopped and gazed out the window at Cozumel.

"I'm a lot more comfortable when we're in port, but when we're at sea all day I get pretty nervous. Because when we were out in the middle of the water, we were boarded by pirates." She made a face. "Pirates, in this day and age, can you imagine it? That's what they called them. No eye patches or parrots, but just as ruthless as the old-fashioned kind." She gave another shudder and continued.

"Our ship stopped. I still don't know what they threatened to do if we didn't. A bunch of men boarded from a ship a little smaller than this one. The Captain, or someone anyway, made an announcement that we should all go to our lifeboat stations. It was spooky, just like the drill they do on the first day of the cruise. Having to go there was scary just because you never think you'll need to do it. At first we all thought we were sinking or stalled or having mechanical trouble. Then we realized it was something completely different."

I was surprised she was telling me all this detail. Paul had implied she wasn't very forthcoming about it. Maybe she was just intimidated by him. I hadn't really expected a detailed answer to my casual inquiry, but I was happy to get it. I'd always been called a sympathetic listener. Lord knows Paul was anything but. Maybe that was why she felt comfortable telling me about it. I wasn't interrupting her with a lot of questions, which may have helped.

"There were a few men with automatic rifles at the doors of the dining room where my parents and I were," she continued. "We weren't able to even get out of the dining room and I remember being scared to death! Then, after a while, it seemed like a long time, we heard another boat approaching and the men ran out. We heard shouting and gunshots. Apparently the good guys won—after a few hours everything seemed to go back to normal. Well, almost normal. It really shook me, though, and I kept thinking someone with a gun would break into our cabin at any time. I think it would have been better for them to tell us what had happened. Instead they kept it rather hush-hush."

"I agree, it usually is better to know. So how did you find out what had happened?" I asked.

"When we got into Galveston the next night, already later than we were supposed to due to the delay at sea, we had to stay an extra night on the ship. They interviewed everybody one by one, even as young as I was. Afterward,

Mom and Dad and I pieced together the information we got in our interviews. The pirates had planned to steal the ship for smuggling and take anything of value on it at the same time. No telling what they would have done with us if the Mexican Federales hadn't stopped them."

Another shudder went through her. Although she dressed and looked the part of a strong and capable young woman, I could see a fragile young person underneath. If pushed far enough, reminded of that earlier cruise and threatened, could she kill somebody? I couldn't quite capture that image.

"I can see how that would be traumatic. It's a pity you've had a violent episode on this cruise as well," I said. Trying to lighten the mood, I added, "Nobody mentions these harrowing kinds of experiences in the brochures, do they?"

"No more brochures or cruises for me, I'll tell you that. Not to mention all the trouble with my cabin. I told you about that, didn't I?" I nodded and she brightened. "But at least I'm having fun with square dancing," she said, obviously trying to change the subject.

I wasn't going to change the subject so quickly. I was working my way up to the murder.

"Remind me about your cabin situation," I said. "Have they gotten everything straightened out?"

"Well, no. My initially assigned cabin still doesn't have working plumbing. The second one, well, I'm not allowed in there now. I'm still housed in sick bay. But with the broken wall safe, I was already having to store anything of importance at the Purser's office so it hasn't made much difference. A federal agent is onboard, and he accompanied one of the crew to get some clothes out of the cabin for me. I don't think I'd like to stay in that cabin now anyway." Her eyes flickered with nervousness. Then she shook her shoulders back and took a breath. "It's not so bad, though. Going to the Purser's office all the time certainly makes me learn my way around the ship."

"So what did you think of the agent?" I asked.

"He scares me. He isn't very sympathetic. He somehow seems to think all this is my fault. Doug told me not to let him worry me. He said that he's met him before. Do you know him?" she asked. I nodded and she continued, "He's cold and I wish I could avoid him."

Clearly she was not impressed with Paul. Although I found his attitude a little frustrating sometimes, I had dubbed him the Harbinville Hunk from the first time we'd met. Well, to each his own. She probably was too upset and traumatized to appreciate just how 'hunky' he was.

"So do you know who the man was in your cabin?" I asked. I omitted the word 'dead.' It just seemed too harsh.

"No. No one will tell me anything. Everybody just asks me questions," she replied.

I saw her shoulders slumping again, so I changed the subject. We talked a little more about nothing in particular, but I couldn't stop thinking about her cabin change. I did think her experience on her earlier cruise was just bad luck, highly unusual, and not connected. But I couldn't stop the nagging feeling that changing cabins earlier in the cruise might be a piece of our puzzle.

When we finished eating and talking, Mandy said she was going back to sick bay to rest. It was still a little before 9:30, so I swung by Joaquim's office. The door had been repaired but was open. Joaquim was at his desk and looked tired.

"Ms. King, I didn't get a chance to thank you the other night. I appreciate your help. I am not sure how long I would have lain here had you not found me," was his greeting. Despite his personal words and obvious fatigue, he was his usual professional self.

"No problem. How are you doing?" I asked.

"The doctor said it was a small concussion only. I still have a sore head and a pounding headache, but otherwise I am okay," he replied. "Captain Rios said he has notified appropriate authorities on the other matter also. It is too bad about the crew member...," he said with a shrug. He seemed to be extremely unconcerned about the 'other matter.' Dismissing the topic, he asked, "Why are you still onboard? Don't you wish to go on shore for a while at least?"

"I'm glad you're okay." I wondered why he thought I knew about the dead crew member, but maybe it was a slip. Or maybe he figured gossip travels fast through a ship's population. "I talked with Agent Harbinville last night, and I was sorry to hear about the crew member. And yes, I am going ashore. In fact, I need to meet my friend soon. But I wondered who the crew member was. Can you tell me?"

"I wish I could. But if you have talked with Agent Harbinville, you know the situation is complicated. I hope you will have an enjoyable day in port today," he said. His statement held a clear note of dismissal.

"I hope so too, thanks," I answered. Joaquim nodded and I headed toward the Purser's office. At the appointed hour I was waiting for Carlotta at the Purser's office. I was still feeling tired and generally disconnected from everything. I replayed my conversation with Mandy, but nothing popped out at me.

After about 15 minutes, still no Carlotta. It occurred to me that she probably had a better offer and had decided to go ashore with Nick. I seriously considered just going back to my cabin. Or maybe I could go to sick bay to talk more to Mandy and, more truthfully, see if Doug was with her there. I was deep in thought when odd Mr. Jarcourt burst around the corner. He really couldn't move fast enough to call it jogging but he was moving as fast as he could. He still clutched the

satchel tight against his chest. Before I could react, he ran
right into me and almost knocked me over.

"Oh, no, oh no. You again? Leave me alone!" Mr.
Jarcourt yelled at me, barely missing a step. That really
stepped on my last nerve.

"Excuse me! You just about knocked me over. Watch
where you are going, sir!" I retorted, a little louder than I
needed to. Mr. Jarcourt didn't seem to notice my response.
He just continued on his way toward the disembarkation
platform. I turned and was ready to head back to my cabin
when I spotted Carlotta.

"Hey Darla! Sorry I'm late! You know that funny little
man with the suitcase? Well, I was on my way here with a
couple of chocolate mocha lattés for us. He bumped into me.
Spilled the lattés all over me. Well, they were a lost cause and
I had to go back and change my clothes, so we don't get to
enjoy those drinks after all! Do you think he has the Hope
Diamond in that bag or what?" Carlotta asked, laughing and
shaking her head, running her words at high speed as always.

Carlotta was dressed in her usual high style. Today it was
bright reds, greens, and blues. She wore solid pants with a
paisley top. As always, she looked like she had just stepped
off a magazine cover. And this was her quick-change
solution. No telling what her original outfit looked like before
she had to change.

"Yeah, he just about bowled me over just now too. I
hope he doesn't go in the same direction we're going. What
direction is that anyway?" I asked as we started toward the
platform and off the ship. I had done limited homework
before the cruise to look up sights and excursions possible,
but about now, all the ruins swam together. I realized I
should have checked the brochures before breakfast this
morning.

"Well, I thought about it after we talked, and I really want to go visit the Mayan ruins. I don't remember which of the ruins it is where the calendar ended in 2012, but I heard so much about how the world was going to end based on that calendar that I want to learn more about it. Most of the ruins are on the mainland. We need to take a ferry and then a bus to get to Tulum. That would be almost two hours in transit in each direction. There are some other ruins right here. I think Nick's enthusiasm for ruins must be contagious. Other than that, well Darla, you know I love to shop," she said with a bright smile and looking like a little kid.

I wanted to just relax and maybe get in a nap on the beach, but I knew Carlotta's energy level wouldn't allow much of that. Besides, the ruins would be educational, I told myself. We arrived at the end of the exit stairway and encountered a long line of taxis, buses, and limos.

"Okay," I said, "that looks like a tour operator right there. Why don't we see what they're selling, and if it fits our schedule," I replied. Most of the offerings were the same trips as those offered on the ship, just a little cheaper. Carlotta started chatting with the man at the first taxi stand who was holding a sign saying 'Mayan tours.' While she chatted, I tried to read all the fine print, or at least the part that was in English. He offered several options including San Gervasio, El Cedral, an Eco Park at Punta Sur, or the Castillo Real. We obviously couldn't do them all and still get in Carlotta's shopping and my beach time.

"Darla, they have a full-day package and a couple of half-day options. What do you think?" asked Carlotta.

"Actually, I'm thinking I'd rather do a half-day of ruins and then head out to the eco park. What is it called?" I suggested.

"Si, la Punta Sur!" the tour operator supplied. He explained that Punta Sur was at the southern most tip of the island and would take an hour or so to get there. This was consistent with the packages I had seen in the ship brochure. We had a dance scheduled for late tonight so I needed to get back in time for a quick nap before I had to call the dance.

"Okay, would you suggest that or San Gervasio?" I asked the tour operator. I looked at Carlotta and shrugged.

The tour operator hesitated. He probably didn't want to give a negative vibe on either. He looked from one of us to the other. "You see ruins before?" he asked. When we nodded, he nodded back and said "Punta sur better then." Carlotta nodded again and the tour operator did a quick tally. We paid for our tickets and he directed us to the correct bus. It was only partially filled. I looked around but didn't see any familiar faces. First we'd visit the eco park and then come back to this general area for a quick lunch. That would leave some time for us to relax and shop before getting back onboard this afternoon. So we were off on our adventure, along with about ten others. Some were from our cruise. Some were from the other cruise ship that had docked right after us. The bus was comfortable, air conditioned, and not very crowded.

Carlotta was her usual bubbly self as we made our way. She talked with the passengers sitting across from us. In the process, she established that the group of people wearing the white and green tags were, in fact, a group from a church. So, my guess on that group was pretty accurate. Carlotta chatted away, and I chimed in with a "Yeah," and "Uh huh" when I could. It was a pleasant ride and the beach did look inviting. The driver provided some commentary and explained that the part of the island we were going to was not as crowded. Shortly, he pulled over to the side and asked if anyone wanted to taste tequila or use the restroom. We all piled off, followed him, and listened to someone explain about agave plants and how tequila was made. Carlotta and I each tried a sample of flavored tequila and used the facilities. Locals hawked their goods as we made it back to the bus.

We stopped again at a beach area with some refreshments. We walked on the beach and then we were off for the eco park. The driver pointed out that our tour included the lighthouse and the maritime museum. We arrived and grabbed a couple of bottles of water. As we walked through the area and toured the museum, I read the brochure.

At the lighthouse, some of our group decided to make the trek to the top. Carlotta and I meandered through the huts with touristy goods. As she looked at an onyx chess set, she commented, "Nick would really like that, but where would we put it?"

"Where would we put it? It's that serious then?" I asked, somewhat surprised even with all the time they spent together. After all, they'd just met earlier this year and I couldn't imagine me making a life-changing decision that quickly. "Is there a wedding in your future then?"

"Not yet, but we have had lots of serious conversations about the future lately, so I guess it's out there somewhere, sometime," she confided. "If and when we do set a date, Darla, you better plan on being there."

"As if that's even a question," I said. "Of course I'll be there! And I better be one of the first people you tell, too. So have you done any of the 'meet the family' stuff yet? Does Nick have family in Texas?"

"So far it's just pillow talk with us, and most of it started around Christmas. Neither one of us was quite ready to do the family thing. Darla, do you realize we've really only known each other three months? I feel like I have known him so much longer," she said with a sigh.

We made our way back to the center as the others started to come back out of the lighthouse. Carlotta looked at me and said, "So… Darla, I know you're feeling upset about Doug and whatever is going on with him and Mandy or him and you. Do you want to talk about it?" ventured Carlotta, a little hesitantly.

"I can't explain it, really, Carlotta. I like Doug, and sometimes I think it would be nice to 'be a couple' with him. To be a couple, period. But that's part of my trouble, I don't know whether it's Doug or my need for someone in my life that's driving my time with him. Most of the time when we're together I feel really comfortable, and I enjoy his company. He's a great guy, stable, caring. What else could I ask for? And I do feel twinges of jealousy when I see him paying attention to other women," I explained.

"But when I try to imagine our relationship moving forward, or if he tries to move it forward, I back away," I continued. "I don't know if it's because the relationship isn't right, or because I'm just scared to get close to anyone. Neurotic, aren't I?" I said with a shrug and sigh.

"Darla, at our age we're all neurotic. Maybe at any age. It's not really any of my business, but you know that doesn't stop me so I'll ask anyway. Have you had this reaction to other guys, or just Doug?" she asked.

"How would I know? I haven't dated much. In fact, no one but Doug, unless you call that one dinner with Harbinville a date. I don't. Clearly the dinner was just to try to get some information, so it really doesn't count," I contended. But I knew Carlotta saw my dinner with Paul as a date. I wasn't ready to admit it, but even thinking about Paul made me blush. I was acutely aware that I did have a very different reaction to Paul than to Doug.

"Well, Darla, I think you need to get out there and do some dating. I like Doug too. He's a good guy. But maybe the uncertainty you feel is because you don't like him exactly the way you want to like him. You and I are radically different, but I know immediately when I feel a serious attraction to a guy. And you might have had the dinner with Harbinville to get information, but it sure seemed like he thought it was more than that. And whether you know it or not, you just blushed when I mentioned his name. How do you feel about him now that you saw him again this week?" she asked.

"Carlotta, he's here on a case, not to see me," I said, avoiding her question.

"Well, that's a non-answer if I ever heard one. I think you just need to get out there some more and give yourself a chance. Lord knows I don't want to get involved in another mystery caper with you," she rolled her eyes. I knew she was talking about the wild ride she and I had taken together the last time we got involved in what the Clearton Gang called 'my' mysteries.

"But with Harbinville on this cruise, there's obviously a mystery here too, and maybe you'll find romance in his direction along the way—if it doesn't kill you, of course." She was joking, wasn't she? At least about dying, if not about dating Paul.

"Or how about one of those online services? You know, eDate or something?" she continued.

I retorted, "You sound like my daughter! Online dating, right! I can just see myself doing that. As for Paul Harbinville and the murder case, right now the only thing I want is to avoid excitement on this cruise and have some fun." Even as I said it, I knew I was lying to myself. I loved a mystery and seldom could keep from trying to solve it. After my years as an investigator, I'd limited myself to puzzles and mysteries in the form of paperback books. Lately, however, I was finding out my curiosity for real-life whodunits hadn't really abated. Not my fault, I told myself. I hadn't asked to be involved in either this mystery onboard or the last one with Carlotta.

Trying to get back to lighter topics, I laughed and added, "The only mystery I'm curious about on this trip is the intriguing question of what Mr. Jarcourt has in that bag of his. Oh, and why someone brought a bunch of porn videos on a cruise."

Carlotta laughed in response and countered with "You're right—enough soul searching. Here comes our driver and we get to go see where the alligators are now!" We followed our driver, a little behind some of our group, down a path through tall greenery. The driver was explaining that this area had many alligators. We gathered on a wooden walkway above the water. He pointed out where there were some alligators. A wooden structure was at one side. Some of the church group climbed up it to get a better view. Cameras came out and we all took turns playing photographer. Then we boarded the bus and headed back to Cozumel.

As we rode the bus, I commented to Carlotta, "You know, Doug probably would have loved this park and been even more enthusiastic than we were. And Nick would have liked the maritime museum. I hope they're enjoying their day."

"I bet they are. I think Sam, Nick, and Doug were all doing one of the beach buggy, zipline, or snorkeling gigs. Those are way too active for me," she laughed.

The bus arrived in what likely passed for downtown. We were still a ways from the port, but it wouldn't be a long walk. We started to walk and Carlotta quipped, "That was a great way to spend the morning, but do you realize it's after 1 o'clock already!" She continued, "I'm exhausted and starving. And that's just with riding the bus and walking around. I'd be ready to eat a horse if I'd been doing strenuous activity all day like they are. Let's find someplace to eat. I hope it's not siesta time with no restaurants or cafés open."

I agreed and we walked down the sidewalk and tried to decide where to have a meal. Most of the places seemed to be bars rather than restaurants. It probably would have been a good idea if we had asked the driver for a recommendation.

"Darla, I'm starving," Carlotta said again. "Here's a café right here, La Copa de Oro. How about if we try it?" Carlotta asked. It kind of looked like a dive, but then it looked like many of the buildings we'd seen.

"Let's see if we can figure out enough of the menu to manage. My Spanish is kind of rusty. Do you see a menu anywhere?" I asked as I searched the windows and walls near the door of the café Carlotta had indicated. Most of the restaurants and cafes posted menus in their windows so tourists like us could choose a place based on food and cost. It didn't appear this one wanted to brag. The windows were dark from window tint or something blocked them. I couldn't see inside. It didn't seem as busy as one of the places we had passed, so I thought we might be able to get in and out quickly.

"No, I don't see a menu but we could go in and ask," Carlotta said as she reached for the door.

"Whoa there, Carlotta." We turned around to see Sam walking toward us in a rush and smiling ear to ear. "Hold up, gals. I don't think you want to be going in that door there. Don't you know enough Spanish to understand that La Copa de Oro is a play on words for a "gentleman's establishment," if you get my drift."

I didn't get his drift, but I searched my mind for a translation. I came up with it about the time Sam explained it.

"Loosely translated, La Copa de Oro means 'golden cup.' In this case, not the kind of 'cup' you drink from," he said with a chuckle. "Can't you tell what kind of establishment this is by the blacked-out windows and lack of advertising out front? Honest, we can't leave you girls alone for one minute without you getting into trouble, can we?" Sam chuckled some more.

Carlotta was all sorts of red and embarrassed. I felt a little awkward too, but we just laughed it off. After all, I'd been ready for an adventure, hadn't I? I didn't think Carlotta and I would have been in serious trouble inside the club, it being on the main tourist thoroughfare. And obviously, we would have figured it out as soon as we walked in. But with my limited Spanish, I hadn't realized where we were soon enough to keep us from being embarrassed at least.

Nick and Doug caught up with Sam as he finished his explanation. Needless to say, they joined in the joke at our expense. Zoe was nowhere to be seen, so I guess she and Sam weren't Velcro-ed together today. Looked like it had truly been a guy's day for them.

Sam continued, "So I'm guessing you ladies haven't eaten yet either. Why don't we all find a nice restaurant," he placed the emphasis on 'nice' with a smile, "and eat together?" He scanned all our faces for some indication.

We all agreed. Doug, Sam, and I walked in the first tier with Carlotta and Nick bringing up the rear. Sam continued to tease, first about La Copa de Oro and then about shopping.

"I thought for sure you gals would be loaded down with shopping bags when we found you," he said. "But it looks like all you have are tiny souvenir bags. Couldn't you find any stores you liked?"

"For your information, we've been partaking of the local history and educational activities this morning," I retorted. "We haven't even had a chance to do any serious shopping yet. But we plan on it."

We arrived at a place that looked like a good candidate for lunch. It was called Las Tortugas. I believed that meant turtles in English, but that didn't make sense. I turned to Sam. "So, Sam, does this one meet your standards?" I asked.

"Looks like it from out here, Darla," he said as he reviewed the menu. "I think it's your basic Mexican deli. Okay with everyone if we give it a try?" he asked the group. We were seated almost immediately and the prices were reasonable. It looked like locals ate here and not just other passengers. That's usually a good sign, and it was this time. The food was delicious. While we ate, we talked about what everyone had done during the morning, and then Carlotta opened a can of worms.

"Hey, Darla and I were talking this morning about the two mysteries we have on the ship," she said. "What do you guys think about them? First of all, we have this odd little man, Mr. Jarcourt, who will not be separated from his bag and thinks everyone's out to get him. He made me spill two lattés this morning and about knocked Darla over," she exclaimed.

"You know, we ran into him too this morning. Not quite as literally like you guys," said Nick. "He was over at Marine Park when we were snorkeling there. He looked like he was dressed for dead of winter in that same sports jacket he always wears and had his case clutched tight. He's always looking around suspiciously and seems generally unpleasant. But I gotta tell you, I think he is just weird, not criminal," Nick commented. "I guess it is a mystery in a sense. But I bet it's something pretty simple and boring," he added. Carlotta made a face at his deflating response.

"And what's the second mystery, Carlotta?" Sam asked, eyes twinkling.

"I'll let Darla tell you about that one," she answered. "Darla, tell them about the…you know!"

I was surprised to realize that I didn't want to talk about it. I enjoyed just being a tourist today. Plus, I knew I couldn't trust myself not to spill more beans than I should. I played the good sport, though, and gave a quick description.

"Oh, just all the mix-ups with the CDs and DVDs and the porn DVDs we found. While it really isn't a mystery if you just think of them as someone's porn collection, it is a mystery if someone's distributing them. I've never heard of porn trafficking on a cruise ship. Especially one headed out of the U.S., not into it. Then someone busted down the door and knocked out Joaquim to get them back," I explained. "I guess it's possible whoever had them thought they could be traced back to them. I don't know if there's a way to trace where a DVD was made," I continued.

"Well, do you think it's likely the two mysteries link up?" asked Nick. "Is it likely that Mr. Jarcourt is the one with the porn DVDs? Maybe that's why he's so nervous and guilty looking? Maybe he has the master porn DVD in his bag?" Nick asked, smiling. None of us took him seriously.

"I suggested it was maybe the Hope Diamond he was hiding," Carlotta said. "And I wasn't serious about that, but I'd believe that quicker than believing that he's connected with porn-trafficking. I am real curious about him though. I think that we need to check out the guests too. The ones who are not square dancers. We need to see who looks like they could be a porn-trafficker. You know it couldn't be a square dancer," chimed in Carlotta. We all laughed.

"Carlotta, my dear, you'll recall the last mystery we tried to solve did involve square dancers. Well, it involved imposters dressed as square dancers. So we can't rule anyone out. And, my dear, just what does a porn-trafficker look like?" Sam countered with one eyebrow raised questioningly. Carlotta shrugged and shook her head, obviously unable to come up with an appropriate description.

"The only clue for the porn stuff is that a lot of it is something about a Snooping Dog or something. I guess that is who produced it," I said, finding myself caught up in the telling despite my earlier reluctance. "But the truth of it is, we turned everything over to Joaquim. He was to give it to the Captain. But then he was assaulted, and now it's gone. So there's no evidence for us to look at unless one of the other entertainers still has one of the DVDs. The Captain notified the authorities, but I don't really know who that would be. I'm not sure if they notify U.S. folks, Mexico folks, or who," I responded, trying to put everything in perspective while still not revealing more than I should.

"Okay, so we have two possible mysteries, and no clues to speak of. Is that the whole of it, Darla?" Nick asked. He sounded for all the world like he was ready to dive into investigation.

"Hey, hey! Who said we should get involved in this thing at all? We're not going to 'look into' anything," said Doug, the voice of reason. "The feds have been called in, and we should just leave it to them. What's this 'evidence for us to look at' thing? It's not our responsibility to look at evidence." He looked over at me. "And you haven't even mentioned the biggest mystery, Darla. What about the murdered crew member?"

I was so taken aback with Doug's question that it must have showed. Paul had asked us not to talk about that. It was the first direct statement Doug had made to me in relation to our time on the deck last night. Doug must have recognized my reaction because he continued hastily.

"Don't worry, Darla, I'm not spilling any beans that came from Harbinville. First of all, he's not hidden on the ship and everyone knows he's a fed. Second, I'm only sharing information that came from Mandy, a friend, not secrets from the esteemed Federal Agent Harbinville." I felt a little better, though I sensed more than a bit of hostility in Doug's comments.

"Yeah, Darla. Doug filled us in earlier today. From what Doug told us, our prickly old friend Harbinville is right in the thick of it again. And he seems to think Mandy is a 'person of interest,' though I don't get why at all," Sam responded. He looked more serious than usual.

"Well, Sam, it did happen in her cabin. It makes sense that she would be considered a suspect," I offered. I noticed that Doug bristled a bit at my suggestion. I realized that I had just defended Paul. That likely explained it. "Doug, did Mandy mention how the crew member died? Do they have the murder weapon? And do you know who he is yet?"

"What? Your good buddy Harbinville didn't share his info with you? I'd have figured you'd have the inside scoop." Doug answered. It was becoming a little tense at the table for my taste.

"I don't know much about it. You know Harbinville, always vague. He listens but doesn't offer much," I hedged, trying to bring the tension level down a notch. "I don't know that any of our mysteries are connected to any of the others. Mandy does seem to be in the mix somehow. Just like Nick was a few months ago. That doesn't mean she's part of anything nefarious," I added, looking over at Nick. I hoped to diffuse the rising tension and get someone else involved in this conversation. To do that, I reminded them that Nick had been an innocent victim, even though he was the one who pulled us into that last situation. It worked, and Nick chimed in.

"Yeah, I can certainly relate to what Mandy must be feeling. Harbinville can be like a dog with a bone, not about to let go," Nick responded. "So Doug, what's your take on Mandy's involvement?" he asked.

"Actually, Mandy mentioned something about smuggling and some kind of excitement related to illegal activities when she took the cruise with her parents some years ago. She said it added excitement to the cruise, but they actually had to stay on the ship one day in port because of it. She seems to be particularly nervous about crew members. Apparently some of the crew were involved the last time," Doug explained. "What her involvement is this time, as well as the dead crew member's, I don't know. She's pretty shook up. She'd have to be a pretty good actress if she's involved. So I'm giving her the benefit of the doubt. We all should," he said, more like a command than an observation.

I felt slightly deflated. Here I thought I was such a good listener, that was the reason Mandy had opened up about her parent's cruise to me. Apparently she had told Doug the same story, true or not. There was an uncomfortable silence before Sam stepped in to lighten things up.

"Here, here, if we don't get going the real mystery will be to figure out how to get back onboard the ship if we're late," interjected Sam. He stood up and that was all we needed to make our way out to the street.

"Coming up with a good explanation why one of the callers isn't there to earn her keep would be tough," I mused. "Carlotta, do you still want to squeeze in some shopping before we head back? I only have about," I checked my watch, "thirty minutes."

"You know me, I can do a lot of damage in thirty minutes of shopping. Let's go!" she said.

With that, we all paid our respective bills, and the guys headed back to the ship. Carlotta and I hit a few stores, and she did do a lot of damage in a short time. It was very tempting to take our time looking at the intricate embroidery on the peasant blouses, and even on the dresses and skirts. Even though I realized it meant I had missed my beach time, by the time I finished shopping I was getting a little antsy to get back to the ship and prep for work tonight. I had to urge Carlotta to speed it up several times, but we finally made our way back to the ship just in time for dinner. It was surprising how quickly time sped by. I didn't have time to think about anything else.

Dinner was spent with everyone at the table talking about their day in port. Doug didn't come down. I couldn't decide if that was a good thing or not. I was relieved not to have to deal with tension. The food was too good to end up with an upset stomach from anxiety. Before I knew it, it was time to rush to my stateroom, clean up, change clothes, and head to the Dreams. It didn't give me any time to think about the continued tension between Doug and me. I was thankful for that. And Carlotta didn't ask about it or comment on it either. Of course, it didn't give me much time to plan what I was going to call at the dance either. I was winging it a lot lately.

The majority of square dancers, particularly the newer and younger ones, would probably not bother with the square dance after a full day on shore for a second day in a row, so we expected a small crowd. But it was a scheduled event, and some of the diehard dancers wouldn't miss a chance for 'skirt work' as we called the lively dancing. I dressed in a basic jean skirt and comfortable t-shirt. With the tension between us on shore, I figured Doug wouldn't be looking for me to dance much. When I arrived at the Dreams, Zach and Slim were in serious conversation with Joaquim and Danny.

"What's up?" I asked, wondering if something else had happened.

"Hey Darla, how are you?" Slim responded. He continued, "While we were all ashore, apparently someone tried to break into our equipment storage. I called Joaquim. He and Danny have checked out the damage. It wasn't just our stuff. All the entertainers that had sound systems had the same kind of thing. Damaged doors or in some cases, open doors on all the entertainment cabinets. Some of the equipment was damaged. Seems a heavy way to communicate not liking the music, so I don't think that's all it was. It looks like the Dreams must have been at the end of the run. Possibly whoever it was got interrupted here. The cabinet lock is broken, but our equipment doesn't look like it was touched. Nothing seems to be missing." He shook his head.

"Hello, Ms. King. I apologize for this inconvenience. I am pleased to say I think everything is fine here. I do not understand what is happening with all these incidents on the ship. The Captain has been notified of the vandalism problem and is in conference at the moment," offered Joaquim, looking pale and worried.

"So you think it was just plain vandalism, not someone looking for something?" I asked, thinking about the porn DVDs and the way Paul had described the condition of Mandy's room.

"Looks to me like vandalism," Slim answered, shaking his head again. Zach remained silent.

"Some of the activities for this evening have been cancelled due to damaged equipment. Since your equipment is in good shape, as I told these gentlemen here, you might have more people at your dance tonight than you expected," Joaquim said. His shoulders rose and fell with an audible sigh. "The vandalism, the death of a crew member, and my office being trashed, I just don't understand," he said.

"Looks like we are still all set to go, guys. I see a few folks coming in the door, so I guess the show goes on," chimed in Zach, nodding in the direction of the door. With the entrance of passengers into the Dreams, Slim moved into management mode and started setting up equipment. Joaquim made a hasty exit, greeting the incoming passengers as he left. Amazingly, he had managed to paste his professional smile and demeanor into place again.

We had decided last night that I would be up first tonight. We were all calling in the same room and would share Slim's equipment setup. I got out my CDs for the first tip feeling a bit ill-prepared, after having rushed getting ready after our late arrival back to the ship. I regretted being the opening caller of the dance. Zach would be up second and had already indicated he was going to call to a current pop song, so I decided to go with a little Jimmy Buffett for both the first and second part of the tip.

The three of us did a quick revamp of the dance schedule to account for new dancers who might be coming from other venues and not been expecting to square dance tonight. I'd call a Mainstream tip first and then Zach'd call a couple of fun tips everyone could dance to. At that point, Slim would be up to call and he could decide how to handle the rest of the night based on the ability of the dancers in the Dreams. Good thing callers are flexible, I thought.

In no time, with about 40 folks milling around, it was time to get going. We assembled on the stage. Grabbing the microphone, I greeted them with, "Good evening! I hope you all enjoyed your day in Cozumel. We'll be doing Mainstream dancing to get warmed up tonight. So let's square 'em up!"

Slim added, "Welcome, everyone! I know some of you folks might be joining us for a square dance for the first time. We're glad to have you at the Dreams Club. If you're a dancer or have had any of the workshops, feel free to square up and dance this first one with us. If you're new to the sport of square dancing, well then just watch these first two songs. See how much fun it is, then we'll invite everyone to dance the next set."

As they formed squares, I looked around to see who was here. I spotted Sam and Zoe, Carlotta and Nick, and Al and Amy that I had met earlier, but no Doug. Hmmm, and no Mandy. At least there was no Paul Harbinville either. I saw a few other familiar faces. I said hello to some of the folks in the squares up front. I thought I recognized a few of the newest dancers as more people filtered in. How many there were would determine how we called the movements. A few curious faces ringed the dance floor. They sat or stood and looked a bit lost. I figured these were first-timers.

When it looked like everyone was set, I started with the familiar call, "Bow to your corner, bow to your partner, circle left." I worked them through a number of moves I knew had been covered in workshops so far during the cruise. I used a tropical Jimmy Buffet song as the background for my patter call portion of the tip.

"That's great! Now, nobody move. We're off to Margaritaville!" I really liked this Buffet classic song. I did the singing call by replacing some of the lyrics with instructions to the dancers. "Okay, great job! Take a short break, and get ready to rock with Zach! This time, everybody up on the dance floor. You don't have to have any square dance background for this one!" I stepped off the stage and retrieved my CD from the sound system as Zach walked up with his.

He gave me a big smile. "Nice job, Darla. Good choice of music as usual," he said. "I'm really enjoying calling on this cruise, despite all the problems they seem to be having. Oh, yeah, and my lack of sleep. I'm trying to fit in way too many activities, but I suspect I'll survive. Anyway, I'm learning a lot from you and Slim." I thanked him, then walked over to Slim and passed on the compliment. Slim still seemed a bit off-kilter from the earlier incident.

"Is everything okay with your equipment and CDs, or did you end up with something missing or damaged after all?" Slim asked me. His forehead was beaded in sweat. He took a sip of water.

"I'm just heading over to check my equipment," I answered him. "I didn't have time to check it before we squared up, and didn't need to since we're using your equipment tonight. So far I am still missing the one CD I noticed earlier." I shrugged my shoulders and added, "but I haven't had a chance to figure out which one it is. I've found ones I wanted to use, so I guess it wasn't all that important. How about the rest of your stuff?"

"Everything looks fine," he said. "The country western singer, Chance, got hit bad. Part of his sound system will likely have to be replaced. In fact, he may have to borrow parts to do the New Year's Eve dance and after party," he added, shaking his head. "I told him we might be able to share and loan him speakers or something. But it just doesn't make sense to me. It's not like our equipment or anyone else's is all that useful to anyone—it's really geared to entertainers."

Slim slung back the rest of his water and looked around for a place to set the cup. He ended up just holding onto it as he continued. "From that point of view, it doesn't seem like one of the other entertainers would be the culprit. It doesn't appear anything was stolen, just damaged. I guess someone could be planning to pawn or sell the equipment for cash, but then why damage it? The whole thing especially doesn't make sense on a cruise ship, with all the security we have here and the difficulty of offloading anything stolen. What did I hear Joaquim say about a crew member being killed? Obviously that's hush-hush, but it sounded like he thought we already knew about it." Slim looked at me expectantly and I felt a little guilty for not sharing what I knew with him, despite my promise to keep quiet.

"Yeah, I can tell you what I know later. It's not exactly anything that we want overheard," I said. "I have no idea who knows, or what's connected and what's not anymore."

While Zach was finishing up his 'fun moves' for everyone on the dance floor, I went to get some water.

"Ms. King, how are you this evening?" I heard from behind me, close enough to startle me. I spilled my cup of water down the front of my blouse. I brushed off as much as possible, then turned around to find myself very close to Paul Harbinville. So close I could smell his aftershave. And then I blushed, although I wasn't certain why. Sure, he was one very nice-looking hunk, but so were a lot of other men. He definitely had a different effect on me than the average man. And he clearly enjoyed being the cause of my discomfort, with the smirk on his face. And he didn't move to increase the distance between us.

All I managed to stammer out was, "Paul, hi. Oh, my gosh!"

"Well, apparently trouble follows you, even on a cruise," he said. He obviously referred to the incidents on the cruise, as well as the situation when we had first met in the fall. "The Mexican and American governments are jointly involved in the investigation of the murder aboard this ship now. They are also looking into the possible pornography situation, which you were apparently the one to point out. I figured I'd stop in and say hello when I saw you in here."

He wanted something, that was clear. What, I wondered.

He continued, "I wasn't exactly sociable last evening. I am still trying to get my sea legs and check out the ship. I had only come onboard about an hour before the ship left the port when I searched you out last night. I will be back by later and you can fill me in from your perspective. You usually have one," he said with a smile. "I spotted Carlotta and some of your other friends. It will be like old home week," he added sarcastically.

Now that was surprising. He gave me information without my having to even ask. I waited for the other shoe to drop.

"How'd you know I was onboard to search me out?" I asked.

"I reviewed both the passenger roster and crew manifest on the way to my assignment. I wouldn't be much of an investigator if I didn't know my opponents, would I? Or my allies, for that matter," he responded. I hoped he included me in the 'allies' category, but I couldn't tell.

My fluttering stomach assured me that I wasn't immune to attractive males, despite my earlier dithering over whether I wanted any relationship these days. I certainly experienced a different feeling when Paul was around, or when I thought about him being around, than I had when I was with Doug. But I wasn't sure if this feeling was one I wanted. It could just be nervousness based on his position as an FBI agent, after all. After Clint's death and my traumatic exit from my job in Florida, I had vowed not to have anything to do with anyone in law enforcement. Yet here I was.

I was definitely attracted to Paul, even though I didn't really know much about him. Not the solid ground to base a relationship on like I had with Doug. I pulled my shoulders back and rolled my head around to stretch my neck. I made myself relax and get my thoughts and emotions under control.

"I'll be glad to talk to you about it," I responded, "but remember I'm working on this cruise. It will have to be after the dance is over." He nodded, and I escaped back up to the stage. I could feel him watching me. Only when I turned back to face the hall did he leave the Dreams Club.

I was barely back up by the stage where Slim was, and Zach's time at the mic was ending, when Doug popped up out of nowhere. I'd checked for him earlier and he was nowhere to be seen. Where had he come from? He stepped up and massaged my shoulders possessively. I wondered if he had seen me talking with Paul, and what prompted his change in attitude from lunch. He was beginning to make me dizzy with his twists and turns of attention and withdrawal. Served me right. I guess I knew how he must feel.

"Care to dance the next tip?" he asked. "I assume Slim is calling, since you and Zach already called," he said. I hesitated

and then agreed. Square dancing was neutral territory. I
didn't think I'd be making any commitment I didn't intend.
He and Slim engaged in some small talk, Doug's hand still on
my shoulder. Then Slim excused himself to call while Doug
led me to a square. Because of the dance level of the crowd,
he opted for another Mainstream instead of a Plus tip. Doug
and I ended up in a strong square, including Zach and a young
lady named Ivette. I had not met her before.

She seemed about Zach's age and was attractive, with
bright eyes. His body posture and expression suggested it
wasn't the first time they'd met. Maybe she was the reason for
his lack of sleep, or at least one of them. There were two
older couples in our square who had been in workshops.
They actually weren't much older than Doug and I but I often
had trouble remembering I was getting there too. Slim did a
great job, keeping it upbeat and challenging. Before I knew it,
it was my turn to call again. One problem with the pace of
square dancing is that there isn't much room for conversation.
Doug said "I'll be back" and took off. I went to work.

"One more set for experienced dancers, then everyone
on the floor again," I announced. I decided to keep up the
pace with Sara Evans' song "Suds in the Bucket" and the
Beatles' song "Hard Day's Night" for my tip. "Square your
sets," I called, and cued up Sara Evans.

"Join hands, circle right," I called. For some reason,
starting right instead of left catches dancers off guard. I heard
the expected groans and chuckles travel through the crowd as
the squares adjusted their direction. As I called, I saw Carlotta
and Nick in a square. Carlotta gave me thumbs up. This was
one of her favorite songs.

"Now circle left," I instructed. I continued with the calls,
but noticed a commotion in a back square. I watched as the
dancers immediately stopped moving but continued holding

hands. I realized that I could see only five heads in the circle instead of eight. Sure sign that someone had fallen.

The folks in that square must be experienced dancers, I thought. They knew the appropriate response when a dancer went down. Usually a dancer hops back up, the square reforms, and the dancers get back into the patterns. If a fall is more serious, however, the standard response is for the remaining dancers in the square to hold hands and form a circle around the fallen dancer. This provides protection against any jostling and also privacy. Usually one person will go to the fallen dancer's aid and one will go for help if it looks like it's needed. That's probably why I spotted only five heads in the circle out of the eight dancers. One dancer was down, one helped, and one sought assistance.

I kept calling while I watched the square to see how serious things were. If it seemed appropriate, I'd stop the tip and ask folks to clear the floor. If not, it was better to keep going and let the situation be handled with as little unnecessary interference as possible. I saw Slim make his way quickly to the unmoving square. Zach also had his eye on it, but he was in a square and kept dancing. Well, he tried to, but he missed a call while his attention was diverted.

A couple of squares nearby had become aware of the trouble and were also distracted. A few dancers crowded around the circle with the fallen dancer. Slim apparently convinced them to act normally. They regrouped and resumed dancing. He looked up at me, put his forefinger in the air, and made circles, motioning me to on with the song. I finished up "Suds" and made a short announcement.

"Folks, we've had a spill over at the far corner. Everything's under control," I hoped I was telling the truth, "and everybody is going to be okay. I ask that you slide your squares a little over to the left on the dance floor for this next dance, though, to give them some air. Now, square 'em up for The Beatles."

I kept the dancing going to prevent rubberneckers from getting in the way of whatever needed to be done. While I called the dance, I watched as Dr. Matisse came in and knelt inside the circle of dancers. Following him, a couple of crew members came in with a stretcher and loaded the fallen dancer. Neither of the crew members looked familiar. The others in the square dissolved to the sidelines, and Slim headed toward the stage. I finished up Hard Day's Night.

"Great dancing, everyone. Take a break and Slim will have a all-dance tip for you coming up," I shot an inquiring glance at Slim and he confirmed with a nod in response. I stepped off the platform and met him as Zach walked up too.

"So," I asked, "what's the situation?"

"Looks like a case of exhaustion," he said. "Not a heart attack or injury, thank goodness. An older man. The doc took him to sick bay, and his wife is with him. Doc didn't seem overly concerned but wanted to make sure he was sufficiently hydrated. Probably just overdid things today," he added.

Sick bay was getting crowded, I thought. First Joaquim, then Mandy, now a dancer. And those were just the ones I knew of. I wondered if cruise sick bays always got this much action, or if our cruise was unusual.

Doug didn't come back until Slim called a Plus tip later in the evening. Not quite sure how he happened to get the timing right, but we danced it together. I did notice that in contrast to other dances, Mandy never came to tonight's dance.

The dance continued pretty much on schedule. It turned out we didn't have a lot of non-dancers after all. The ones who had stopped in faded out quickly. I guess there were plenty of things to do onboard even if some of the entertainment had been cancelled. The three of us finished out the evening calling together on a three-song tip that included "Thumbing My Way to Mexico," "Ghost Riders in the Sky," and "God Bless the USA," all thanks to Zach's great selection of CDs. We did it as a 'tag team' call, handing off the mic after each set of moves. It's not always an easy chore to rearrange someone else's arrangement of dancers, but I enjoyed the challenge and it livened things up a bit.

Paul never made it back to the club, and that was probably best. After the final thank you's, we were back to packing everything up. The events of the day and concerns with the vandalism earlier in the evening now had to be considered.

"I am just not sure I want to leave my stuff here tonight," Slim said. He tapped his foot as he thought.

Doug came up and stood beside me again. At his puzzled expression Slim related the problems with all the entertainer cabinets. After some discussion, Slim offered to take at least some of the stuff, including all the CDs, to his cabin for the night. He took some of the smaller equipment as a precaution. He was beat and didn't plan to stay up. Zach and I thanked him and he headed off with the main sound system. Zach took off to continue his evening, but didn't really say what that entailed. I guessed Ivette figured in there somewhere.

"Doug, you go on if you want to. I need to check out my equipment. We used Slim's sound system to call tonight. I haven't had a chance to make sure mine is all there. I need to do that and let Joaquim know if there's any problem," I said.

"Not a chance, Darla. With everything going on around here, I'm stuck to you." Oh great, I thought, another twist and turn of affection. I wasn't sure I wanted Doug stuck to me.

"Just let me know how I can help and then we'll go have some fun," he finished.

My sound system turned out to be fine. In fact, it didn't even look like it had been touched since the last time I'd put it away. I figured I'd leave it where it was and that would split equipment between Slim's cabin and the Dreams. At least one system would be safe.

I hadn't given much thought to my plans for the rest of the evening. Sometime during the evening, I needed to check my email to touch base with Heather. Despite the unpredictability of her college lifestyle, my 20-year-old daughter seemed to be the most stable thing in my life right now. Odd. She was still glad to hear from her mom, and for that I was grateful. I wanted to do my best to keep the lines of communication open with her, especially after our last few years had been rough.

As Doug and I headed for the doors to leave the Dreams, we saw Carlotta, Nick, Zoe, and Sam headed our way. The Clearton Gang sticks together, I thought. I wondered if Zoe would become part of the gang even though she wasn't actually from Clearton.

"Thought you might still be here," Carlotta said to Doug and me. She gestured to Sam and Zoe as she continued, "Look who I found wandering the hallways! All of you guys gotta come with Nick and me to listen to the DJ in the club next door," invited Carlotta. "He's funny, but best of all, he plays great dancing music. He's been mixing it up with a little bit of everything."

"Man, Carlotta, you have the energy of a power line," said Sam with a smile. "We'll go with you, but I don't know how much Zoe and I'll be on the dance floor after the calling Darla put us through," he laughed.

I figured it was Zoe who wouldn't have the energy—I'd never known Sam to wind down. She smiled. It was obvious that even if she didn't plan on doing much more dancing she wanted to hang out with Sam and our little crowd. I was tired and even my small box of a cabin might be heaven right now, but I thought it would be fun to go with everyone for a while. I had heard about this DJ since the first night. So far I hadn't had much time or energy to just spend time on this cruise like a real person. The week was rapidly coming to a close, so if I was ever going to do it, it better be soon.

Doug responded before I could, and I felt a little miffed that he felt entitled to answer for me. "You sit 'em out, Sam," he said. "But Darla and I would love some more dancing tonight." He had his arm around me and he gave a gentle squeeze.

So off we went, with me feeling more than a little off-balance. Doug still didn't mention anything about the missing Mandy or our earlier tension on the beach or on deck last night. The DJ was quite good, and the music he selected was just right. Doug and I two-stepped and waltzed. That was all I needed to start to feel comfortable with him again. I was being silly, I thought. I was making too much of a little squeeze or a kiss. Doug was just Doug, and I was just me. Life was just life. No reason to think I could control any of it. That thought made me smile, laughing as much at myself as actually feeling happy.

"So, what's the smile for?" Doug asked as he returned with drinks. I tried to think of a flirty retort, what he might want me to say, but couldn't come up with anything.

"Uh, just musing about life," was all I could come up with. Doug handed me my drink and set his on the table between us. Then he walked around behind my chair. He placed his hands on either side of my neck. All the others in the group were out on the dance floor. We were alone at the table. He began a gentle massage. This was getting to be a habit of his, I thought. I should like it, but immediately my defenses were triggered and I tensed up instead of relaxing. Doug's hands stopped moving. Almost as quickly, I relaxed a little. After a heartbeat, Doug began kneading my muscles again. This time I willed my shoulders to relax under his touch. After a few seconds, Doug slid his right hand up to the back of my skull. He pushed slowly forward and I felt a welcome stretch along the top of my shoulders.

I thought I heard Doug say something, but it was so low I wasn't sure. I started to turn to ask him, but his left hand slid outward and pushed down on the top of my left arm to keep me in place.

"Resist," he said.

My brain tried to interpret his meaning, testing other possible words that he might have said when it couldn't grasp the meaning of the one it thought it heard.

"Resist my hand. Push your head back against it," he explained.

"Oh." I followed instructions. I pushed back against his hand, bringing my shoulders down for more leverage.

"Now relax," he said in a low voice.

I relaxed, and heard my upper spine crackle like popcorn. Tension drained out of my muscles. It felt terrific. Doug's hands didn't move.

"Resist, again."

This time I responded without confusion and firmly pressed my head into his splayed fingers.

"Relax," he commanded.

I relaxed. I felt warmth flood my neck and shoulders. I sat still, enjoying the absence of tension after weeks of being keyed up. Doug moved his right hand beside my neck and inched his left in to mirror it on the other side. I felt him lean in toward my back and realized his lips were just behind my left ear. He spoke low and soft.

145

"Resistance is good. But only if you eventually relax," he said. I knew he wasn't talking about massage anymore. I searched for a response, but couldn't form one quickly enough. I felt a soft breeze and turned around to see his back as he walked toward the lounge area.

"Doug, wait!" I yelled over the music.

He raised his hand in acknowledgement. It wasn't really a wave, but more a gesture of half-surrender. I watched him walk away through the doorway, then disappear out on deck. Confused again, I just stared at the door, and thought about following him. I didn't. I shifted my gaze to the dance floor. Carlotta and Nick were dancing, as were Sam and Zoe. I didn't want to explain Doug's absence when they got back to the table and was about to make a quick exit when I felt pressure on my shoulder again. The touch was firm and when I turned around, this time it was Paul, not Doug. This balancing act could get confusing.

"Ms. King, how are you?" he asked, somewhat formally I thought.

"Doing fine, Paul, and you? Taking in a little music are you?" I asked vacantly. My mind was still trying to get a grip on what was happening with Doug.

"You know, Darla, one of these times, I'm going to have to show you that I really can dance. Pretty good at it in fact. I'm not all work and no play," he retorted. My god, I thought, he really is flirting with me! Even I couldn't mistake it this time. This cruise atmosphere must be getting to everyone.

"In the meantime," he continued, "I need to talk to you a little more about this crew member and Ms. Myers. Your friend Mr. Weathers isn't exactly forthcoming with information."

"Well, I'm not sure what else I can tell you. Sam and I talked to her briefly as we were boarding the ship." He leaned forward to hear me as I continued. "She said she was on a similar cruise some years ago with her parents. There was some kind of problem. Doug mentioned it might be smuggling. She didn't explain then what it was, simply that it was why she was taking this cruise, but I told you that already," I related. "This morning, she had breakfast with me and told me more."

I quickly added, "It was her choice, not mine," as he started to say something. I figured he was going to accuse me of interfering with his investigation. He said nothing, and I continued.

"She told me about the earlier cruise." I filled him in on Mandy's story. "But I really think she is leaving something out. I wonder what might have happened while she and her parents were stuck in the dining room. But that's just intuition on my part, or maybe my relentless curiosity or vivid imagination."

"I'm well aware of relentless curiosity," he retorted. I ignored him.

Something that had been nagging at me finally clicked in my mind and I spit it out before the thought formed completely.

"Something's been bugging me about the change in her cabin location, Paul. It has nothing to do with the previous cruise, of course. She's mentioned a couple of times that she was initially in one cabin and had to move. The plumbing was broken and couldn't be fixed in time. So they put her in the cabin where the murder occurred. Maybe there was, or still is, something about the cabin where she is now. She said no one was usually assigned to it. She said that's what she was told by Danny, one of Joaquim's assistants. It seems to me that the person or persons who trashed her cabin might have been looking for the same thing as the people who damaged all the sound equipment," I said, assuming that he knew about the equipment being damaged.

"Maybe this isn't vandalism, maybe they were looking for something," I went on, now completely absorbed in my own theory. "Or looking for a different person they thought might be in the cabin. Or something in the cabin. Oh oh, in the safe! Mandy said she couldn't use the wall safe in her current cabin. Said it was broken or jammed. Could there be something in it?"

I hesitated, but he maintained his usual silence. I was sure he'd respond to my suggestion about the wall safe, but he didn't. Or at least give me grief for running on at the mouth. I harrumphed with frustration at his silence and bland expression. At least that got a response.

"Okay, I appreciate you sharing this information and your ideas," he said. His lack of enthusiasm was underwhelming. "You've raised some questions, and I'll certainly follow up on them when possible. If you or any of your friends can offer any other information about Ms. Myers or anything else related to the investigation, I'm sure I can count on you to come directly to me," he said.

I wasn't sure he really thought that, but I took it at face value. It did occur to me that he put a little emphasis on the word 'directly.' I wondered if he suspected any of the crew. I liked Joaquim and Danny. I hoped he wasn't implying that either of them had anything to do with all the goings-on. Without another word, he walked away. I seemed to be having that effect on men tonight. At the same time, Carlotta and Nick headed off the dance floor toward the table.

Carlotta smiled and winked with this 'I told you so' look as she rolled her eyes toward Paul's retreating back. Nick commented, "Wasn't that the agent guy? Harbinville? Where's Doug, did he chase him away?"

"No, of course not. Doug left before Paul came in. Paul just wanted to know if I knew anything about Mandy and the crew member who was murdered," I explained.

"Unfortunately, I couldn't help. After all, I didn't go to the buffet with you guys the first night. If you remember anything that might be helpful, he'd like to talk to you," I added.

Both Carlotta and Nick shook their heads and shrugged.

"Sorry, Darla. I'd like to help out, but we, um, weren't exactly paying much attention to Mandy," Nick quipped and tightened his arm around Carlotta's waist. I was surprised to see Carlotta blush a bit. That must have been some night.

Sam and Zoe came back to the table, and I repeated the request. Sam just shrugged and agreed. Then he and Zoe made a graceful exit. Carlotta, Nick, and I chatted a little more, mostly about the sad state of affairs on what was supposed to be a carefree and relaxing trip. As they went back out to the dance floor I headed to my stateroom for some sleep, assuming that was possible. Between the massage episode with Doug, the flirting incarnation of Paul, all the mysteries onboard, and the box-like nature of my cabin I figured I'd be lucky to get even 4 winks, much less 40. I was hoping my glass of wine and my level of exhaustion, physical and emotional, would help.

CHAPTER 7

The dawn of New Year's Eve brought with it another day on shore, this time in Belize City, and therefore another day off the ship and, thankfully, out of my small stateroom. Belize was popular for its outdoor activities and barrier reef, and the guys would be off early to get their snorkeling and scuba diving in once again. This time Carlotta went with them. I was invited but declined.

On principle, I don't like the way I look in a bathing suit, so I didn't bring one with me. And, I don't particularly like swimming, for another. I know that seems strange, but I'm not good at it and never feel safe in any water over my head. Or in water that isn't contained, like a bathtub or pool. While I lived in Florida I considered taking swimming lessons. But all the others in the class I signed up for were under 12, and the instructor wasn't much older. I felt a bit awkward and out of place, so I didn't go back.

Nevertheless, since I had missed out on it in both Progreso and Cozumel, I planned for a little downtime just kicking back on a beach. Nick and Sam had rattled on and on about their intended activities in port after the snorkeling, but Doug hadn't said much. I guessed, rightly or wrongly, that he planned to spend time with Mandy. Of course, I hadn't asked him to spend time with me, had I?

At breakfast, I met up with Carlotta. She again told me she thought Paul was interested in more than my mind. She followed that with her usual pep talk and told me I should just live a little. She bolted down more calories from the buffet than I could afford to eat in a week. Then she jumped up and was off to meet up with Nick and Sam. That left me to my own devices. First I found a comfortable lounge chair on the upper deck with lots of open space and a prime spot for people watching. There was no set time for my excursion to the beach.

Actually, it turned out to be excellent for sleeping as well, and I didn't even feel bad about snoozing. I was tired from the emotional rollercoaster of the night before, in addition to the lack of sleep caused by my claustrophobia. I woke up about an hour later. I decided it was good timing. I hoped the crowds leaving the ship had slimmed. I went back to my tiny box of a room just long enough to collect everything I needed so I could go do a little sight-seeing, then get my long-delayed time on the beach. I checked the room safe, hoisted my backpack full of maps and beach things, and headed out.

As I passed the library, I remembered to stop and use the internet to check my email and wish Heather an early Happy New Year. She had responded to my previous email with an "lol." She wrote on about how she and Micah were going to a party, but that they would be careful and that they weren't going to be drinking. I wasn't sure I believed her, though they were both under age. I did appreciate her trying to reassure me. My mom guilt kicked in, but I squelched it. She didn't need her mom holding her hand, I told myself. I wrote her we were in Belize, and to have a safe, but good time. I had a few other emails from square dance clubs asking if I was available for this or that date. I didn't need to deal with those, so I just left them. I'd be home soon enough to respond to them.

Signing off, I headed for the debarkation area. For this port, the ship was anchored away from the mainland. A large barrier reef prevented the ship from getting closer to shore. All morning the announcements about the tenders and such had repeated at regular intervals. I still wasn't quite clear what a tender was. On my way out, my curiosity flared up but not in the direction of the tenders. I headed by Joaquim's office.

"Good morning, Joaquim. I talked with Mr. Harbinville last night. I guess you're spending a lot of your time in port with officials today. Is it always like this?" I prompted him, hoping he would fill in some of the details.

"Good day yourself, Ms. King. I've never had a cruise like this one for sure. I hope to never have another. My office is still a disaster," he added, waving his hand at the barely repaired door and other temporary fixes, "and we have a cabin that is a mess as well. Your friend the agent and the Federales have not allowed us to clean it up. We have three more days, two of those mostly at sea, and no extra cabin. And we still have to find acceptable accommodations for your agent and Ms. Myers. So far he has been staying in the Captain's quarters, and she is in the long-term part of sick bay. That is not really suitable, do you think?"

His normally bright face looked dull and he was developing dark circles under his eyes. I also noticed that somehow Paul had become 'my agent' in Joaquim's mind.

"I'm sorry about the crew member, Joaquim, was he a friend?" I asked, trying to sound sincere and not just curious.

"Oh, no, I barely knew him. Will was a last-minute hire, not one of our regular crew," he answered. "Besides, I really have little to do with most of the crew." Ah hah! It was Willie that was killed. I felt some satisfaction that I had ferreted out the name, although I wouldn't have been able to tell you why I felt satisfied. Knowing his name didn't tell me anything. It didn't explain Mandy's involvement or who had an interest in killing him.

Joaquim continued, "I do wish that if any of the crew were bothering Ms. Myers she would have told me. I was not happy to hear that two of the crew were annoying her and following her. Maybe we could have avoided some of this. We could have taken some action against the crew members involved or kept them below the public decks." He closed his eyes briefly and shook his head as if to clear it.

"What? Mandy was being stalked?" I asked, suddenly feeling a bit silly. This information put Doug's protective stance in relation to Mandy in a new light. Perhaps he was just being protective, and not romantic at all. Something to think about. I remembered Sam mentioning that the crew members made her nervous, but I hadn't realized it had gone beyond that.

"Yes, Ms. King, I assumed you knew. Oh dear, I am so sorry if I upset you. I am getting careless with my words. As soon as we locate the other crew member that came aboard with the man, we will restrict his movements. For now, though, I need to get to work and help search for him. Then I need to talk to your agent some more," he added as he walked around his desk and edged me efficiently and politely out the door of his office. "I hope you enjoy your day in Belize City. I believe you have a busy evening ahead, no?" he asked before he turned to go.

"Yes, Joaquim, a busy evening. Have a good day, yourself!" I responded as I once again headed for the tenders. Like yesterday, I was later than the masses leaving the ship so it went very smoothly. It was a little more complicated though because I had to clear the debarkation and then get on a tender boat. Just getting off the ship, it seemed like there were more officials and the crew were checking identification more carefully than yesterday. Although there were two levels of benches on the tender, there were only about 10 of us this trip. It was a pretty short ride and then the boat was at the dock.

Only one tour bus was still waiting, and it looked about ready to depart. I read the sign and talked to the vendor, and this one was the basic city tour and visit to an ancient Mayan site. I thought about securing a private taxi, but wasn't sure enough of myself to pick a legitimate one. So I decided the tour sounded good and I'd to go to the ruins and then catch the beach. I bought my ticket and boarded the bus, and found a window seat about midway down the bus.

The guide immediately asked us to be seated, greeted us, and started telling us about the highlights of the city as the bus took off. We went through the business district as well as the historical areas. The bus stopped for a photo op near the Old Belize Capital area, which had a lovely combination of colonial buildings and modern architecture. It was picturesque and a contrast to some of the poorer areas that we drove through.

I simply clicked a few shots through the window and stayed on the bus to wait for everyone who got off. While I waited, I checked out the other tourists. Very few of them were faces I recognized from square dancing, but they seemed friendly. I visited with the woman in the seat ahead of me, who had also opted to stay on the bus. She traveled alone but said she found the cruise relaxing and the other passengers friendly.

When we were on the road again, I talked to the couple across the aisle. They were also on the cruise and enjoying themselves. Obviously, they had no idea about the crew member, the vandalism, or the porn DVDs. I managed to keep from asking if they knew anything about the events and in so doing ruining their vacation. I was proud of myself.

As we rode along through the city, the guide pointed out schools and other landmarks. He remarked about the poverty and low level of education in Belize. My mind wandered with the motion of the bus and his voice became background noise. I thought about all the very strange things going on aboard the ship and missed part of what he shared. There was Mr. Jarcourt and his satchel. The mishap with the entertainers' music that led to discovery of the pornographic DVDs. Were either of these related to the three crew members and some of the entertainers from a different ship being assigned last minute to our ship? Joaquim's assault seemed most connected to the DVDs. How did any of these connect to the subsequent vandalism of the entertainers' equipment? The vandalism of Mandy's stateroom and the dead crew member might be linked to the other vandalism, I thought. Did the change in Mandy's stateroom connect somehow? That seemed more likely than any connection to an incident ten years ago. I struggled to see how anything was connected. I had an especially difficult time fitting Jarcourt into the puzzle, so I put him aside.

With that decision, I realized there were four events that might be connected. Four parts, just like dance squares with four couples. Just like the four end dancers and four center dancers for Load the Boat. I started looking at the four events and trying to 'move' the pieces around in my head, just like when I mentally 'move' dancers through their paces when I'm learning a dance movement.

One, the crew exchange with the other ship and the change in Mandy's stateroom. These two events both had to do with ship management. Two, Joaquim's attack was possibly the means to recovering the pornographic DVDs. It made sense to link the vandalism of the equipment and Mandy's new room. I questioned if either was actually vandalism or someone searching for something. Either way the result was the same. That left the dead crew member. If I could just get my mental 'dancers' in the right place and 'call' the right moves I imagined I could untangle the dance. Assuming I had all the pieces. Unfortunately, in this case I had a few extra pieces, namely Mr. Jarcourt and Mandy's previous cruise.

I tried thinking it through from a different angle. Joaquim had said he'd never experienced a cruise like this one. Well, I would hope not! The first change from past cruises, at least that I knew of, was the last-minute change in crew members and entertainers. I'd come on at the last minute for Tom, too. With these changes, confusion ensued in baggage checking and handling. From everything I'd heard, last-minute changes and baggage handling that left loose objects were pretty uncommon. The common denominator among the four parts might have to do with the unexpected transfer from the other ship to our ship. I was brought back to the present by a shout from one of the other guests.

"Gerald, look over there! It's that obnoxious little man scurrying around. I really do think there is something seriously wrong with him," the woman across the aisle said to the man with her, obviously Gerald. Her voice was shrill and carried easily throughout the bus. Her companion just shrugged, but her comment prompted me to look out the window. Sure enough, she was talking about Mr. Jarcourt. He was making his way down the street, his suitcase clutched to his chest. I didn't have much time to think about it, as the guide announced that we were leaving the city and moving on. He explained that we would be traveling on the northern highway for about 45 minutes and that he would point out some of the local fauna on the way.

I zoned out again and went back to my mental 'dance.' I wasn't sure what had caused the last-minute transfer or who had decided which crew members and entertainers would be transferred. Maybe they just took whoever volunteered. I certainly didn't know which entertainer had suddenly been added. I didn't know who that person had replaced. I'd have to ask Paul or Joaquim about that, assuming I'd get an answer from either of them.

I wished for my home computer. I wanted to access information on smuggling or pirating incidents around the time of Mandy's first cruise. I might be able to find out about the backgrounds of crew members on the cruise line through some databases I knew about. That would be difficult without full names, and real names, I thought. For sure I'd be able to search for info on Snooping Dog, Mr. Jarcourt, and so on. Given the nature of my searches, I really didn't want to try to access records on the cruise line's computers, not to mention the charges that would incur. Charges for internet use on my cell phone would be exorbitant here as well. I discounted that possibility even though the phone was burning a hole in my backpack. Uh oh, I realized I was inserting myself into a mystery that wasn't my business…again. Oh, yes it was, I countered. It was my CD and equipment and safety that were involved. I felt better.

The landscape flew by outside the window, and eventually I came back to the present. What was I doing, I thought? Surely, I didn't want to waste my time in this beautiful country on daydreaming or speculating. This was a gorgeous place, and who knew when or if I would ever get to see it again. I watched the beautiful green countryside roll past. Occasionally we passed locals as they walked along the road. I saw very few cars, and the ones I did see were clunkers. Somehow the old cars and locals seemed to fit the setting. With the jungle-like atmosphere, I thought of the Kathleen Turner movie, Romancing the Stone.

I was surprised how quickly the time went by and we arrived at the Altun Ha Mayan ruins. It was a good thing, I thought, because I felt nature calling me. As we approached the parking area, the guide pointed out the path and explained the markings on the temples. He directed any of us interested to the stone steps to get to the top of three main temples. Some of the people climbed up to get photos of the surrounding area, including the rainforests. Fortunately, he also pointed out restrooms. We had about an hour to make our way through the ruins and then we were to meet back at the bus.

I left the bus, found the restrooms, and then located the steps to the top of the major temple. There were places to stop and look out and around among the many steps to get to the top. I needed the breaks, and the view was breathtaking. It was somewhat surprising that parts of the other temples were not excavated. The guide had explained that the ruins were discovered when someone tried to level the land. The explosions had uncovered, and inadvertently destroyed, parts of the temples. I stood there for a while appreciating the history and archeology. Then made my way equally as slowly back down the steps.

As I came down, I noticed someone below me off the steps and in the wooded area. He looked out of place and inappropriately dressed for the location. Then it hit me. Of course, it was Mr. Jarcourt! I couldn't tell what he was doing, but he had his ever-present satchel with him. By the time I made it farther down the steps and closer to where he had been standing, he was gone. I knew he wasn't on my bus. He must have been with a different group or, more likely, on his own.

I looked around as I made my way to the bottom of the steps, but I never saw him again. When I checked the time, I decided I better grab something to drink and get back on the bus. Altogether it was a relaxing morning, and pretty soon we headed back to the dock. It was a quiet ride back and the guide really didn't add much. He had some suggestions about other tours we might want to take. Many of the sights sounded good, and I was thinking more and more about ditching my beach plans. Some of the comments I'd heard made me a little shy about finding a beach on my own. Besides, my mind and curiosity were in overdrive.

In place of the beach, I decided to head back onboard and make some notes to see if I could make any sense of what was going on. I decided I would go to the library and use the computers there to do some research. I'd limit myself to an hour to limit the expense. With any luck, I wouldn't get interrupted. I soothed my suspicious nature by assuring myself I'd take care to delete any searches when I finished. That way the cruise line couldn't track who accessed what. Maybe I could gain some information. It occurred to me that I should go see how Mandy was doing. My first stop, though, was going to be Deck 11 and lunch.

With that in mind, I got off the bus and headed for the ship. Usually, getting back onboard was fairly benign. There's an official at the beginning of the walkway to check your passport and you check in with your stateroom key. Then the inevitable security check with xrays of your bags. If it's last minute, there may be a long line, but it really had been pretty simple. Of course, this time there was the tender boat business. Under a tent on the pier, I joined several other passengers to wait for the tender. When it arrived, a few people got off. Then we all lined up to board. Two officials, one U.S. and one Belize, stood and checked passports as we boarded the tender.

The tender left within about 5 minutes and we were back at the Journey. As I stepped off the boat, I dug out my stateroom key for the check in. I inserted my key into the security checkpoint. It beeped as it should, but the ship officer signaled me to hold up. He held a clipboard with a computer printout and scanned it briefly before speaking.

"Ma'am, what is your name and stateroom number?" a crew member with a clipboard asked.

"Darla King, cabin 4234," I answered, wondering why there was an extra step boarding this time. All that information was on the stateroom key and was linked to the photos from the first day.

"Can I see some identification, Ms. King?" he asked.

Getting out my passport again, I asked, "Is there a problem?"

"No, ma'am, but we are checking all passengers today as they reboard. Sorry for any inconvenience," he responded. He made notes on his clipboard and returned my passport. I wondered if this was in part due to this being the last port before returning to U.S. waters. Or, more likely, it had to do with what I'd single-mindedly started thinking of as 'my' mysteries.

My calves gave me a little grief as I took the stairs to my cabin on the fourth deck before heading to Deck 11 for some food. Taking the stairs was my compensation for the food I planned to eat. Deck 11 was laid out like a very large, mall-type food court. As you walked around the deck, there were different options—all buffet style from hot meals to pizza to deli sandwiches, and oh, yeah, desserts. I got myself a burger, fries, and coke. I sat down by the window to do some more people watching as I ate. It was about two o'clock and there was the constant come and go of the tenders. Every so often there seemed to be a hiccup in the movement. I wondered if it was as passengers were stopped at the entrance to the ship as I had been, but doubted it.

"Mind if I join you, Darla?" Paul asked as he sat himself down with a healthy salad. His meal made me feel guilty about my burger and fries, even if I had walked several flights of stairs.

"Well, I guess so. Make yourself at home. Oh, you already did," I answered. He smiled and ignored my sarcasm.

"Didn't you go ashore today? Belize is really a very beautiful place, you know, once you get out of the city," he said.

"Yes, I did go ashore for a bit, and yes, it is beautiful. I'm working tonight though. We have a New Year's Eve square dance. I wanted to come back, relax, take a nap, and get ready," I explained. I intentionally omitted the part about searching the internet to see if I could get some answers. As soon as I finished talking, I wondered why I was explaining myself to him. I changed the subject.

"So Paul, have you figured out the pornography angle? Mandy's cabin being trashed? The dead crew member? Joaquim's attack?" I asked before taking another bite of my burger. My curiosity hadn't waned from the morning, and a girl could hope for information, right?

Grabbing one of the fries off my plate, Paul sighed and said, "Well, I suppose some of it is common knowledge already or at least fodder for gossip. You probably know it already. Ms. Myers is staying in sick bay since her cabin is a crime scene now, not to mention a mess. The Captain has told her they'll have another cabin ready for her soon. She indicated that there wasn't anything stolen. As you already found out from Joaquim…," he hesitated and gave me a sharp look. I wondered how he already knew I'd talked to Joaquim. The man was utterly omniscient! He continued, "…she was being followed, stalked actually, by two crew members. She did identify the one in her cabin as one of them. And before you ask, no, she doesn't know why they were following her. At least that is her story."

"It sounds like you don't believe her?" I asked. I wondered what he was basing his lack of trust on. Of course, in his business, maybe he just immediately assumed everyone was hiding something.

Paul shrugged in answer to my question, gazed out the window and stole another one of my fries. After working on his salad for a bit, he looked at me and said, "So Darla, I did talk to a few of the crew. The only passenger they could identify as 'odd' or standing out was some older gentleman, who is rather rude, and a bit compulsive. Do you know who that might be? I respect your intuition about people." Really? He did? You could have fooled me. I burst out laughing.

"Mr. Jarcourt?" I asked. "Short, older man with a satchel always clutched to his chest, always nervous, and yes, very rude? He definitely stands out, but unless that crew member tried to get that bag and took it to Mandy's room, I can't imagine him killing anyone!"

"Hmmph. Joaquim didn't remember seeing him this morning," Paul said.

"Mr. Jarcourt was in the capital area of Belize. I saw him. And someone else on the bus spotted him too, so I know I wasn't mistaken. He still had that case with him, still scurrying like a busy squirrel trying to find the right place to hide his acorns. Also in the Altun Ha ruins," I offered.

"Okay, so maybe he likely had nothing to do with Ms. Myers' cabin or the dead crew member. Could he be involved in the pornography thing, do you think?" was his retort.

I laughed again, and said, "Possibly I guess, but I really doubt it. I think you're pulling at straws. Is the man weird? Yes. Is he criminal? I don't think so."

"Okay, so what about your friend Mr. Weathers? He's been spending a lot of time with Ms. Myers since this happened." Well, that was hitting below the belt. He had to know Doug and I were close. He might not know how close. Then, again, he might, given his omniscience. Did he want to know about Doug in relation to the case, or in relation to me? He seemed to be fishing as he waited for my response.

I hesitated. Not because I doubted Doug, but because I wondered what Paul knew, or at least thought he knew about my relationship with Doug. Not that we had that kind of relationship, well not yet, but I was hoping. Well, sometimes I was hoping. Sheesh, what was I, a teenager?

Getting my thoughts under control, I said, "Well, I can't really tell you how Doug has spent his time. I'm not exactly his keeper, just his friend," I added with emphasis. "If he's been spending time with Mandy, it may be because she was nervous and upset from that other cruise. Or nervous because those guys were following her. Doug's a good guy like that. He even rescues people who are left for dead on his property!" The last part was a dig directly at Paul related to the first time we had met, when Nick was found beat up and unconscious on Doug's ranch.

This time it was Paul's turn to laugh. A little more seriously asked, "Darla, you have any other ideas on this popping around in your pretty head?"

A little taken aback at the blatant compliment, I stammered, "I don't know, Paul." Ah, that was an insightful comment, wasn't it? I didn't usually sound empty-headed. I confessed, "I am a little curious about something you said, though. Joaquim indicated the cruise ship was completely full. He said there were no vacant staterooms. He said that was why Mandy was still in sick bay. He even mentioned you were staying with the Captain because they didn't have any open staterooms. So where did the empty stateroom come from at this late date?"

Paul laughed, winked, and asked, "Gee, Darla are you offering me a place to stay?" I blushed and my embarrassment was obvious. He took hold of my hand, and came close to an apology.

"Sorry if that was inappropriate, Darla, I couldn't help myself. Not to worry, the Captain has a suite with plenty of room for me. I did check into the cabin change you mentioned. As for the open stateroom, the couple in the stateroom next to Mandy's, well, they heard about the problems going on and took issue with them. The Captain made arrangements for them to leave the ship here in Belize. Flight home courtesy of the cruise line. Needless to say, the cruise line is working very hard to keep the guests satisfied and, in most cases, in the dark."

I really couldn't think of a response, though it occurred to me that if either one of that couple had killed the crew member, they just got a 'get out of jail free' card.

As I finished my lunch in silence, Paul asked, "Would you mind coming to the Promenade deck and hanging around as an extra pair of eyes? There will be many activities starting as it gets closer to time to leave Belize. Looking for Jim, and Pete for sure, but if you could help identify other entertainers or tell me any intuitive suspicions you have, that would be helpful."

"Well, yeah, I guess so," I answered, surprised he had asked for my help and that Jim was a 'person of interest.' I mean, after all, how could I refuse when perhaps it would satisfy my own curiosity as well. I pushed my plate with its remaining fries toward him with lifted eyebrows. He nodded and he took another few off the plate. I grabbed my coke and the two of us went down to the Promenade deck. We easily found a bench that allowed us to see the stairs and elevators, and watch as people walked around. There was a Christmas tree at one end and a number of different shops, a bar, and a coffee and snack shop. I had almost forgotten how recent Christmas was.

"So, Paul, how often have you been to Belize?" I asked, picking up on his previous comment about how beautiful it was, and trying to make small talk.

"Oh, I've been here a few times in the past ten years. Sometimes on business, and sometimes on pleasure. I like the beaches and the snorkeling the best. But mostly the quiet that comes with the snorkeling. You can't really appreciate the reef without snorkeling, and there are a lot of other activities besides. Where did your visit take you? A tour, I presume?" was his response.

I related where I had been and told him a few more details about my Jarcourt sighting. He took me more seriously than I thought it was worth. Then he asked me to relate all of the interactions I'd had or seen with Jarcourt. So I did, starting with getting on the ship and the incident with Mandy when we boarded, his run-in with the Purser, accusations, and generally obnoxious demeanor.

"So it's safe to say he wasn't trying to keep from being seen. Was he at any of the square dances? How about any of these folks?" he added, indicating a group of about twenty that was congregated at the elevators.

"Hmm…well, it's hard to tell, but I don't recognize any faces in that group. Jarcourt definitely hasn't been at the dances or my workshops, although I can't speak for Zach or Slim and their workshops. I kinda suspect if he had though, they would have mentioned it. It's hard to square dance holding a satchel against your chest," I answered to his first question.

I pointed to a man in the group. "See that tag around his neck? Some of the others are wearing it too. I saw some other passengers with similar tags at my workshops. I can't tell for sure, but it looks like they identify a specific group on the cruise. The ones I saw in my workshops were from a church in Louisiana. I think there may be more than one group though. They don't look like they're all traveling together. Carlotta talked to a church group on our tour bus, I don't recognize them." Paul nodded and watched attentively. The group reached the Christmas tree and took a lot of pictures. More passengers started to mill around. The coffee shop was full as were the tables outside the bar.

As I noticed Zach and Slim heading for the elevators, I pointed them out, although I was sure Paul knew who they were. I could identify some of the square dancers who walked by. The ones from Clearton Squares said hello and looked curiously at Paul. I could point out some from other clubs or that I'd seen at dances. I mentioned the ones that I'd seen wearing club outfits, which identified them as experienced dancers.

I couldn't figure out how any of this would help him in his investigation, but it was pleasant sitting by him and chatting almost like an equal. As we sat there, I became very aware of the physical warmth radiating from Paul. At least once, when our eyes met, I felt myself blushing. He did some version of the adolescent Danny Zuko move in Grease, the yawn and stretch, and his arm was behind me.

"Relax, Darla," he offered in soft tones, but of course, it really had the opposite effect on me. "We're just watching and taking note of possible interactions. It's not high espionage." I did relax some. Well, at least tried to. I let him pull me closer into his side and his arm moved further around my shoulders. We just sat there, close together. I guessed to everyone else we looked like a romantic couple taking a few moments together, I'm sure. That was probably his plan so we would blend in. Occasionally we commented on some of the passengers. Then one in particular in the distance caught my attention and I hopped up out of the bench.

"Oh, my gosh! There's Mr. Jarcourt. The tweedy type jacket, ill-fitting clothes, see him, Paul? But he doesn't look as frantic as usual. Wait, he's not holding on to his satchel! What happened to the satchel?" I tried to keep my voice down, but clearly I broke any romantic mood we'd developed. I didn't mean to draw attention to us, but a few faces looked over at us. Sure enough, there was Mr. Jarcourt walking down the promenade, almost smiling. For once, he didn't seem to have a problem, and he was not carrying his satchel. Smiling might be too strong a word. I wouldn't say he was grinning, but his face was definitely relaxed and he seemed at ease.

"He looks like he needs a good clothier, but he doesn't look quite as bizarre as you and Joaquim and others led me to believe. By sight he doesn't fit the profile for any of the incidents either. Doesn't look a candidate for the vandalism and burglary, the porn, or the murder," conceded Paul.

Sitting back down, I added, "No, I don't know what was in that satchel, but I doubt it has anything to do with the rest of the weird things going on." It was odd to see him without it, though. We continued to sit for a little while longer, Paul deep in thought and me watching. I pointed out other entertainers and square dancers as they boarded, but mostly we just sat there. His arm didn't go around me again and we remained separated by a little space. As it approached four o'clock, I said, "This has been fun, but I really do need to get some rest, shower, change, and get ready to work tonight."

"Thanks for sitting with me, and giving me your insight," he responded. I couldn't tell if he was genuinely grateful or if his comment was laced with sarcasm. He raised one eyebrow and continued, "Maybe we can catch up with each other later tonight, like around midnight. After all, it is New Year's Eve."

"Anything's possible, I guess," I blurted out. Wrong tone, I thought, especially after sitting in his arms for so long. "I mean, you know where I'll be. I don't know what my schedule will be." I shuffled off to my cabin feeling like a romantically immature clod. I managed to sleep for a bit and then headed to dinner. I didn't see Paul again and dinner was pretty much everyone talking about the reef, the snorkeling, or some other activity. Oh, yeah, and I wasn't the only one who noticed the extra security. I headed back to my cabin to dress before the square dance at 9:00 that evening, not sure what the evening would bring or how it would end up. Doug hadn't mentioned if he would be at the dance or not.

Even as a teenager, I knew it wasn't fun to not have someone to kiss come midnight on New Year's Eve. The fact that I was working didn't make the thought feel any less lonely now.

CHAPTER 8

As I dressed in my favorite prairie skirt, I shook off my funk and was feeling pretty good. With a basic black background and thin metallic ribbons of royal blue, gold, and red woven into the fabric, the movement of the skirt created a symphony of color as the skirt moved. I topped off the skirt with a shimmering royal blue scoop-neck top and black belt. I took extra care on my makeup and for a change was feeling surprisingly good about how I looked. For some reason I was more confident than I had been in a while. Even my hair somewhat cooperated tonight.

I had a pretty good idea that only experienced dancers would choose the square dance as their venue for tonight, but we planned for all levels of ability anyway. Square dancing isn't how most people choose to spend New Year's Eve, but everybody has to go somewhere. There were other dance and entertainment venues on the ship, but many square dancers choose squares over ballroom, two-step, polka, or swing dancing. Square dancing doesn't really require rhythm or the ability to feel the beat of the music. The caller tells the dancers what to do and when. If you can follow directions and know left from right, you can do okay at a square dance.

But that's not the only reason I didn't expect a big crowd. Most people associate drinking with the New Year's Eve celebration. There is no drinking at a square dance, at least not until the dance ends. Even on New Year's Eve. All the promotional material for the square dance had made that clear, so I knew some people would go elsewhere simply for that reason. The square dance would go until midnight, when we would celebrate with noisemakers, streamers, and confetti. Then the Dreams would close down. Everyone could go to alternate venues to continue celebrating. I was getting myself psyched up and mentally planning what songs I would use, especially for the midnight dance, when there was a knock at my door.

"Hey, Carlotta! What's up?" I asked when I opened the door and saw who it was. She was dressed in what I knew was her favorite square dance outfit. She wore a blue and white paisley "big skirt" with silver sequins with a matching sequined t-shirt, silver crinoline and, I supposed, silver pettipants underneath.

"Hi yourself! Just checking up on you. Making sure you hadn't gotten into any trouble today," she quipped.

"Relatively quiet day, actually. Short tour of Belize, and then came back to the ship," I offered as I gathered what I would need to take with me. Slim still had all my CDs, so I didn't have to carry them or any equipment. But there seemed like a lot of personal stuff I wanted to have with me. I made sure to include a change of shoes in case we went two-stepping after the square dance. And after Mandy's troubles, I stashed all the things I didn't want to leave in the cabin in my bag as well. Since I was calling, I could safely stash it behind the stage area.

Carlotta made herself at home and sat on the bed, or at least tried to with stiff crinolines fluffing up all around her. Then she went into talk mode while she waited on me.

"I had a great time today," she said. "I ended up serving as the caddy for all the stuff the guys took with them. I didn't actually get in the water, but it was fun being around all the action. And did you get a load of all the extra security as we were reboarding today? Did you see and find out anything? I am just dying to know what is happening. Did you see Harbinville around?"

I laughed out loud at her constant energy. I related what I knew and that, yes, I had run into Paul over lunch. I told her we had talked about the murder, burglary, and porn as we watched folks on the Promenade Deck. I left out the personal part, how I felt sitting so close to him. Even though Carlotta was my best friend, I wasn't ready to delve into it with her.

"What really surprised me was when Mr. Jarcourt came back onboard he didn't have his satchel," I added as I finished my story, leaving out the part about Paul's arm around my shoulders or my reaction to him.

"What? You're kidding me, right? What do you think happened to the bag? Did he look upset about losing it or something?" she asked as she jumped up from the bed.

"Actually, Carlotta, he was smiling and looked relieved to be rid of the bag," I said. "But I know he had it when I saw him in Belize. It's a puzzle."

"Well, it would be exciting if he was a mule for a drug dealer and now that he made the drop, his family is safe or something like that," she responded, her fertile imagination running wild instead of mine for a change. "So did you see Mandy and Doug? Nick and I were on shore, but we didn't run into either of them," she continued.

I told her I had not. Her face reddened as she realized she had automatically paired Doug and Mandy. She stammered, "I didn't mean Doug and Mandy—I meant Doug or Mandy. Either one, you know? Not both. I mean...."

I interrupted her and smiled my best on-stage smile. "It's okay, Carlotta," I said. "I didn't see either one or both, for that matter. No big deal, really. I enjoyed my day and it sounds like you enjoyed yours."

I thought about my time with Paul, as we people-watched and talked, and realized it had been one of the most enjoyable parts of the day. And I wouldn't have had the chance if I was with Doug. I kept that revelation to myself, not quite sure where to go with it.

"Now we have a square dance…" I continued, "…and I bet your partner is waiting for you! I expect that Sam and Zoe will be there as well. Besides, Slim and Zach will be waiting for me!"

I still wasn't quite finished getting ready and told her I would meet her there. She gave me a quick hug and headed off to the Dreams. After she left, I took a final look in the mirror to make sure I was ready to take the stage. I also practiced holding my smile in place no matter what came my way tonight.

As I walked through the passageway on my way to the Dreams, I noticed Mr. Jarcourt sitting by himself in one of the lounge chairs near a window. His back was toward me and he was slumped over facing the window. He wore the same heavy tweed jacket with elbow patches that he had worn since I first saw him on the boarding ramp. What a funny little man, I thought. As I passed him, he straightened up, then slid down so that the back of his head was against the top edge of the chair. It was the first time I had seen him that he didn't look agitated. In fact, he looked exactly the opposite. He looked much too calm. Sad, removed from reality, like he wasn't even there.

Keep walking, I told myself. Don't stop, he's never expressed any interest in having a conversation. He accused you of being a stalker. Don't let your curiosity get the better of you. Too late, I answered myself. I walked toward his chair. Sometimes I could be so maddening.

"Are you okay, sir?" No answer, his eyes were closed. "Mr. Jarcourt?" I scanned the floor, but I didn't see his satchel.

He jerked and opened his eyes. They were distant, his look faraway. "Yes?"

"Are you alright, Mr. Jarcourt? I thought you might need help. Can I do anything for you?" I was a little concerned with his lack of energy and his subdued demeanor. Every other time I had seen him he had been quite energetic, if annoying.

"No, no. It is already done," he said, and closed his eyes again.

I detected a slight accent, maybe German or Czech, I thought. What was done, I wondered? My imagination followed my curiosity to center stage. It occurred to me that he acted like someone who had taken pills and waited for them to take effect like an overdose. Was that what he meant he had done? Is that why he looked like he had given up? I sat down in the chair next to him and leaned toward him.

"What's done, Mr. Jarcourt? Is everything okay?" I asked softly, looking for any clue in his face.

He sat up straighter and looked at me appraisingly. "It's a long story," he said. "Long and sad. Beautiful, but sad. You ask, but are you sure you want to hear it?"

I looked at my watch. I wasn't due in the Dreams for a half-hour yet. Surely it couldn't be that long of a story, could it? And I really didn't feel I should leave him until I was sure he was alright.

"Of course," I said. "If you want to tell me, that is."

"If you are sure," he said. I nodded.

He took a breath and began. "Many years ago I married my teenage sweetheart. She was beautiful, wonderful. We lived in Poland. Times were harsh and we were poor. We both worked hard. After we were married for several years, we found we were expecting our first child. We talked about it and decided we would like to raise our family in America. So we left both our parents and came to the United States, where we lived in Chicago with her uncle until we could get on our feet. Again, we both worked hard. We raised three loving and productive children together."

I would have expected talk of his family to bring a smile to his face, but it remained heartbreakingly sad. He looked out at the green-blue water that sparkled in the Caribbean sun.

"All grown now. Families and responsibilities of their own. I don't see them very often," he continued. "Maybe ten, twelve years ago, my daughter and her husband took a vacation to Belize. She brought many many pictures to show us. She said Belize was the most beautiful place in the world. She told us we must take a trip there ourselves. Of course, we never did. Time moves so fast as you get older. Last year, my wonderful children got together and bought this cruise for us. For our fiftieth anniversary. Fifty years, we could not believe it. We have been married fifty years!" He paused, looked out at the water, looked down at his hands.

"That is the beautiful part," he said. "Are you sure you want to hear the rest?"

The rest. That would be the sad part. But I couldn't stop him now, nor did I want to. He hadn't boarded the ship with his wife, so I thought I knew where the story was headed. I was only partially right.

"Yes, go on," I said.

"So of course we were excited to come and see the most beautiful place in the world. We were so proud of our children. Proud and grateful that they would give us this magnificent trip. We made plans."

Again he looked out at the water. Again he took a breath. I waited. "Six months ago..." His voice trailed off and he had to begin again. "Six months ago we found out my wife was sick. Cancer. There was nothing that could be done, it had progressed too far. She was brave, stoic. I thought we would at least have this cruise together. Six weeks ago, she told me she did not think she would be able to come on the cruise. 'Of course you will,' I told her. 'I will not go without you.' But then she gave me a job to do. Made me promise to do it."

He stopped talking and looked at me. To see if I was listening, I guess. Maybe to see if I had figured out the ending to his story. His strong accent and lyrical way of speaking had mesmerized me, and I said nothing to break the spell. He picked it back up.

"'You're right, we will go together,' she said. 'One way or the other. If I don't make it long enough, take me with you. I want my ashes to be scattered in the most beautiful place in the world.' Yesterday was our fiftieth anniversary. Today I scattered her ashes in the most beautiful place in the world. So you see, now it is done. The most beautiful woman in the world will spend eternity in the most beautiful place in the world."

Tears ran down his cheeks as he finished his story. I could feel them in my eyes as well. How could I respond to such a beautiful and sad story as the one he had just shared with me?

"I'm sorry for your loss," I said. So pat, so inadequate. I struggled to find something to add. "You are a very strong man, and you have done what your wife wanted."

A small smile finally turned up the corner of his mouth. "Thank you for listening," he said. "It makes it more real, more final. But it also makes it a little less painful."

The satchel, I thought. That's what was in it, his wife's ashes. It explained why he was so protective of it, worried about it. I hesitated to ask more questions, but I couldn't help myself.

"What about El Corchito?" I asked. "Why did you go there, and take your wife's ashes with you?"

A rueful smile bent his lips. "Well, you see, I didn't know where the most beautiful place in the world was exactly. Was it El Corchito? Was it Altun Ha? I didn't know.

Everywhere I went, I thought people looked at me, mocked me. I was afraid to leave her on the ship, afraid to take her with me. I took her to El Corchito with me, but it didn't seem right. When I got to the ruins, I knew that was the place."

My heart broke for the odd little man. I could identify with a grief as deep as his and with a sense of loss that confused one's thoughts.

"You're on a cruise. You've done what you came to do. Now you should at least experience a little of what your daughter told you about," I said. "Try some activities. I'm a square dance caller. Please come to the dance tonight. You don't need any experience, it's for anyone. You don't even need to dance, just come and listen to the music and watch the people. It's very entertaining, I promise! Maybe it will help ease your pain."

"I don't think I can do that," he said.

"Well, just think about it," I replied. I sat with him a few minutes longer, then told him goodbye and headed for the club. I left him still staring out the window, but he seemed to be a little more alive than when I had first seen him. I hoped so. Probably he wasn't an odd little man at all. He was just a very sad and lost man dealing with an enormous load of grief. I hoped he would come to the dance tonight.

When I arrived at the Dreams Club, I saw that the dance area had been decorated with typical New Year's decorations. There were streamers, faces of the Baby New Year, clocks, and cartoon champagne glasses. Some of the crew were arranging snacks. I noted these were not the crew members who had helped with the dance on the first night. The snacks were extensive enough to pass for dinner. The water looked cool and refreshing in sweating jugs filled to the top. I noticed a box under the table, and a quick look inside confirmed the usual New Year's hats, rattles, and horns. Zach and Slim were seated at the table that held our sound equipment. I pulled up a chair and joined them.

"We've got three levels of dancers we have to please tonight," said Slim. "The experienced dancers, who want to have fun with challenging moves and lively calling. The new dancers, who've taken workshops on this cruise and need slower, easier calling. And we need to throw in a few fun tips for non-dancers who choose to spend New Year's Eve with us."

"I've been thinking about that," Zach said. "I have a suggestion. If we get a projector setup like the one the country-western DJ uses next door, we could display a schedule of tips. I've worked up a DVD I think shows it in a fun way that everyone will understand. They'll be able to tell which dances apply to them. Here, I'll show you."

Zach opened his laptop and pushed a few keys. A video popped up showing a square dance in progress.

"This is a video of the Phoenix Fours dance club," he said. "I've used it as a background." As if by command, the video faded into the background and an animated male square dancer dressed in boots, bandana, and hat held up a cartoon sign that said 'Plus tip in progress—experienced dancers. Next tip—everyone dances, no experience needed.'"

"I've made up a slide for every dance schedule combination I can think of, but I can make others if I've missed any. Then we just put up the appropriate slide between tips and everyone can see what's going on and what's coming up," Zach explained, obviously pleased with himself and his plan.

"Zach, that's terrific," I said. "I do think we should schedule a block of time just for experienced dancers, though. Can you make up a slide that says something like '10 to 11 p.m.—Mainstream with Announced Plus for experienced dancers'? What do you guys think about the timeframe on that segment?" I asked.

Slim liked both our ideas, and we agreed that we would hold the experienced dancer segment from 10 to 11 o'clock as I'd suggested. The rest of the evening we would go with a rotation of tips for everyone, then beginners, then experienced dancers, and finally Plus dancers. Slim and I would each call for an entire rotation, then Zach would call three of the four and hand off to Slim or me for a Plus call.

"I'll make sure I have the slides we need," said Zach. "When we start the dance, I'll show you how to pull them up on the screen. Right now, however, I better go see Joaquim and secure the projection setup."

Zach took off to get the projector and screen. Slim and I chose our music and chatted about mutual friends, including his brother, Tom. He commented that he had emailed Tom and shared the problems we'd encountered on the cruise. Slim seemed a little more relaxed than he had been the night before. He told me there hadn't been any more issues with entertainment equipment. When I asked about his day, he said he had gone into Belize, done some shopping, and caught a tour.

Zach came back with a crew member who installed the screen and helped him hook in his laptop. As he was getting that all set, I spotted the country-western DJ going into the studio next door. Slim saw me watching him and commented, "With his equipment damaged, he wasn't sure how he was going to do the dance and after party tonight. I lent him some of my extra gear, and so did a bunch of the others. Joaquim found some additional stuff somewhere and the DJ managed to cob together a whole system."

"It's nice that everyone helped him make the best of the situation," I answered. I hadn't spent much time with the other entertainers, so I didn't know them all that well. I was a little surprised, but heartened by what Slim said.

The dance was scheduled to start at 8 o'clock, and people started filtering in about 7:30. I had already selected the songs I'd use, so I mingled and tried to make people feel welcome. About 7:45 I saw Carlotta, Nick, Sam, and Zoe come in. Doug wasn't with them. Neither was Mandy. I finished up my conversation and headed their way.

"Hi guys. Happy New Year!" I greeted them with hugs all around. "Who'd have thought this was where we'd be spending New Year's Eve, huh?"

"Ain't that just the truth, Darla Darlin'," replied Sam with his arm around Zoe.

"Thanks to you, Darla, we're all having a fabulous New Year's Eve," said Carlotta. "How's this dance going to work tonight? Regular dance or fun night?"

I explained the plan we'd devised and waited for their reaction. They all thought it sounded like a superb idea. Of course, there isn't much this group would object to as long as they got to dance.

"Just watch which DVD you're playing up there. You don't want to get one of those racy ones!" laughed Carlotta.

I laughed in return and headed up to the stage. Slim got the dance going.

"Welcome, everyone! Happy New Year! Glad to have you all at our New Year's Eve dance," he said. "Tonight we will be calling tips for everyone at every dance level, so you will all get a chance to dance. Just keep your eyes on the screen behind me and you'll see who's at the plate and who's in the batter's box. For you non-sports fans, that means you can see what type of tip we're calling at the time and what type is coming up." He gestured to the screen behind him, which was currently showing the cartoon dancer bowing to the audience, then continued.

"Any of you experienced dancers that might want to strut your stuff, notice that we'll have an extended set for you from 10 to 11 o'clock. And, of course, everyone meet back here before midnight. We've got a special treat to ring in the new year. Now, let's dance!" Slim finished his announcements and called, "Square 'em up!"

Zach pulled up the first slide. Slim pointed to it and announced that the first tip would be a fun dance for everyone, followed by a beginner-level tip. He got the night rolling by calling a no-experience-required tip to two classics, "Bingo the Dog" and "Fishing in a Crawdad Hole." Then Slim took over for his tip. While Slim called, Zach showed me how to pull up his slides as I needed them.

I was up next, and I put on "Sea Cruise" as my first song. In the middle of my patter call, I saw a passenger walk in the door wearing a bright flowered Hawaiian shirt and did a double-take. Oh my gosh, that was Mr. Jarcourt. I stumbled on my call, then recovered. I tried to watch where he headed, but I needed to concentrate on getting the dancers where they belonged. I ended my tip with an old favorite, "Another Saturday Night." When I finished calling my full rotation, I made a beeline off the stage in search of the bright yellow flowers. I found him in a chair at the edge of the dance floor.

"Mr. Jarcourt, so glad you decided to come," I said. "You look wonderful, very touristy." I was rewarded with a small smile.

"After our talk earlier, I looked around and realized I was very out of place," he said. "I stopped by the shops and picked up a few things. I've seldom shopped for clothes without my wife, but the sales clerk helped me." He looked down at his shirt and shorts. "I think maybe she steered me a little wrong."

"No, not at all. You look fine. Did you enjoy watching the dance?" I asked, tickled that he had taken my suggestion and stopped by.

"Yes, I am. It reminds me of the folk dancing we used to do in Poland when I was young. I'm surprised at the number of older folks out there. I would expect it to be all young people," he answered somewhat wistfully.

"Oh no. The dancers can move as energetically or as calmly as they need to, so all ages can enjoy square dancing. It's good exercise no matter how old you are," I told him. Zach rounded up everyone for the next fun dance, a big circle dance like the one on the first night. I noticed Mandy come in the door and waved her over.

"Mr. Jarcourt, do you remember Mandy? We all met on the ramp when we boarded the first day of the cruise," I said. He looked a little lost, then I could see the memory coming back. He looked embarrassed. Mandy just looked surprised.

"Hello, Mr. Jarcourt." Mandy looked at me questioningly. I wasn't sure she was going to like what I said next.

"Mandy, why don't you be Mr. Jarcourt's partner for this time around?" I asked. He immediately protested, and I thought Mandy was going to do the same. She came through like a trouper though, like a true square dancer.

"Well, sure," she said. "I'm a new dancer, too, Mr. Jarcourt. I just learned on this cruise. I'm not very good, but I'll show you what I know." I watched Mandy drag him into the circle of dancers and thought for the millionth time how much value and healing there is in human contact, music, and dance.

The night went smoothly. Zach managed to get in some oldies and some George Strait, and we cycled through our calling rotation again. I noticed that Mr. Jarcourt left sometime during the hour for experienced dancers. During that hour, at one point I noticed that Mandy had left as well, but she was back before the hour was up.

As midnight approached I found myself looking around for Doug, and yes, for Paul. I had seen Doug dance with Mandy early in the evening, but not after that. He hadn't come to find me to dance a Plus dance with him anytime during the evening. I was getting ready to call the first dance of my last tip before midnight when I saw Doug walk into the club with another male dancer. They were laughing and talking, then the man split off and Doug looked up at the stage and waved. I waved back, ridiculously pleased that Mandy wasn't with him.

He searched the room, spotted the square with Carlotta, Nick, Sam, and Zoe, and headed over their way. I saw him hesitate and check the screen to see what was coming up. My Mainstream tip was up next, and would be the last dance before the midnight countdown. I noticed Slim and Zach get out the hats and other stuff and pass them out to the dancers. Doug turned back toward the tables in the back of the club, and I refocused my attention on the dancers and wound up the tip.

"Ladies and gentlemen, we are about to start the last dance of the year," I announced. "It's a Mainstream tip, so grab your partner and square 'em up."

Slim stepped up to the mic. "This may be the last dance of the year," he said, "but it's not the end of the evening. After this tip, everyone is invited onto the dance floor for the midnight countdown followed by a special treat from your callers. So don't go away!"

He handed the mic back to me. I spotted the Clearton Gang in a square just in front of me, and Carlotta waved happily. Doug was partnered with a woman I didn't know. Carlotta danced with Nick as usual. Sam and Zoe made up the third couple, and the fourth was a couple I didn't recognize.

I called the tip to 'God Bless America' and 'When the Saints Come Marching In.'" Since they both used standard square dance calls, Slim and Zach chimed in on the choruses. When I finished, Slim took the mic again.

"Okay, everyone, we've somehow managed to actually time this thing right. Midnight and a brand new year are only 5 minutes away. So everyone out on the floor!" He waited until the crowd milling slowed a little, then continued.

"And as much as we love calling square dances, you might have noticed your callers also enjoy harmonizing on a good song now and then. So as soon as that clock over there," he pointed to the wall clock, "reaches the midnight hour, we will help you celebrate by serenading you with 'Auld Lang Syne.' Now, here we go! Everyone got their hats, noisemakers, and confetti? 10…9…8…7...6…5...4…3…2…1…Happy New Year, everyone!"

Zach and I picked up our mics and joined Slim at the front of the stage. The dance floor was chaos, with everyone hugging and kissing. I noticed the only ones kissing in the Clearton square were Nick and Carlotta.

We waited just a minute before Slim nodded and we broke into our rendition of the traditional New Year's favorite. Within a few seconds, the dancers went completely quiet and everyone turned to face us. Watching the serious upturned faces, I felt almost as if we were singing a hymn. When we finished, though, the dancers hooted, hollered, and clapped and the jubilant chaos returned.

I hugged Slim and Zach and said, "I'll be right back." I stepped down to the dance floor and went over to the Clearton Gang, although not without numerous stops and good wishes along my way. The crowd was thinning out, and

Doug spotted me on my way over. He came toward me and gave me an enthusiastic hug. A long hug, but only a hug. When he pulled back a little, I faced him and smiled, giving him every opportunity for a New Year's kiss. None.

Why was it, I wondered, that I can take charge of the rest of my life but not my love life? I can't even take charge of a kiss. There was absolutely no reason I had to wait for him to kiss me. I could kiss him. But I didn't, and the moment passed. Carlotta, Nick, Sam, and Zoe came up and we all wished each other Happy New Year through multiple hugs.

Finally I said, "Guys, I've gotta pack up my equipment so I'll catch up with you later." I went back up on stage and began putting equipment and CD s into cases. We still had a couple of dances left before the cruise ended, so I could leave the equipment in the club. Slim locked it up in the cabinet that had been repaired after the break-in. Doug was waiting for me at the foot of the stage when I finished.

"Hi," I said, "what's the plan tonight?" As we walked out the door of the Dreams Club, he started to answer me but Paul walked up.

"Listen, Harbinville, you've already taken up a lot of my time this evening. Give it a rest, okay," Doug just about spit at him. I could almost see the testosterone in the air.

"Not interested in you, Mr. Weathers. Ms. King, may I see you for a moment?" he asked formally. I looked at him, hoping to read what he wanted, but his face told me nothing. Doug stayed by my side. I wondered just what had transpired between Doug and Paul, and how this related to the murder or me.

"Sure," I said. "What's up?"

Looking at Doug, he said, "There's something rather confidential I need to show you." Doug hesitated and looked at me. I shrugged and nodded, so Doug took off down the hallway.

"There are some couches over there, Darla. Let's use them," said Paul. We walked into a small alcove hidden from the hallway. As I started to sit down, he put a hand gently on each of my shoulders. He pulled me into him. Then he kissed me. Darn the man, he did everything well!

After the first instant of surprise, I started smiling. Actually, grinning. The grin was so wide it interfered with our kiss, and he stepped back. I'm sure I looked like a grinning idiot.

"Wow," was all I could say. I was gratified he didn't look very composed himself.

"Yes, wow," he echoed. "I'm afraid I used a bit of a ruse. What I needed to show you in confidence was how I felt about you."

"Can we try that again?" I asked. "I promise to do better."

"You did fine the first time," he said, but he didn't resist when I stepped up to him and put my hand behind his head to pull his lips down to mine. Hmmm, I thought, I guess I can take charge of a kiss after all.

When we finally ended the kiss this time, Paul pulled me down next to him to sit on the couch. He held my hand and neither of us said anything for a few minutes.

"So." I said.

"So." He agreed.

"What happens next?" I asked.

"Darla, I'll probably be tied up all day the next few days wrapping up the loose ends of everything that's happened here. I haven't worked it all out, actually, so there's more to be done before we make port, if possible. Once we go into port, the case falls apart and multiple agencies will be vying for the lead. I'm closing in on it and hope to clear it all up tomorrow. Plus, the paperwork will take days, I'm sure. But I want to see you again. See you in a social setting, and preferably with no burglaries, smugglers, or murders," he added with a small smile.

"Do you have my number? Oh wait, you probably have ways of getting it, don't you?" I teased.

"I don't think that would be a very appropriate use of taxpayer money, do you?" he retorted. "Yes, actually, I kept it from the last time we worked together."

"I don't have yours," I said, remembering that I had to reach him through Sheriff Lorys the time I called him for dinner.

"You will when I call you. Now let me walk you to your stateroom." He thought a second or two, then said, "If that's where you're going." Although I wasn't sure, he seemed to be asking if I was going to join the Clearton Gang, and Doug, at the after party.

"For now, yes." I said somewhat evasively, and we headed off to my stateroom. Once we got there, I was happy to share a few more kisses with him, then he said he had to go.

I sat on my tiny bunk in my tiny room, confused and tired but happy. I still wasn't sure what was happening with my love life, or with Doug and me, but I knew a kiss from Doug never left me feeling like Paul's had. That should tell me something.

I decided not to go out again, and checked my phone to see if we were back in U.S. range. We were, so I texted Carlotta, Nick, Doug, and Sam 'Happy New Year without me, I'm for bed.' Then I texted Heather with Happy New Year, took a shower in my tiny bathroom, and collapsed onto my tiny bed in my tiny room. This time the cabin's size didn't bother me one whit, and it didn't take me any time at all to fall soundly asleep, and despite the fact that I hadn't even had a glass of champagne. I'd also missed my black-eyed peas and cornbread, but I figured I would get them the next day.

Load the Boat

CHAPTER 9

I awoke and checked my phone for the time: 8:00 a.m. I had a text from Heather wishing me a Happy New Year. Apparently my phone had dinged sometime in the night and I had slept through it. Good, I needed some solid rest.

I really wanted to hear Heather's voice, but even though we were in range she might still be asleep and I hated to wake her. I knew, as much I like to think of myself as a modern mother, I would be very uncomfortable if I called Heather this early and Micah answered. So I settled for a text sending her my love, and headed for breakfast.

I was feeling a little giddy and decided to blame it on not eating much last night, as opposed to anything else. I avoided thinking it could be from my midnight kisses. Even though we were at sea, no workshops were scheduled today so I had the day to myself until the dance tonight. I took my time getting dressed and, no longer feeling the need to make a good first impression, I decided to go with jeans instead of a skirt. With all my dawdling, it was about 11:00 when I finally headed out to get some food.

New Year's Day brunch in the dining room was a lavish buffet, complete with mimosa drinks and champagne, for anyone who didn't have enough of the latter the night before. Black eyed peas and cornbread, too. As I walked down the hallway and past guests and crew, I was struck again by the fact that most of the passengers were probably completely unaware of the dead crew member and were just enjoying their cruise and New Year's Day at sea. When I got to the dining room, I joined some of the other square dancers and listened to them talk about the various activities and excursions they liked, and the ones they didn't like. Carlotta and Nick came in and sat at the large table with us.

"Did you get some sleep finally, Darla?" Carlotta asked. "It's almost noon and we are just getting around to eating breakfast. I guess it really is brunch!"

"I got up early, but took it slow and just got here myself. It sure does feel good not to have to get anywhere right away. We have the dance tonight, and then one workshop and the final dance tomorrow night, and we'll be back in Galveston. Can you believe it?" I responded.

"Hardly. The time just has just flown by. Darla, did I see you talking to Mr. Jarcourt last night at the dance? What a surprise! Have you solved the mystery of the satchel?" she asked, her eyes twinkling. As I told her about his wife and the ashes, the table gradually became quiet as the others listened to the story. They became subdued and several people's eyes welled up with tears. After some silence, one of the other square dancers said, "Well, I feel bad now. I think we all thought he was just a crazy person, maybe carrying something like his life savings in that bag. I guess on an emotional level, he really was."

In an effort to cheer everyone up, I asked a general question about the after parties. I had missed the country western DJ and the singer, Chance, that I'd met earlier. I said I hoped they had both found the equipment they needed, and asked if anyone had heard them. Carlotta was the first to answer.

"Oh, Darla, you missed a great time," she said. "We went to hear the country-western singer instead of the DJ. He was great! I mean, the DJ the other night was pretty good, but this singer, Chance something, was terrific. He apparently wasn't originally scheduled on this cruise, but I bet they have him back again. There was a good crowd to begin with. I'd guess probably about 100 people so it was crowded and a bit noisy. By about 2 o'clock, it had dwindled down some. Then

Chance took requests from those of us still hanging around." Carlotta threw out all the information at her usual fast pace.

I envied Carlotta that she could have so little sleep and still look like she could take on the world. I made a mental note that Chance must be the entertainer that came onboard from the other ship, along with those three crew members.

A man named Al chimed in. "We were one of those couples that dwindled away," he laughed. "Darla, he was good for sure, but you just wore us out at the dance. We didn't make it to the wee hours of the morning like some others did," he teased Carlotta and Nick.

The conversation continued, and I finally found a break to make my exit. I wanted to check in with Slim and Zach about tonight, and I wanted to check my email. On my way to the library, I decided to stop and see Joaquim. Maybe I could get some more information from him about the crew changes.

Joaquim's door was open, and as I approached I heard him in conversation with someone.

"I am trying to get information on this employee. He is not a regular crew member on this ship." After a pause, he said, "No I don't know which ship he is usually on. Please try to find his employment packet and get back to me." I waited at the door as he concluded his call with "thank you." It reminded me that I'd never gotten around to doing my computer research and perhaps I could do that after I emailed Heather.

"Hello, Joaquim. Happy New Year! How are you doing this morning?" I asked. I opted for small talk instead of launching into questions right away. Judging from the part of the conversation I had heard, he may not even know the answers to them anyway.

"Good morning, Miss King. Happy New Year to you. It is a pleasure to see you and I hope you are doing well," he responded, always the professional.

"Oh, yes, relaxing a bit today. The cruise seems to have gone by very quickly. Hard to believe we have been gone for a week," I offered.

"Yes it is hard to believe. We will be back in Galveston in less than two days, and you will be on your way home, I assume," he added with a smile and nod.

"Ummm. I have to say I am looking forward to my own house and the same familiar old routine," I responded with a chuckle. "And what about you? Do you have time off between cruises? When will you go out again? I guess I don't know how that all works. You must get days off, but, come to think of it, doesn't this cruise just turn around and go back out again?" This last fact had just dawned on me. Even if the lower level of crew members changed out frequently, the officers and such would likely stay with the ship.

"Actually, no, depending on our job, we don't have time off between cruises. We usually work in 3 or 6 month cycles, sometimes changing ships or itineraries. So, yes, we will get everyone off the ship early in the morning, and we would normally then prepare for the next set of passengers to arrive and board in the late afternoon," he explained.

"Is that true of everyone on the ship?" I asked.

"Well, depending on when we were hired on determines our time on and off. And sometimes we have to get updated on trainings and such. So some of the crew will remain and some will leave. The Captain, Social Coordinator, Purser, Chef, and some others would be continuing, for example. But we would get new medical personnel coming aboard. And some of the same entertainers and some new entertainers. And then sometimes special event entertainers like you, of course," he continued with a shrug of his shoulders. I really couldn't tell if he thought that was good or not, probably just the way it was.

It sounded like the normal process wouldn't happen this time. "Joaquim, you said 'you would' – does that mean that you're not continuing on the next cruise?" I asked.

Joaquim sighed and explained, "No, Miss King, with the crew member dead, this ship will not be able to turn around and leave as scheduled. I have not been advised of what will happen with most of the crew. Captain Rios and your agent have already indicated that several of us, myself included, will need to stay in Galveston until these issues get resolved."

"Oh, I'm sure it will work out, but that must affect your schedule long term, doesn't?" I asked, not quite sure what to say. I wondered if he and any others detained would get paid.

"You said you weren't sure about the crew," I plowed on. "Are all the crew on the same kind of cycles? Like housekeeping, waiters, and such? What happens when someone decides to leave, or in the case of the crew member who died?" I knew that I was probably scrunching up my eyes or knitting my brows so to speak, but I was having trouble fathoming this.

"It is very complicated but human resources takes care of all that or at least that is the usual protocol." He shrugged again, and continued, "This last time, because of an issue on another ship, late docking and other issues, corporate tried to find places for everyone who needed a position somewhere. If someone had already been promised work more or less and they could fill a job we had open.... They have an obligation to honor the contract and would rather have them working somewhere, instead of paying them to do nothing."

"I see, so it was a corporate decision who got picked to come to this ship? Not the Captain or someone onboard", I surmised aloud.

"Actually, the way it works is that corporate provides the Purser, my assistant Danny, and I with the list, what the qualifications are, job assignments, and then we can select who would best fit. We give them a list of preferred help, and then get notified who we actually get. Ms. King, I am not sure why you are concerned with this. Sorry, I am sure I am going into much more detail than you need. Most of the time, it is just business as usual," he explained, again shrugging.

"Joaquim, the country-western singer at the dance last night, Chance, mentioned in his show that he wasn't originally scheduled to be on this cruise. Did that work the same way?" I asked, trying to sound as innocent as I possibly could. I could tell he was getting a little weary of me.

"Not quite. As you know, contracts for entertainers are very clear and if you don't show up or work, you don't get paid. Sometimes, an entertainer can't make it and they provide us with a replacement—as with you yourself. Other times, they cancel their contract and we have a list of entertainers to contact. Now, Ms. King, do you have any other questions?" he asked somewhat tersely.

He continued without waiting for me to respond, "I hope you have a good day and that you will come back and cruise with us again, with less excitement." With that, he glanced down at his desk, the signal that our conversation was over.

"Well, thank you, Joaquim, for satisfying my curiosity. I'd never given much thought to how cruises employ people. It is very interesting." I gave him my best smile and went out to the deck to reflect on what I had just learned or not learned. It did make sense that the ship would be held over. Paul had mentioned it, too. They'd have to process Mandy's cabin and talk to those they considered critical to any investigation. I still couldn't quite figure out which parts would be in the jurisdiction of U.S. officials and which the jurisdiction of the Mexican Federales.

I walked out onto the deck to digest what I had learned. The weather was a bit nippy, but sunny, and my sweater was enough to keep the chill off. There was a slight breeze, possibly enhanced by the movement of the ship. As I glanced down the deck, there were others scattered around similarly looking out at the sea. I suspected that many, like me, were a bit claustrophobic on the ship. This was as close as we were going to get to 'space' until we reached Galveston.

As I considered what Joaquim had told me, I immediately thought of all the issues cruise employees must have with regard to family. To not see my daughter, Heather, for three to six months would be more than I could handle. I had trouble with the fact that she was just an hour or more away from me. This possibly contributed to the fact that most of the administrative types on the cruise were all held by men. In fact, the Captain, medical personnel, Purser, various other management positions were all male. Unlike my memories of the show "Love Boat" with Julie as the social director, even the social director on this cruise, Joaquim, was male.

"Enjoying the view, Darla?" whispered Paul, behind me. I started, and in doing so almost ended up in his arms. I definitely could feel his breath on my cheek and turned around. I could easily get caught in his teasing eyes.

"Yes, I am, and what are doing out here?" I countered, trying to put a little distance between us so I wouldn't be so aware of his body heat.

"I am enjoying the view as well," was his retort as he did an exaggerated survey of me, not the sea.

Feeling myself blush, I decided I needed to get on safer verbal ground at least, and asked, "I thought I wasn't going to see you today. Does that mean you've wrapped everything up? Did you ever find out any more about the cruise with

Mandy's parents? Or who selected those particular three guys to be added to this cruise at the last minute?

Paul laughed, and I realized I had fired the questions at him at a rapid pace. He shook his head, and leaned in toward me. I could feel my insides respond and couldn't quite figure out whether to enjoy the feeling or panic.

"Always avoid the personal, don't you?" he noted. "Well then, Darla, you didn't ask about Mr. Jarcourt. Are you holding out on me?" he asked with one brow raised and a twinkle in his eye.

"Uh, well, it kinda slipped my mind," I responded sheepishly. "How about a deal? I'll tell you about Mr. Jarcourt and you answer one of my questions."

"How about you share what you know, and I'll reward you accordingly," was his response with a step closer and his voice dropped to a whisper.

Stammering, I decided I would share my information. When it came down to it, I was eager to tell him about Mr. Jarcourt, even though it had nothing to do with his case. It truly sounded like he didn't know the story, and I was a little smug about knowing something he didn't. I related the story yet again, having some trouble not tearing up as I did. I added how Mr. Jarcourt had bought some clothes and even come to the square dance.

When I finished the beautiful but sad story, he was gratifyingly quiet. After a while, he said, "Yes, that is a sad story. As we suspected, he is unlikely to be related to this investigation." As before, I wondered about his use of 'we.' Did he mean him and me, his fellow feds, or was he just used to being part of a team?

"Okay, so now I get my reward? An answer to my questions?" I asked, not sure that was really what I wanted for my reward with him standing so close.

"I do have the answer to at least one of those questions…but that wasn't the reward I had in mind." Paul responded, speaking again almost in a whisper, and clearly teasing me.

I smiled back and waited for his next move, hopefully getting my curiosity satisfied. At least I told myself it was curiosity I was trying to get satisfied. But I couldn't help baiting him in the meantime.

He hesitated for a moment, read my eyes, then lightly kissed me. Quickly he stepped back and continued talking.

"After you shared the information Mandy told you about her earlier cruise, I easily located the cruise records. Turns out it wasn't this cruise line. Commander Cruise Lines has only been sailing out of Galveston for about a year. Very few passenger ships sailed out of Galveston before that. So it was obviously not this ship. The names on cruise ships tend to all sound similar, so she must have looked for a similar itinerary, and then Journey seemed like the right name. But she wasn't exaggerating. Although I was skeptical when you first told me, the ship was actually boarded by pirates. The Mexican Federales and U.S. law enforcement agencies cooperated efficiently, for once, to cap the thing before anyone could be hurt, except the pirates of course. They managed to keep it quiet, too. I've gone over everything with the appropriate officials, and talked to Mandy again. I can say with relative certainty that it's not connected to anything happening on this cruise."

"That's it? That's your one thing? Hardly worth my trade, in my opinion," I said, partly in jest.

"Well, I did throw in a kiss," he teased. "If it makes you feel better, Darla, I got the sense, like you, that she wasn't especially forthcoming about what went down in that dining room. She skirted my questions in some cases, so I am wondering myself if she didn't see something happen or get assaulted herself. That could be why she's been so vague about it with anyone when she mentioned it. I'm also wondering if that may be why she was so quick after a few comments at the buffet to think she was being stalked."

At my somewhat confused expression, he continued, "Your friends weren't much help, but the manager of the buffet remembered her, your friends, and the two crew members. They were Willie and Pete. Apparently they did try to flirt with her, called her 'babe,' and leered no end. But the manager said they basically were just womanizers and acted like that about any woman under about 40. He laughed, talking about how they tried to get your friend Carlotta's attention, with no luck whatsoever. He said he thought it was Mandy's imagination that they were targeting her in particular." He shrugged his shoulders, his usual response to just about everything.

"Huh, so maybe she wasn't being stalked at all?" I asked. He nodded and shrugged again.

"You know, Darla, I said 'at least' one answer. The other has to do with your pornographic DVDs. But I may need some motivation," he said with smile. While it was just like him to hold out on the good stuff, I was seeing a whole new side of him as he teased me. I wasn't sure I like it. He leaned in for a long and very pleasant kiss. On the other hand, I thought, I liked it more all the time.

"So fess up," I said when we came up for air. "What's your other answer, or other answers, about the DVDs?"

"Turns out we were able to weed out another aspect of the case as unrelated, too. The porn issue. It seems a few teen entrepreneurs were trying to make some money and the thing blew up in their faces," he said with a sigh.

He explained that a couple of teens coming on the cruise with their parents had decided they could make money by selling porn DVDs to the other kids on the ship. Their street-savvy and tech-savvy friends had been all too willing to take part in an amateur video shoot for a cut of the profits.

"Technology makes this sort of thing way too easy these days," Paul said. "And teens don't really seem to understand the gravity of it. They send each other pictures of themselves nude and in suggestive positions, and don't realize it's pornography or that the person they send it to can piece it together and distribute it. Same with cyber bullying. It is definitely a downside to our expanding technology capabilities." He sighed as he said this last bit. I wondered just how often he's had first-hand experience with these issues.

"But how did those discs get mixed up with everyone else's?" I asked, still not understanding how I had ended up with one of the porn DVDs.

"Bureaucratic screw-up," he said.

From his description, apparently U.S. Customs had caught the DVDs on the way through inspection. One of the Snooping Dog DVDs fell out of a bag and had a picture on the sleeve that made them question the contents. They confiscated it, viewed it, and flagged it. Officials subsequently flagged any CD or DVD bound for this cruise as suspicious, so a random selection of discs went through an in-depth manual inspection in the same room as the Snooping Dog ones.

"At the change in shift…" Paul said, "…the outgoing inspectors failed to tell the incoming Customs workers which discs had been reviewed and which ones hadn't. All the storage cases were left open with reviews in progress. Then the late ship, the rush to get substitute crew cleared and on board, and the Customs staff got pulled over to check folks coming in. When they finally returned to inspecting items for your outgoing ship, the cruise line was putting pressure on them to speed up and get the ship cleared. The inspectors began a spot-check and any loose discs got put back into whatever case they fit. It seems the last Customs staff in line didn't get the message that there were any pornographic discs in the bunch, because all they had seen were music discs. So they passed all of them through, mixed up together as they were. It wasn't just in the baggage of entertainers. But most passengers probably don't pack CDs or DVDs in checked or shipped baggage." He stopped and took a breath.

"Bureaucratic screw-up, plain and simple," he repeated. "But apparently unrelated to the murder and assault. The teens, who we've now identified, admit to breaking into the entertainers' equipment cabinets to see if they could reclaim any DVDs. They disclaim any involvement with the attack on Mr. Gonzales, the death of the crew member, or any involvement with Ms. Myers. I believe them on those counts. Unfortunately, the porn activity will result in charges I think they didn't expect. And needless to say, their parents weren't particularly thrilled with the anticipation of getting off the cruise with the first stop the Galveston Police Department. They'll be detained there pending further action."

He shook his head. "I must say, Darla, this is the oddest assortment of unrelated stories I've seen in a good while. You sure know how to get into the middle of things, don't you?"

"Me? How am I in the middle of things? Okay, maybe I am," I admitted. "But it's purely circumstantial, really. They just happened around me. Well, that and my curiosity. Speaking of being in the middle of things, I've been thinking." I could see Paul take a deep breath as if he had to brace himself for any outcome my thinking might produce. I bristled a little, but kept going.

"I was thinking about this situation in relation to one of my square dance workshops. You know, to figure out who the 'perps' are." Another deep breath on his part, but I plunged ahead.

"There's a movement called Load the Boat. I've been teaching it here for obvious reasons, given the name. Anyway, Load the Boat looks very complicated, but the end result is simple. If you just focus on where you need to be when the call is over, none of the dancers need to take more than a few steps. The complicated part is all for show." I finally had his attention. He was listening at least, but looked a little confused as to how this would relate to the various happenings on this cruise. I could understand his confusion, but hurried to tie it together best as I could.

"So, in this situation, maybe we, uh, I mean you, could just look for the end result being achieved and that will lead you to the perps." Paul smiled at my continued use of the slang term. I could tell he was still a bit skeptical.

"So what's your point, Darla? Do you have any idea what the end result here is? Why the crew member was killed?" he asked.

"Well, no," I admitted sheepishly, but I forged ahead. "Now that you've weeded out the unrelated matters, it should be easier to figure out, don't you think? In Load the Boat, the end dancers really just walk around to the other end of the line, passing each other, but not really interacting. That's kind of like Mr. Jarcourt and the pornography. But the center dancers, they have to interact with each other. They twist and turn and are closer together. I think that's the case with the dead crew member, the assault on Joaquim, and Mandy's trashed cabin. Somehow those are closely tied together and they all interact." I stopped and waited for his response. As usual, it was slow in coming as he processed what I'd said. I half expected him to just brush me off.

"Load the Boat, huh? I don't know how you got here from there, Darla, but I must say you've refocused my thinking. I was feeling a little all over the place with all the players and their connections, but you've given me renewed inspiration. And a fourth piece that likely is part of your centers is Pete. He is still missing, but there's no way he ever got off this ship. You are a surprising woman. And I do like surprises, believe it or not."

I was also a little surprised myself. Not only had I heard more actual words from Paul in this conversation than I had since we'd met, he ended up actually complimenting me. I felt warmth crawling up my neck into my face, and I'm sure my cheeks blushed pink. Whether the blush was from satisfaction or awkwardness, or something else, I wasn't sure.

He kissed me again, lightly this time, barely brushing my lips. "Darla, I hate to say it, but I need to get back to work. Maybe we can pick up later where we're leaving off now." He stared at my face intently for a few seconds, then turned and walked away. I watched his back until he disappeared inside. Then I turned back toward the sea and continued to contemplate the murdered crew member, the vandalized cabin, cruise employment practices, and the upcoming dance. My head hurt. Rather than trying to find Slim and Zach, or even the library with its tempting computers, I followed my usual head-in-the-sand routine and decided to take a nap before dinner to see if I could fend off a full-blown headache.

Back at my stateroom, I tossed and turned. I still didn't even know how Will had been killed. Surely someone would have heard a gunshot. And surely security would have detected a gun. My best guess was the old standby of 'blunt force trauma' but as I looked around my cabin I didn't see many things that weren't bolted down. That would mean that whoever killed Will had to have brought the weapon, whatever it was, with him.

I thought about Mandy and her belief that the crew members were stalking her. I had to concede that it was possible she felt threatened and hit Will, killed him by accident. But why was he in her cabin to begin with? And would she lie about finding him later? Finding out about her previous cruise from Paul really hadn't helped one way or the other. But, I just didn't think it was her, or maybe I didn't want to think that an anxious librarian could kill someone, accidentally or not. I realized I was assuming she hadn't told Doug what she'd relayed to Paul. That would give him another reason to be protective and to bristle at Paul.

Sleep just wasn't coming. Okay then, what if Will, and possibly whoever killed him, were looking for something. Would they be the same ones who attacked Joaquim and vandalized his office? I'd been thinking the other crew member involved was Pete, who I now knew was missing. But what about Jim? Both Jim and the singer Chance were also late assignments. Were they involved? I liked both of them, so I didn't want them to be involved, but were they? And did whoever killed Will find what he was looking for in Mandy's cabin, if that's what he was doing there? Or was the killer still trying to find whatever it was? Maybe it was a good thing Mandy was still in sick bay.

As questions flew around in my brain, I consoled myself that at least I could weed out a few events. We now knew Mr. Jarcourt wasn't involved in anything illegal, and the pornography twist was resolved. At that point in my litany, I finally managed to doze off. I woke just in time to dress for the dance and grab a quick bite on Deck 11 on my way back to Dreams. I'd missed another dinner, but fortunately my headache was on hold.

I normally look forward to calling a dance. I think it is the performer in me. But after a week of dance after dance and workshop after workshop, this definitely felt more like work. Judging by Slim and Zach's moods, as I joined them in the club, they were also ready to finish this up. We were scheduled for this dance, a workshop tomorrow, and then the last dance tomorrow night. We'd dock at Galveston during the night tomorrow, so the following day would just be going ashore and home. I was ready.

As the three of us tried to get motivated, Zach didn't seem very focused and that was a first for him. We decided Slim would start out the calling tonight, then Zach, and then I'd do a Plus tip. We would keep up that rotation for the three hours. We really didn't expect a lot of folks. If we took long breaks we could limit the number of tips we called. We figured the dancers would be tired as well.

As the dancers came in, it was no surprise that most of them were long-time club dancers rather than newer dancers. I smiled and hugged first Carlotta and Nick, and then Sam and Zoe. I hadn't seen Doug since last night, and when he came in I felt myself tense up. I intentionally turned to Slim to make conversation, but Slim immediately commented, "Hey Darla, here comes Doug," followed by "How you doing Doug? Happy New Year!"

"Hi Slim. Hi Darla," he said with a smile and a hug for each of us. "Sorry you two didn't make it for the after party last night. Our friend Zach here sure seemed to be having a good time," he teased as Zach stopped fiddling with the equipment and came over to join us.

"Heck, I decided I needed to see if I could win playing Texas Hold 'Em," said Slim. "Unfortunately, it didn't quite work out the way I planned." Slim grinned, rubbing his fingers together to indicate money, or the loss of it, I guessed. He continued, "I've walked through the casino a lot in the past week, but I bet they pull in the most money in these last two days at sea. Man, it took a while just to get a seat at a game. I should've taken that as a sign." Slim shook his head while we all laughed at his hang-dog expression.

Some of the crew had laid out refreshments and jugs of water as usual. The dancers were already starting to square up, so Slim excused himself, grabbed the mic, and the square dance was off once more with "Okay, square 'em up!"

Doug asked if I wanted to dance and we joined a square. Slim finished his tip without any problems. During the break Doug and I went over to talk to the other Clearton dancers. I hadn't figured out which CD to use for my Plus tip, so I excused myself and joined Slim while Zach did his tip. I commented that Zach didn't quite seem his usual energetic self, and Slim just shrugged. Zach finished up a lackluster set, and I stepped up to the mic for my set. Somewhere between my patter call and singing call, Mandy came into the dance.

Since most of the dancers were seasoned, Slim decided to do back-to-back Plus tips. He made an announcement and waited while the dancers shuffled themselves according to who wanted to dance Plus and who didn't. I danced with Doug again. The good and bad thing about square dancing is that you don't have to, and well, you actually can't, make conversation when you're moving.

Zach was up next, and while he called I stepped outside for air. To be honest, I was avoiding Doug and hoped Paul might find me out there. I wondered if he would stop by the dance. No luck, and I was up to call. This time I opted to call a Mainstream tip since Slim had called double Plus tips. We seemed to be free forming it tonight instead of sticking to our calling plan, but the dancers were responding well.

Doug and Mandy were partnered up for my tip, and for many of the others for the rest of the night. It became a pattern that if it was a Plus tip and not one I was calling, Doug came to get me as a partner. I realized at some point while Zach was calling that I wasn't as bothered by the fact that Doug was dancing so much with Mandy anymore. Mandy had a frailty to her, and Doug was a caring person.

Though we were all tired, the dance was probably more typical of one back in our home clubs. Having danced together so many days in a row, everyone seemed to know and be comfortable with each other. Quite a few folks sat out tips just so they could visit with each other.

After the dance, the Clearton Gang, along with Zoe and Mandy, headed for a quick bite with no more mysteries to deal with except what to eat. I still hadn't heard much about the after party I missed. As everyone chattered, I again heard about how great a singer Chance was. After that, most of the conversation focused on getting back to Galveston. Carlotta regaled the group with all the different activities that were going on the next day, our last day at sea.

I finally called it a night. Back in my stateroom I tried to will myself to sleep despite the cabin size and my nap earlier. I was getting tired of the increasingly closed-in feeling I had being out to sea and on the ship for so long. While I waited for sleep to come, I pondered my feelings for Doug. When we'd first come on the cruise, and he paid attention to Mandy, it bugged me. I had thought being on this cruise, being so 'available' to each other, would cement my future with Doug. I thought about our infrequent dates over the past year, and the rollercoaster of feelings on both our parts this week.

I realized that Carlotta may have a point—maybe Doug and I were destined to be friends rather than sweethearts or lovers. Certainly, my continuing to analyze things over and over and over again wasn't a good sign. If there was terrific chemistry or an obvious attraction, I shouldn't have to think about it, right? Doug was a really good guy. He was settled, fun, and caring. He was even giving up part of his ranch to create an equine-therapy camp for kids. He was a real catch. Maybe just not my catch.

I finally dozed off, feeling a little more comfortable about my intentions with regard to Doug. Now I just had to figure out how to let him in on the arrangement. My last thought though was of Paul.

CHAPTER 10

Our last workshop was scheduled for late morning, this last full day of the cruise, as we continued toward Galveston and home. Personally, I was glad to see it come and go. I had expected a relaxing cruise with a little work here and there. Instead, there had been a busy work schedule and the tension between Doug and me. Tomorrow I'd be sleeping in my own bed, and I was more than ready for it.

Slim had suggested we wait and see who showed up before we tried to figure out how we'd structure the workshop today. It was not likely that we would have dancers who needed the Basic program. Anyone who was interested would probably already have taken the earlier workshops. If there was enough interest, Slim might do a workshop on dancing-by-definition, or DBD as dancers called it, where dancers practiced how to perform square dance moves from any position in the square, not considering 'men' or 'ladies' positions. DBD was not something I could handle yet.

I actually managed to sleep in instead of being up at the crack of dawn, so I was feeling rested. I grabbed a quick bite to eat and went to the library to email Heather. She had responded to my last email yesterday, mostly she assured me she was okay. I walked along the outer part of the deck. It was quiet and calming as the ship continued on its way. Then on to Dreams. When I got there, Zach was idly flipping through his case of discs.

"Good morning, Zach. How're you today? We're on the home stretch now, huh?" I said, relief in my voice.

"Yeah, good morning, Darla. You sound chipper. That makes one of us. I'm feeling rough today. I guess I've burned the candle a little too much during this cruise," he said. Now that I noticed, he looked a little green around the gills. He certainly didn't look like the put-together young man I'd met a week ago.

"You need me to cover for you today?" I asked. "Slim and I can take the workshops. There probably won't be many folks."

"Nope, I can do it," he responded. "I just might not be my regular clever self!" He made an effort at an unsuccessful smile.

"Well, you just let me know if you need to leave. This isn't a marathon, you know," I told him.

Slim arrived and we mapped out our plan for the day. As we anticipated, there weren't many folks interested in workshops, though Carlotta, Nick, Sam, and Zoe arrived early. With so few, Slim convinced Zach to take the morning off and get some shut-eye. I took the Plus workshop and Slim did a DBD session. We each had about three squares, with no extras. If any dancers sat out for a break, there was one less square.

Carlotta and Nick decided to go to the DBD workshop, but Sam and Zoe stayed with me to do Plus. Doug showed up and decided on Plus, too. Even with Doug, we were short a male in the third square, so Zach hung in as a novice Plus dancer. He'd wanted a chance to learn Plus, I thought. As I watched the dancers, I wasn't sure it was such a good idea. He was looking paler by the minute.

I asked the dancers which Plus calls they wanted to workshop. Not surprising, they asked for Spin-Chain-Exchange the Gears, Crossfire, Fan the Top, and Coordinate to start. These are some of the more complicated calls on the Plus menu. Zach managed to hang in and didn't do too bad on the dancing either.

As the workshop broke up, Carlotta and Nick asked if I wanted to join them for a late lunch. I knew that Slim, Zach, and I needed to plan the last dance—our finale—but I'd eaten light at breakfast and Zach already was headed to his stateroom to lay down. I opted to go with them for lunch. I could get together with Slim and Zach later.

As soon as we got our food and sat down, Carlotta was on me like icing on a cake. "I have to tell you more about the after party the other night. And I want to hear about this 'confidential' thing with Harbinville. Oh, and this casserole is delicious. I gotta figure out how they make it," she said without taking a breath.

As we sat and ate our food, Carlotta talked nonstop about the after party, but this time not about Chance. She talked more about the romances she was building up in her head. She cataloged the goings-on of Sam and Zoe, but I already knew about them. Then she described Zach and a young woman from Oklahoma, Ivette. She bet Zach would likely be spending a lot of time up in Oklahoma in the future. She started to talk about Doug and Mandy, but cut her comments short. I suspected she limited the comments about them for my benefit. It didn't slow her down, though, and it didn't take long before she was on to another topic.

"Now, Darla, Doug was a little miffed that you didn't come to the after party. He seemed to think that it had to do with this 'confidential' business Harbinville said he had. He didn't blame you, of course, just Harbinville. He was also miffed that Harbinville grilled him about Mandy and about his whereabouts the night that crew member was killed. So, what the heck was this confidential business? Give!" she said, ending with a broad smile.

"Well," I stammered, not prepared for Carlotta's questions, "he just wanted to have a private conversation." As I felt myself blushing, I added, "He and Doug have had some issues related to Mandy as a 'person of interest,' you know. I'm sure that's what Doug was upset about." I intentionally tried to divert attention away from Paul's confidential meeting but to no avail.

"Now, Nick, would you guess from the rising color in Darla's face that this 'private' conversation was business or personal?" she teased.

Nick laughed and said, "Carlotta, I'm not going there. No how, no way." He forked a load of mashed potatoes into his mouth.

Deciding a change of topic was in order, I interjected, "Oh, I forgot the salt and pepper. Be right back."

I hopped up and went back to the buffet line for said salt and pepper. The area was crowded with others getting a bite as well. Some were getting brunch, others a full lunch at the buffet line. Looking around, I saw Danny in conversation with the missing crew member. Well, at least the last I heard he was missing. Pete, I remembered was his name. Curiosity got the better of me, as always, I got my salt and pepper packets and slipped over to the juice counter. This way I thought I would be close enough to hear their conversation.

I could hear okay, but it was all in Spanish. My Spanish was too rusty to understand, but I caught a few words. Policia—the police. Pasaporte—passport. Primo —cousin. Based on everything that had been going on aboard this ship, I decided the conversation justified some investigation. Not mine, though. I looked around for Paul or even Joaquim. Not a chance.

I remembered Nick's fluent Spanish with the man at Progreso. He could get the gist of the conversation. Then we could let Paul or Joaquim or even the Captain know if it seemed important. Keeping my eye on Danny and Pete, I got some juice and went back to Carlotta and Nick.

"Nick, would you do me a favor? See the crew member over there talking to Danny? Remember him from that first night? No, don't be obvious!" I said. "Don't let them see you looking over there. Anyway, I picked up a few words in Spanish from their conversation, and it sounded suspicious to me. I'd like to know what they're saying, but it's in all in rapid Spanish. We can hear them from the juice bar. Would you come with me? We can make like we're getting more juice for our table so it won't look so obvious."

Carlotta spoke up, "Don't do it, Nick! She'll rope you into the investigation. You'll be sorry."

Nick smiled back at her. "You know me, Car, I've got just as much curiosity as Darla does. We're only going to the juice bar. How dangerous can that be? Be right back," he said, chuckling. "Besides, somebody has to watch out for Darla," he added over his shoulder.

As we walked toward the juice bar, I talked slightly louder than normal about the great orange juice. "It tasted fresh-squeezed, didn't it? What kind of oranges do you think they used? Do you think they bought them fresh in port?"

Nick simply smiled indulgently and shook his head, refusing to play his part. When we got to the counter, I stopped talking so he could overhear their conversation. I also made a big show of getting three glasses of orange juice. I fiddled with the ice machine and filled the glasses, very slowly.

Danny looked up and I was sure he saw me. Maybe the loud-talking cover hadn't been such a good idea after all. He said something low to Pete and they separated. Pete headed out the door and Danny came toward us. I looked at Nick. Nick's face was serious, but he didn't have time to say anything before Danny walked up.

"Ms. King, so glad to see you. One of the crew was just relaying a message from Mr. Gonzales. He needs to see you right away. Please come with me," Danny said, in his usual professional tone. He looked very serious with a hint of anger I hadn't noticed before. Nick answered before I could speak.

"Ms. King hasn't finished her meal yet. In a while we will be on our way to the Dreams Club," Nick said. It was obviously a dodge, so I realized he was telling me not to go with Danny. "Mr. Gonzales could meet Ms. King there," he finished.

Danny turned to me. "No, no, that will not work. Mr. Gonzales apparently has something he must show you urgently. He asked me to bring you to him." To Nick he said, "You are welcome to come also, sir."

"I'm sorry, we just can't right now," I said. "I can't imagine what Mr. Gonzales needs to see me about. You might ask him if Mr. Harbinville would be a better choice if he has something related to that other incident."

"Oh yes, Mr. Harbinville is already there," he said a little too quickly. "The crew member indicated they both asked for you. I'm sure it will only take a few minutes of your time."

I was weakening and thinking that maybe he wasn't lying. If Paul was with Joaquim, my safety wouldn't be in question. But that was a big 'if' given that his story kept changing. At the same time, I didn't know what Nick had overheard and he seemed more than hesitant to go with Danny. On the other hand, I might find out some valuable information and if I could help I really should go. I seesawed for a minute, then caution, and Nick, prevailed.

"I can't come right now," I repeated. "Please give Joaquim my regrets. He can reach me later in the Dreams Club if he still needs me. Mr. Harbinville as well."

Danny looked from me to Nick and back. "Oh dear. Well, yes, I will tell him. Have a nice day," he said as he turned sharply, obviously not pleased that we had declined his invitation. He headed toward the same door Pete had used.

I turned to Nick. "Well?"

"I didn't have time to hear much," he said. "But what I did hear sounded pretty fishy. Something about family, immigration, and Danny not trusting him. He said they'd meet up before we got to Galveston tomorrow to give him 'the papers.' Danny said 'at the stateroom' as if the crew member would know what that meant. The crew guy said the stateroom was too dangerous. That's when Danny noticed you, cut off the conversation, and came over to us. I didn't hear the last thing he told him, his voice was too low. What do you think it means?"

"I don't know. But I'm beginning to think Danny might not be the well-behaved staff member he appears," I said. "I've got a feeling he's a big part of the whole mess. We've got to find Paul and let him know what you heard. If Danny is involved, then we might not be able to trust Joaquim either," I added, remembering Paul's earlier warning to give information directly to him. Perhaps he already had suspicions about Joaquim and Danny.

As we walked back to our table, Nick said, "You're right. We need to alert someone. Let's go get Carlotta," he said.

"Nope, I learned my lesson," Carlotta answered with a chuckle when we told her what we discovered and what we planned to do. Carlotta's curiosity didn't drive her as hard as mine did. I figured our wild ride earlier this year quelled it even more. Despite Nick's imploring look, she declined to come with us. She finished her lunch as we talked. I envied her. Nick and I each ate only part of our food. As Carlotta took off to the pool deck, Nick and I went to track down Paul.

I wasn't sure where to look for him, but I remembered Joaquim had mentioned that he was staying in the Captain's quarters and Paul mentioned there was lots of room there. If we headed there, we might at least find Captain Rios. I doubted we would catch Paul at the Captain's quarters, but the Captain would do. Joaquim might know where to locate Paul. If we went to Joaquim's office, we wouldn't have to tell him anything really. I could just say I was looking for 'my' agent. If Danny told the truth and they both wanted to see me, they might even be together in Joaquim's office anyway. It was worth a shot, and we really didn't have any other ideas.

We headed down the narrow carpeted hallway to Joaquim's office. As we rounded a corner, a hand grabbed my elbow roughly from behind and jerked me up short. I turned to face Danny and Pete.

"I really must insist, Ms. King, that you come with us," Danny said through gritted teeth.

"We can't do that, Danny. We are on our way to Joaquim's office. You're welcome to come with us. You told us he wanted to see us," I replied with what I hoped passed for a smile despite the pain in my elbow and fear in my heart.

Danny jerked his head toward Nick. Pete stepped closer and pulled Nick's arms tight.

"Hey, back off!" Nick yelled. It got him an immediate response, just not the one he intended. Pete pulled Nick's arms even tighter behind him and I heard Nick suck in his breath. Nick might be a good insurance man and actuary, but he wasn't particularly athletic. His slight build suggested that he would be hard pressed to take on these two. Danny spoke up.

"Ms. King, you and your friend here obviously figured out that was a ruse. You just should have left it alone and minded your own business. Now, it is too late for games," Danny warned. "Neither of you will make a sound or act as if anything is wrong. You will come with us and I will explain the entire matter." He nodded to Pete, who released one of Nick's arms and produced a gun from under his shirt. "If you do not cooperate, the consequences will not be so pleasant. Do you understand?"

I looked at Nick, and we both gave a nod. Danny pushed me into a walk. Pete followed, the gun hidden against the edge of the narrow walkway but clearly aimed at Nick's back. I tried to think what to do. Our little group would look fairly normal to any passerby. Most groups bunch up to walk down the ship's small halls, so it was unlikely somebody would notice anything odd. Our only hope would be if a passenger or crew member stopped Danny to ask for something, but I couldn't count on that.

The hallway had been empty, but several yards up I now saw a crew member enter the hall from a crossway hall with a room service cart. Danny must have seen it too. He jerked my arm as warning. Pete murmured, "Silencio!" and I heard Nick grunt.

As we got closer, I saw the crew member knock on the stateroom door, wait for an instant, then position the cart in front of the door. He walked away from us down the hall, but not before I recognized him. It was Jim, the third crew member borrowed from the other ship. I didn't see any looks pass between Jim and our captors so I hoped he wasn't part of whatever Danny was orchestrating. Jim didn't seem to pay any attention to us or even notice us. It wasn't looking good. I was pretty sure that if they got us wherever Danny was headed, the outcome for us would not be favorable.

We approached the room service cart, and the smell of fresh brewed coffee was strong. I scanned the cart and saw a carafe of what I hoped was steaming hot coffee. I thought about all the self-defense classes I had taken in my life time, but with the gun on Nick, I was hesitant to trust any big maneuvers. I remembered my instructors telling us to use what we had. I had coffee, hopefully scalding hot.

As far as I could tell, Danny didn't have a weapon. That meant Pete was the one I needed to divert. It would be tough to nail him with the coffee without getting Nick caught in the spray, but I had to try. It was the only thing I could come up with. I was smart enough to know Danny wasn't going to just 'explain the entire matter' and let us go. Action was called for, and there might not be another opportunity.

When we got almost to the cart, I stumbled forward. On my stumble toward the cart, I reached out as if for support and nabbed the carafe. Nick reached forward to steady me, not realizing my fall was on purpose. It gave me just the opening I needed. I wrenched my other arm from Danny. I pulled my arm back and then forward, its contents aimed at Pete.

Bullseye! Pete screamed and dropped the gun as his hands covered his face. My movement caught Danny by surprise and he hit the corner of the cart but recovered quickly. We both dropped to our knees on the floor and tried to get the gun. I heard a sound, then felt Danny's full weight flatten me to the carpet. I struggled to look up. Nick stood over Danny with a heavy pottery platter in his hand. Scrambled eggs and bacon lay everywhere and on everyone. Danny was out cold, but Pete was whimpering and moving as quickly as he could down the hall.

Adrenaline was still pumping through me and I managed to throw Danny's body off me easily. I crawled over to pick up the gun as Nick tried to help me up.

"Don't worry about me, I'm fine," I said. "Just make sure he doesn't get away. If he comes to, smack him again." I stood up, braced my feet, and took my best two-handed aim with the gun pointed it at Pete. It had been a while since I had been to the range, but the gun felt comfortable in my hand. I knew how to use it if I had to.

"Freeze," I hollered.

"Freeze," came an echo.

Behind Pete, Paul aimed his weapon directly down the hall in our direction. Pete froze. Looking from one of us to the other, he simply fell to his knees and put his forehead on the floor, hands still coddling his scalded face and neck.

"Darla?" Paul's voice held more than a tinge of disbelief. "You okay? Where'd you get the gun? Do you know how to use it? Is it loaded?"

"Yes," I said. "Yes I'm okay, and yes I know how to use it. It came from Pete, and I don't really know if it's loaded or not." Pointing to the man huddled between us, I said, "That's Pete, the missing crew member you were looking for."

Paul lowered his gun and walked up to stand over Pete. I changed my aim to Danny, who hadn't moved.

"You hit him pretty hard," I said to Nick, impressed that Danny was still out cold.

"The adrenaline," he answered with wide eyes and a shake of his head. I think he was a little surprised himself.

"How'd you get here?" I asked Paul as he joined us, with Pete in tow.

"I had just run into your friend Carlotta who said the two of you were looking for me. She didn't know where you were. In the meantime, a crew member saw you and thought something was wrong," he said. "He got hold of the Cruise Director, Joaquim, and told him something was going on. Joaquim notified me, and they led me here," he explained.

Nick and I still stood over Danny. I raised my eyes toward Paul, who quickly handcuffed Pete. Behind him I could see the tops of two faces barely peeking around the walkway into the hall. Jim and Joaquim, I imagined.

"We're going to need the doctor," Paul said over his shoulder, without looking up. "Would one of you go get him?" The upper head, Joaquim, I supposed, spoke to the lower head and they both disappeared.

"Would you come watch this guy," Paul said to Nick, gesturing at Pete. Nick complied quickly. Paul moved over to check out Danny. With a shadow of a smile Paul added, "You can stand down now, Ms. King."

I relaxed and let the gun fall to my side, but didn't put it down. I didn't know where to put it. Somehow the room service cart didn't seem quite right. Paul put out his hand and solved my dilemma with a "I'll take that—it may be evidence." I handed it to him.

As I looked at the mess on the cart and the eggs and bacon all over floor, the stateroom door behind the cart opened slightly. An eye appeared in the crack and a man's voice said, "Um, do I need to call anyone?"

I looked at Paul, who shook his head. He was busy handcuffing the still-inert body of Danny. I realized the whole episode had taken only a few minutes. It seemed much longer.

"Not for us," I answered the man. "But you'll want to order room service again."

CHAPTER 11

Paul sent Nick and I to the Captain's quarters to debrief. Paul was right, the Captain's lodging was quite expansive and more like a couple of combined hotel suites. We were made comfortable in what passed for a living room while Paul went to deposit Pete and Danny somewhere. I wasn't sure where. The Captain was more courteous to me than previously, and he asked fewer questions than I expected. There was less paperwork than I had experienced in other situations as well. I supposed that being on a ship, even if we were back in U.S. waters, limited the number of law enforcement authorities compelled to have forms in triplicate.

As I wound up writing my story for the record, Paul walked in.

"Are you really okay, Darla?" he asked. "Do you need anything?"

"Yes, I'm really okay. Although I'd just as soon not have another afternoon like this one ever again. You got time to talk?" I asked.

"Not now, no. How about I come by your stateroom in about an hour or so?" he asked.

"I'm going to scout out some food," I said, "then I'll be back in my stateroom. I never did get to eat my lunch." I risked a small smile, which he didn't return. "You have my number," I said, hoping to get a response. Still no smile, but I got the reward of a head-shake at least.

I didn't see how the whole thing fit together, or how Danny and Pete ended up on the wrong side of this mess. I couldn't figure out where this 'piece' was supposed to end up in my choreography using Load the Boat as a guide. Maybe I was way off base thinking real life mirrored a square dance move.

I filled a plate back up on Deck 11 where it had all begun earlier this afternoon. It was fairly deserted at this hour and that was a good thing. Once I finished my food, I went to my stateroom. It seemed, other than work, all I was doing on this cruise was eating and sleeping, or trying to sleep. I'd have to work off extra pounds when I got home, I knew. At the moment, though, I wasn't sleepy so I turned to the ship's channel on television. At least I learned a little about how we would get off the ship. After that, I packed up as much as I could so I'd be ready to head out tomorrow when we pulled into Galveston. That really didn't take very long in the small room. I still needed to leave out clothes for the formal dinner and last dance.

When I finished packing, I unfortunately had time to think. That was when I realized how close Nick and I had come to being toast. My knees went weak and I sat down on the bunk. Part of me wanted to know why I'd been attacked. The other part knew it was because I had stumbled on to something. I just didn't know what. My patience was waning and my curiosity piqued. I was about to erupt when Paul finally showed up. The first thing he did when he closed the door was grab me and kiss me. Yep, still just as good.

"Darla, you have got to stop giving me heart attacks," he said. "The first time you got yourself kidnapped, and this time almost killed and maybe buried at sea." He shook his head and looked oh, so serious. And so seriously sexy.

"Hey, not my fault," I said. "I don't go looking for international espionage, thieves, and murderers like you do. Honest, I try to avoid them. That's why I became a square dance caller. Now, tell me the parts I don't know. Why did Nick and I almost get killed?"

"Because you're you, and as usual you take a friend into the fray with you," he said. I made a face.

"Okay, I can tell you the basics without revealing confidential case information. Danny was the key, as you discovered. He was the one who selected the three extra crew members from the ship coming into port. That was Pete, Willie, and Jim. Jim appears to be simply an uninvolved crew member so far. We're double checking that. Pete and Willie wanted entrance into the U.S. without going through the necessary channels. Whether they intentionally caused the other ship to come in late and therefore rushed the crew transfer, and whether Danny intentionally caused the openings on this ship, we don't know yet. The investigation isn't over." He hesitated and added, "But your part definitely is."

"Hey, you were the one who knew Danny was trouble and didn't tell me. Anyway, go on. What else?" I asked, intrigued with the story so far.

"Well, apparently Danny has the reputation for running an illegal entry operation and has done this type of thing before. He has the connections to get forged papers and a human pipeline around Customs. Pete and Willie are undocumented workers with criminal records from Peru. Danny was smuggling them into the United States via the Port of Galveston. He made the arrangements for them to be the ones transferred to this ship. We think he even created the last-minute openings by paying off the 'ailing' crew members that needed to be replaced."

Paul paused before he continued. "Pete was desperate to get to the States because his sister and her family are here. One of his nieces has some form of cancer, leukemia, I think. He had it in his head that he could be a donor. He didn't seem to know what he would be donating, but somehow had understood that a donor was needed. A good motive, but not the best way to approach entry. He probably could have gotten an emergency visa if he had applied, given the circumstances. But so many have been rejected that he thought it would be easier to pay a 'broker' in their country to arrange his immigration. Will, on the other hand, likely doesn't have a humane bone in his body. He was in trouble with the authorities in Peru, and he needed to get out of Peru fast. He was part of the criminal element and that was the loose screw in the deal."

Paul went on to explain that Danny stashed the forged papers required to pass Customs in the safe in what was supposed to be an empty stateroom. That was the room they moved Mandy into when her cabin's plumbing malfunctioned. Danny knew that cabin was usually not assigned to travelers, so he felt confident in storing papers there. He also set his own combination to the safe. Danny wasn't involved in cabin assignments, and didn't realize she'd been assigned to the cabin until she was already moved in.

Once Mandy was moved into the cabin, however, she asked why the safe wouldn't work. Danny had to remove the papers and figure out another place to put them. He had Pete and Willie keep an eye on Mandy to determine the best time to go into her room. Only to her, that seemed as if they were stalking her. Like stalkers, they watched her whereabouts and positioned themselves near her cabin frequently.

"Get to the punchline, Paul," I demanded impatiently. "How did Willie end up dead in Mandy's stateroom?"

"I'm waiting for the full story from Danny and Pete. But from my preliminary interviews with them, it sounds like Danny, Pete, and Willie were in Mandy's room to remove the papers and discuss what to do next. Danny and Willie had a disagreement and got into a fight," he said.

"How did he die?" I asked. "That question has been bugging me."

"Not sure yet. Sounds like Willie wanted to steal what they could from Mandy. He figured they were already there and it would be easy to make it look like a robbery or vandalism. Pete wasn't in favor of that. He didn't want any part of burglary or the like. He just wanted to get into the country and help his niece and sister if he could. He also didn't want to risk being found out. Danny, apparently, also didn't agree with the stealing. He was afraid it would draw more attention to them and blow the immigration deal. He wanted to get the papers from the safe and avoid any appearance of anyone being in the room. We'll know more later, but my bet is that Willie started to trash the cabin looking for anything valuable, the argument got heated, and either Danny or Pete killed Will. Not sure if it was intentional or not. They probably finished trashing the room to divert attention."

"Yes, but how? You still haven't told me," I said.

"Oh, you mean cause of death? A full autopsy is yet to be conducted. He had a significant contusion on his temple, so I'd say that probably caused his death. I won't go into detail. In fact, as usual I've already told you more than I should. But Will didn't die quickly. There was little blood in the stateroom, but there was evidence he had tried to reach the cabin door. Sorry to be so graphic, but you asked," he finished up.

"So, blunt force trauma after all," I said, not caring that I felt a little ghoulish. "That's what I'd guessed, but I appreciate you appeasing my curiosity." That good-listener stuff was a powerful thing. People almost always ended up telling me more than they intended to.

Paul went on to speculate that after Will's death, Danny had to come up with a safe place for the forged papers. He decided to hide them in plain sight, in with all the other official papers in Joaquim's office. He nearly made it, but didn't expect Joaquim to still be in his cabin. Joaquim was there late as he tried to figure out what to do with those DVDs. When he discovered Joaquim was there, Danny was

223

the one who knocked Joaquim out. He didn't want to have to explain why he was there. If Joaquim hadn't been in his office, Danny most likely would have just filed the papers in the filing cabinet. If Joaquim had come across the papers accidentally, he wouldn't have known what they were for or that they were forged. The attack had nothing to do with the port DVDs after all.

I couldn't stay quiet. The puzzle was falling into place for me, and I picked up the narrative at that point.

"So after Will was killed, Pete laid low and stayed out of Danny's way. In fact, he stayed out of sight in general, probably scared to death," I guessed. "That was why you had so much trouble finding him. But he had to confer with Danny prior to reaching Galveston to find out the plan and get his paperwork. That was the conversation Nick and I overheard. Somehow as the whole thing unraveled, Danny thought we knew more than we really did. Danny needed to get rid of us, just in case. Involving Pete was one way to be sure he kept his mouth shut." Paul nodded and interrupted me.

"I also think Danny saw you with me the day before. Joaquim knew that you talked to me about all the various incidents. I'm sure he innocently mentioned that to Danny," said Paul as he added the wrap-up to the story. "I take part of the blame for putting you in harm's way. But only part, you know. You could have stayed out of it," he added with the stern expression back in place.

"Once you get to know me better, you'll know I couldn't have stayed out of it," I said. He smiled.

"So I will get to know you better?" he asked, smile broadening.

My answer was another kiss. Despite the circumstances, it made my insides flutter.

"But now both of us have commitments we have to meet," I said. "I really hate to say this, but you have to go. Last dinner, formal night, and I've got to get ready for the last dance of the cruise. The show must go on!"

Paul started for the door and I stopped him. "But wait, one more question. Is there any way Immigration will let Pete stay at least long enough to find out if he could be a donor, and if so, do what is needed for his niece?" I asked, fully expecting that it would not be possible.

"That will probably depend a lot on what we find out about who actually killed Will. If Danny confesses, then there is some slim chance that it could be arranged, slim is better than none," he said, shrugging his shoulders as usual.

"Okay, now go, so I can get dressed!" He laughed, kissed me again and left.

No sooner had Paul left than Carlotta, Nick, Doug, and Sam came pounding on the door. I was halfway through getting dressed.

"Give me a minute!" I called.

I pulled on my skirt and top and went to the door. Obviously, my square dance prairie skirt was going to have to have to be sufficient for the formal night. Doug was the first one to rush through.

"Damn it, Darla! Are you okay? Why didn't you call me? Nick told us what happened. You could have been killed!" Doug put his arms around me and held me longer than a hug. It felt good. Safe.

"I'm fine," I said into his shoulder. I backed up and looked at Nick.

"How are you, Nick? You saved my life and I haven't even had the chance to thank you," I said. I moved over and gave him a grateful squeeze.

"Darla, darlin', you never cease to amaze me," said Sam, eyes sparkling.

Carlotta didn't say anything, she just looked at me with tears in her eyes.

"It's okay, Carlotta. Really," I said. "Nick and I are both fine." I looked over at Nick to see if he would contradict me. He didn't. "And we helped solve all the mysterious doings on the ship," I said, trying to be cheerful about the entire thing. I didn't feel cheerful. I felt vulnerable and thrown off balance. But I don't usually show my feelings, and I didn't think it would help to do so this time.

"So, Darla, you gonna tell us about all those mysterious happenings over dinner?" asked Sam.

"I'll tell you what I can," I said. "But not at dinner. I have one more dance to call. Just promise me you won't leave me alone any time soon."

"Don't worry about that, Darla. But we're all too curious to wait too long. And I think I deserve the full story, don't you?" I couldn't tell if Nick was smiling or scowling. "After the dance tonight, we can all get together so you and I can compare notes. And you can bring us all up to speed," he continued. They all nodded in agreement. One by one they hugged me again, and then filed out of the crowded room so I could finish dressing.

We all trooped down to dinner. I managed to bypass all the photographers. As we made easy conversation with others at the table, the bar steward brought over a bottle of champagne. He opened it and signaled to the waiter to provide champagne flutes all around. He explained simply, "Compliments of the Captain, Ms. King, Mr. Tricot." Not wanting to get into the details in the dining room, we just smiled and offered our thanks. We made a toast to friendships so as not to waste the bubbly, but I didn't drink up. I still had a dance to call!

The final dance was scheduled for 8 o'clock, and it was open to everyone who wanted to dance. Like the workshops,

I didn't expect to see many new faces. I figured anyone interested in square dancing already checked it out before tonight. It was certainly possible that a few people were still curious about square dancing and just hadn't had the time, especially with all the other activities available onboard. But I doubted it.

Somehow I kept my concentration and made it through the dance. I think I sloughed off some of my calling to Zach and Slim. Zach seemed to be feeling better, although his attention was scattered. Slim pulled the heaviest duty, but then, he was the most experienced caller, I told myself.

On my last tip I reminded the dancers of the first night's dance, and called 'Load the Boat' as part of my tip. I ended the tip with Glen Campbell's song, 'Galveston, Oh Galveston.' We finished up about 10 o'clock with Slim saying our goodbyes.

"On behalf of Darla King, Zach Jameson, and myself I just want to say we enjoyed calling for you on this cruise. We hope you'll join us for another dance cruise in the near future. If you've enjoyed it half as much as we have, we'll see you sooner rather than later." He was greeted by a wave of applause. All the dancers faced us, bowed, and said 'thank you.' Slim waited for the floor to calm down.

"Have a safe trip home and we'll see you in a square," he added. Zach and I joined him in waving the crowd of dancers out. When the last few stragglers left, we began packing our equipment.

"Slim, do we take the equipment ourselves, or ship it home like we shipped it here?" I asked.

"You can do either one," he answered gruffly. "But after all the problems we've had here, I'm taking mine with me."

Zach and I decided that was a good idea, and I piled my stuff on a rolling cart to take with me to my cabin. I'd have to figure out how to carry all this tomorrow morning. Sam and I had agreed to do the self offload option so we could get an early start.

"Slim, Zach, I don't know if I'll get a chance to see you again before we leave in the morning," I said. "But I want to tell you guys, you have made this job a pleasure. Thanks so much!" The three of us exchanged compliments and hugs all around.

The Clearton Gang showed up and reminded me that they were not letting me off the hook or letting me go back to my stateroom alone. The whole bunch of us headed out of the Dreams Dance Club for the last time while I went over in my head which parts of the story I could tell without overstepping my confidentiality promise to Paul.

First to my room to drop off my sound system, and then to the midnight buffet that really started at 11:00. I was ready for some downtime but it didn't look like I'd get it right now.

After we unloaded all my music and equipment in my stateroom, making it feel even smaller than before, we headed up to the buffet. I was pretty surprised just how many people were up there. While the rest of us took the first shift getting food, Doug and Sam scouted out a table near the windows and off from the buffet. The plan was to be off to ourselves for a better place to talk. After we made it to the table, Doug and Sam made their run through the food line.

"Don't say a word until we get back, Darla Darlin'," warned Sam. "I want to hear the whole story, even if it takes 'til morning!"

When they returned, I obediently waited until Sam got settled. Nick was more impatient.

"Okay Darla, we're all here now. Finish chewing, and start talking. I was involved in this mess, and I still don't know what the story is," Nick prompted.

I gave them the condensed version, not with all the details. I wasn't quite sure how much I was supposed to share, but Nick at least should have some explanation for the gun in his back. I gave a brief combined story of my deductions and Paul's findings.

The story got sidetracked with a semi-political and philosophical discussion of illegals coming into the country and what to do about it. We chewed over several theories along with our food. We balanced opinions on the problems with the fact that United States history is pretty much all based on immigration. The conversation was getting a little heavy, but fortunately Sam created a diversion.

"So now Darla, I have to admit I've been spending a lot of time with Zoe…" here he gave Sam's version of a leer, but it just came out comical, "…and I might have missed something, but I swear I saw that Mr. Jarcourt man at the dance last night. In point of fact, I'm pretty sure I saw you talk to him and Mandy dance with him. You know his story, too, I'm sure, and I'm curious about it. What's up with him?" Sam ventured.

This prompted my telling them the sad but beautiful story once again. Carlotta made lots of oohs and ahs, and got a little teary-eyed even though she'd heard the story already.

Doug coughed and we all looked to him and then to where he was nodding. Mandy was looking toward our table but seemed a little hesitant to join us. Nick was closest and called her to join us. At the same time, he quickly got up and grabbed another chair. She sat down with her plate and said hello.

"I don't want to barge in," she said. We all assured her she was welcome, and she was. She thanked us and continued, "I'm sorry I missed the last dance, Darla. I am going to keep up the square dancing, though. It's fun," she said.

"Oh, you'll find it's not half as much fun if you're not dancing with us!" Sam joked. "Now, Mandy, I know you've had a helluva time this week. Did you get to enjoy any of this cruise?" Sam asked.

"Yes, Sam, I did. Mostly thanks to you guys, I must say. I came on this cruise to get past a previous bad experience, and ... well, let's just say I don't think I'll do a cruise again. But I will square dance again. That's one good thing from this. That and meeting all of you and lots of other nice people," she said somewhat wistfully.

We were all quiet for a bit, not really knowing what to say in response to her bittersweet assessment of the cruise. Finally Carlotta piped up that Mandy would see us all again at regional or state dances if she kept with it. Nick and Carlotta were the first to leave the table, Carlotta commenting on the monumental task of getting all her petticoats and skirts back into her suitcases.

Shortly after them, I decided I would leave too, but first made plans with Sam where I would meet him. We decided to meet after we cleared Customs so we could make our way to his car together. I remembered to warn him that I would have my part of the sound system this trip and headed for the elevator back to my stateroom. Doug followed me.

"Darla, do you have a minute?" he asked.

"Sure," I answered, not feeling sure at all.

"Mind stepping out over here a little?" he asked as he guided me through the doors and onto the outer deck. It was a clear night, but a bit chilly.

"Darla, I just want to clear the air a little here, okay?" he continued. He looked very serious. I nodded and he continued, "I got to know you when Clint was killed. With that history between us, I think we can be very honest with each other, don't you?"

I agreed and nodded.

"And then you moved to Texas and we've been pretty good friends all along. We enjoy some of the same things, not just square dancing, but going to shows and museums."

He hesitated and I wasn't sure what to say. I found myself staying on safe ground. "You're right Doug, we enjoy the same things and I enjoy your company and conversation. You're a good friend."

"Darla, I've been giving this some thought the last few days of this cruise. The way I've always seen things, when a man and a woman enjoy time together, and neither of them is married or anything, maybe things change, you know? Then again, maybe they don't. That's what I've been struggling with. Well, I think what I've figured out is that for me, at least right now, maybe friends is where we're supposed to be. Good friends, but just friends. I would never want to hurt you. I'm sorry if I made you uncomfortable or anything on this cruise, that's all. I hope we can still be friends."

He let out a deep breath and looked at me expectantly.

"Doug, you don't have anything to apologize for. You haven't been inappropriate or pushy. Yes, you made it clear, you wanted more, but…." I paused, not quite knowing where to go from there.

"Okay, I just want to make sure we're okay. I think that whole incident in the fall, with you in danger and all, made me realize how much I care about you and value that friendship. But try as I might on this cruise, instead of moving toward romance and closeness, I was feeling like we were getting farther apart. Then you go and get yourself in a mess again, and I get worried about you all over again," he said, shaking his head and smiling.

I laughed and said, "Yeah, well, it appears I can't get involved in a mystery without you and the rest of the gang around."

"I'm getting old, Darla. I don't know how many more of your mysteries my old heart can take," he teased.

"Hogwash, Doug. If you're old, I'm old. And I'm certainly not admitting that. But I'll try to keep my adventures on the tamer side, as much as I can!" I promised.

"Good," he said. "Now give me a hug, and I'll walk you to your stateroom. Sam is hoping to catch up with Zoe one last time and I don't want to get in his way," he said, smiling.

When we arrived at my cabin, I turned to him and said, "I couldn't ask for a better friend than you, Doug."

"Back at ya, Darla." He gave me a hug and headed back down the hall to the elevator.

Opening the door, I realized I felt more relaxed than I had for several days. I think I was, and maybe Doug was too, trying to make something out of our friendship that really wasn't in the cards. I remembered that Carlotta had asked me if I felt 'that way' about Doug. I think the excitement and possibility of something, of not being lonely, was alluring. But in the end there really wasn't that kind of chemistry. Hopefully, he meant what he said about being friends.

I walked into the stateroom, and there on my bunk was Paul. Now, talk about chemistry!

"How'd you…? Oh, never mind, I'm sure you could get into any room you wanted. I keep thinking I won't get to see you again, and then there you are," I tried not to smile too broadly.

"Sorry, Darla, I got tired of waiting outside in the hall, no place to sit down, other cruise folk looking at me oddly, so …" he said with that shoulder shrug, and continued, "here I am. I don't know if you've noticed, but there isn't a whole lot of room in here."

"Oh, that is for sure! So… to what do I owe this pleasure?" I asked a little concerned he might be moving a little faster than I was with our tentative romance. I was a bit on the old-fashioned side.

"Pleasure, huh? Glad to hear it," he answered. "Really, I just wanted to talk to you again. I am probably not going to be around in the morning. Lots of loose ends to tie up. You want to sit down?" he asked patting the mattress next to him.

I sat, and waited for him to continue. "First, based on the information we got from both Pete and Danny, Will's death does appear to be accidental. Danny was trying to stop him from stealing and trashing the room, and in the scuffle Will hit his head on the counter edge. Dr. Matisse isn't a coroner, but he is pretty sure that when they process the blood and hair on the counter edge, it will be Will's. Thought you might want to know," he said.

"Thanks," I told him. "I appreciate you telling me. You're getting to know the bounds of my curiosity, aren't you?" He shrugged and continued.

"Of course, even though it was an accident, neither Danny nor Pete sought medical help. So in addition to all the other charges, they'll be facing that one, too. It's a mess and I don't know how long I will be hung up here. This ship will be held in port, and the cabin will have to be processed. And the various agencies, both from the U.S. and Mexico, haven't been able to sort out who needs to do what on the murder. It may come down to time of death, but this cruise line is under the authority of the U.S., with corporate headquarters here in Galveston, so it may not make a difference. And, of course, the FBI is involved, which is why I'm here."

"This cruise was supposed to turn around and go back out tomorrow," I said. "Joaquim told me that he and some others had been told the ship would not be going out, but what happens with the passengers who think they are going on a cruise?" I asked.

"They likely won't even notice the difference. It will be a different ship, but their itinerary will be the same. I don't know the details. Commander Cruise Lines is going to make a substitution, come up with some excuse why this ship can't turn around. Because we are detaining Joaquim, Jim, and a few other of the crew, there will be some changes to personnel," he explained. I guess maybe changes in personnel were more common than I thought, after all.

Putting his arm around me, he continued, "I assume you are heading back home to Isquith, right?"

I nodded, loving the warmth of his embrace, and added, "Sam and I drove down together, so he'll drop me back at home and then he'll drive on to Clearton." He straightened up and his arm slid away from me.

"Wait!" I said. "Leave that arm where it was."

He smiled and reached around my shoulders again.

"So, what's up with us?" I asked him.

"That's why I stopped by to see you. Okay, I really stopped by just to see you. But I also wanted to make sure you were safe and to make sure we are clear on a few things," he said.

I waited, not quite sure where he was going.

He continued, "Darla, like I told you before, I have wanted to get to know you ever since that incident at the Weathers ranch. The reality of it is, though, I didn't figure there was any point. I live in Dallas most of the time, and Virginia part of the time. I don't always know where I'm going to be or for how long. Makes it kind of hard to have any kind of relationship. But I am so glad to have had this opportunity to get to know you better..." here he laughed, "even if it was in the middle of another investigation. I want to give it a try if you're game. I'll understand if you decide that isn't what you want."

He paused, and when I didn't say anything he continued, "Can I give you a call, then, on that basis? Hopefully in the next week but I can't promise."

He stood up, taking my hand and pulling me up beside him. He put his arms around me and did that wonderful kissing thing that made my insides churn and toes curl. "I hope that motivates you to say yes and to answer when I call. What do you say?" he asked.

"Paul, you haven't even started to get to know me. I have more baggage than you see in this cabin, and I don't mean suitcases. I mean emotional baggage. I fight relationships all the way to Sunday and back. But you do make me tingle all the way to my toes, and that's worth some kind of risk. Call me, I'll probably answer," I teased. "Then we'll see if you still want me to."

"I'm pretty sure I will," he said, and he walked out of my cabin.

Even though I had come to the cabin relaxed after my talk with Doug, I found it tough to get to sleep. But it wasn't the size of the cabin that kept me awake this time.

CHAPTER 12

Early the next morning, the ship's bells sounded and the television clicked on of its own accord. We were all reminded that we had arrived back at the Port of Galveston. We didn't need to fly anywhere from here to get home so Sam and I opted for the quicker self-debarkation option. I didn't leave my sound equipment and luggage outside the door for the crew to pick up and transport to the terminal. Of course, part of the reason was concerns with how the bags and equipment were handled.

I managed to stack the sound equipment on the two roller bags and tied them in place. The rollers were now pretty heavy, but I was able to drag them behind me. Those of us doing the 'self' option were the first to get off, so I headed to Deck 3 with only few collisions with the roller bags. A lot of passengers obviously used this option and I snagged a cup of coffee while I waited. We eventually formed lines but the lines moved slowly to exit the ship. From there, we followed cruise personnel and pier security as we snaked our way to Customs and Immigration Services.

I looked around for anyone I knew or had met, but couldn't spot any of the Clearton gang. As I passed by a wall of windows, I could just see across to the drop off and street in front of the Pier Terminal. There were a lot of official vehicles over there. The Galveston Police, Texas Rangers, Homeland Security, and Immigration Services were the ones with identifying information I could see. I figured the black SUV parked next to them might be FBI. Paul would be having a fun time today, bless his heart.

I detailed my Customs form with my souvenirs and the few clothes I'd purchased, and cleared that hurdle with no hitches. Once outside the terminal, I waited on Sam, my two bags and sound system stacked next to me. Last night when we talked, he seemed to think we could handle both my stuff and his on the bus to the parking lot. He wanted to avoid the hassle of him going for the car and coming back to pick me up.

He hated dealing with the traffic up to the terminal and pier, and then working his way out of the area. As he said, he was like a horse to the barn on its way home. He didn't want to waste any time getting on the road. I wasn't too sure riding the bus would save us any time. I knew my arms were killing me. With his help, we could probably bypass the bus. But the bus looked pretty good to me about then.

The horse analogy was apt. As I waited, passengers piled out of the terminal like horses suddenly freed from a corral. Some of the square dancers spotted me, came over, and gave me a hug on their way to the bus or their cars. I consider myself unremarkable, and I'm always surprised when people recognize me. Square dancers are a friendly group and they seem to remember who I am, even when I'm off stage.

I kept my eyes peeled for Sam. I didn't want to miss connecting with him. I hoped I might see Paul, but reminded myself he had said he would be tied up. Just as I spotted Sam and waved to him, I heard a voice yell, "Mom, over here!"

At first I didn't respond to the shout. I heard the words, but just figured it was someone else's daughter. Then the familiarity of the voice worked its way to my brain, and I turned to see Heather getting out of a Honda. What a surprise and what a sight for sore eyes!

"Heather, it's great to see you, but what are you doing here?" I stammered. "How did you know when to get here?" She ran up and gave me a hug. Her current boyfriend, Micah, left his car idling at the curb and joined us. I didn't know Micah all that well, but I gave him a quick hug too. They were both in t-shirts and jeans, and looked wonderful to me.

About that time Sam and Doug walked up behind me, and I made introductions all around. Heather already knew Doug and Sam, but they didn't know Micah.

"Mom, I knew you were worried about me, and I figured you'd keep fretting until you laid eyes on me." Sometimes she knew me a little too well. She continued, "Micah and I were bored and decided to take a road trip. What better place than here to meet your ship? It's not all that far from Austin to Galveston. As for figuring out when, that was easy. It's on the 'net and Micah has a smart phone. Did you have a good time?" Heather's glance included Sam and Doug in her last question.

"You probably already know this, young lady, but going anywhere with your mother is an adventure." Sam rolled his eyes, then looked at me and asked, "So I guess you won't be needing a ride, Darla?"

Before I could answer, Heather looked a little taken aback, and jumped in with, "Uh, actually she will."

While she knew me a little too well, I was frequently confused by my daughter. As I looked at her a bit perplexed, she explained, "Micah has never been to Moody Gardens or anyplace else down here, so we are staying the night. We just wanted to surprise you and say hi and be sure you knew we survived New Year's Eve in good shape! So we're not heading back this afternoon."

Our conversation was cut short by the police officer instructing us to please move along. I wasn't pleased that she and Micah were staying overnight together, in a single hotel room, no doubt, but she was almost grown and this wasn't the place to argue it. I tried to stay out of her decisions when I could. Sometimes I did better than other times. This time I just smiled, hugged them both again, and told her to have a good time. Holding her line of sight, I told her to be safe. She nodded and, I swear, blushed. That helped.

Doug gave Sam and me a quick hug and took off to find Carlotta and Nick. They had driven down together and Nick would be driving them back to Clearton before heading for the Dallas area.

"Where are you parked?" Heather asked.

After I explained the parking situation, Micah said, "You don't need to take the bus. We can just load your stuff into our car and zip you over to yours." I liked this kid better all the time. He seemed courteous despite his scraggy hair and ragged clothes. Besides, Heather looked happier than she had in years. That realization sparked my guilt, but I set it aside to think about later. We took Micah up on his offer. He and Sam loaded all our stuff into the trunk. We rode to the parking lot, and then transferred everything to Sam's car.

"Sam, just how much are you pulling at the bit?" I asked.

"You know me, Darla Darlin', I'm ready to get home. What'cha got in mind?"

"I was thinking, if Heather and Micah have time, if it's okay with you I might be able to bribe them to stay long enough for us to grab a cup of coffee…or breakfast." I raised my eyebrows at Heather, who answered without even glancing at Micah.

"Great! I haven't seen you in what feels like months," Heather said. "Feels like Christmas was a long time ago." She apparently remembered Micah was driving and looked over at him. He shrugged agreement.

As Sam and I were about to climb into Sam's car and head out to locate a coffee shop, Sam stopped still and pointed. He didn't say a word, and I didn't understand what he was pointing at. I followed his finger and saw Mr. Jarcourt. He had on the flowered shirt and shorts from the ship's gift shop, even though it wasn't as warm today as it had been when we left. But he seemed happy and calm, and seemingly warm enough. Then I realized what Sam was showing me.

Mr. Jarcourt was getting into an old model sedan, something like a Ford Fairlane. It was the very same car that had almost run us off the road on the way to Galveston!

"Now, Darla Darlin', you just cool your heels a minute. We are going to wait until he is well ahead of us and stay very far away from that man. I don't care if he is all calm and cool now, I just don't trust his driving. We don't have another spare left in the car," drawled Sam with a broad smile.

Once Sam felt he had given Mr. Jarcourt enough of a head start, Heather and Micah followed us to first Starbucks we saw. Sam and I related the bare essentials of the excitement of the cruise. The story of course started with the explanation of Sam's comment about Mr. Jarcourt in the parking lot. I promised Heather I'd give her a detailed explanation later, although I wasn't sure how much of the personal stuff I'd include.

We talked about some of the things we each had done in the week since we'd seen each other and the general cruise experience. For her part, Heather talked about the party they had gone to and some of the places they were going to go to while in Galveston. She promised to call me when she got back to Austin and said she'd probably come to Isquith for a few days before her next semester started.

Sam, ever the square dance ambassador, encouraged her and Micah to come to a square dance. The eyeroll response was predictable. With hugs and handshakes, they headed off to see the sights on the island, and Sam and I headed for Isquith.

On the way to I-45, Sam pointed out exactly where Mr. Jarcourt had forced us off the road. I had the feeling he was practicing for the next time he told the story, which I expected would have grown just like a good fish tale. We talked a lot about the dances, the mysteries, and the people on the cruise. Then Sam got serious.

"Darla, you know I'm prone to speak my mind, right?" he asked. I nodded and he continued, "Some years ago, after my wife died, I spent a lot of time alone and lonely. I even stopped square dancing for a while, if you can believe it. But like you, I found that square dancing was a nice safe place to get past the loneliness," he said and then looked my way. I nodded again, and he looked back at the road.

"It took a while, but I finally realized that I didn't have to be alone," he continued. "I found I could enjoy a lady's company, have a good time, and the world wouldn't end. And it wouldn't tarnish the memory of my wife. I didn't have to feel guilty, although even though I knew that, it took me awhile to feel it." I could feel my eyes tearing up, but didn't say anything. I wasn't quite sure where he was going and I wasn't used to the serious side of Sam.

"Darla darlin', I'm worried about you, plain and simple. You've grieved for some five years now. I was kinda tickled whenever I caught you and Doug holding hands," he said without looking at me, "but I'm thinking that on this cruise, you and he… well, let's just say, Doug tells me you guys made peace last night and I'm glad. It was clear there was some tension between you two. That's between you and Doug. But, girl, you have to give yourself a chance for some happiness or you're gonna just be miserable. Let yourself have some fun, and maybe do something frivolous once in a while, huh? Take a vacation without any dead bodies or mysteries, maybe?" he ended with a smile and wink.

I knew he meant well, but he'd caught me off guard. At least he had ended on a humorous note so I responded in kind.

"Actually, Sam, I don't know when or what I'll do for vacations, but I am definitely through with mysteries…until the next one, of course!" Sam chuckled.

I added, "I hear what you're saying, and I'm working on it. Really, I am. As you say, it's a tough thing to get the knowledge and the feelings to match up. And you aren't alone. Carlotta and even Heather, believe it or not, are on my case as well. We'll see, Sam, but I've got some serious walls I gotta knock down first. I do appreciate your concern. I have to say it was great to see you enjoying Zoe's company. So I'll turn the tables on you. Any romance there?"

"Ya just never know, girl. We didn't make any plans, but I've got to admit I feel like a teenager again when I'm with her. Probably not, she's from up north, but it sure made the cruise fun," he said.

For the rest of the drive, we talked mostly about Heather and her studies, Micah, and my need to get a grip on how to do the motherhood thing for a grown-up daughter. We made it to Highway 45 and up the easy stretch to Isquith without incident. We got to my house by about 2 in the afternoon. Sam helped me with all the bags, and as we approached the door, I noticed a long white box on the front step.

"Huh, what's that? I didn't order anything," I commented as I moved the box out of the way to open the door. "I wonder how long it's been sitting there."

"Now Darla, was my heart-to-heart talk with you for naught? That there is a florist box as sure as I know my own name," Sam responded. "And the card is addressed to one Ms. Darla King," he added with a raised eyebrow as he picked up the box and followed me into the house. He handed me the box and then went to get my bags from the porch. I stood there frozen and stared at the box.

He returned and set down the bags. "Well hell, Darla, aren't you going to open the box or even read the card? They don't usually bite."

I opened the card, blushed at Paul's note that he'd be in touch, and then opened the box. Inside were a dozen red roses. I just looked at them, and then at Sam.

"They look fresh enough," he said. "They're not from Doug, are they? After all my blustering, you didn't let out a peep about this. What haven't you told me?"

"Oh no, I told you, Sam. I told you I have a lot of walls to knock down." I looked at the roses again. "But these roses are better than a pick-axe at knocking out a chink in them. I'll tell you about them later," I said.

I managed to salvage basic courtesy, and asked him if he wanted a cup of coffee, but he declined. I thanked him for the ride, and the advice. He gave me a hug and said he'd see me next Tuesday when I'd be back in Clearton calling once again. At least that part of my life would continue to be predictable. Clearly the rest of my 'simple' life was not going to be simple any longer.

I put the roses in water and set them in the kitchen window. I swear they glowed. I was pretty sure I did too.

www.ingramcontent.com/pod-product-compliance
Lightning Source LLC
Chambersburg PA
CBHW070917180626
46817CB00003B/1094